LARA DELOZA

Winning

HARPER TEEN

An Imprint of HarperCollinsPublishers

For Wendy, my sister from another mister,
who gives me the courage to keep typing.

HarperTeen is an imprint of HarperCollins Publishers.

Winning
Copyright © 2016 by HarperCollins Publishers
All rights reserved. Printed in the United States of America.
No part of this book may be used or reproduced in any manner whatsoever
without written permission except in the case of brief quotations embodied
in critical articles and reviews. For information address HarperCollins
Children's Books, a division of HarperCollins Publishers, 195 Broadway,
New York, NY 10007.
www.epicreads.com

Library of Congress Control Number: 2015952520
ISBN 978-0-06-239669-3 (trade bdg.)

Typography by Sarah Creech
16 17 18 19 20   PC/RRDH   10 9 8 7 6 5 4 3 2 1

First Edition

ONE

Alexandra

Some girls are born to wear a baseball cap without an ounce of irony. Think of those long-legged, gamine creatures whose tans are never fake-baked, whose shoulders are broader than those of their boyfriends, and who tend to have a pair of blindingly white sneakers they save for "dress up."

Some girls are born to wear a beret, or its sloppy cousin the beanie. Universal symbols that scream "I'm a bohemian—no, really, I am!" These are the girls who believe they belong in the spotlight, only to end up in someone else's shadow every single time.

Some girls are born wanting so desperately to blend in that they spend hours trying to coax their locks into one of those messy-bun-and-elastic-headband combos that are so on-trend. Only these girls a) look like every third person and b) are not fooling anyone because the amount of effort they exert in trying to look effortless is obvious.

And I won't even talk about those girls hiding behind thick bangs, dyed black and ironed straight. As if a curtain of hair could mask the pain and self-loathing that run so deep, they've turned parts of their bodies into lines of scar tissue.

You may wonder why I have such strong opinions about such seemingly trivial things.

It's because I have to. It's my job to size people up. To see what's hiding beneath the surface—and then use that to my advantage.

You see, I am not like any of those girls.

No, *I* was born to wear a crown.

TWO

Alexandra

I spend fifth period the way I always spend fifth period: stuck in a mint-green box of a cafeteria, besieged by an army of clichés.

Samantha and I are seated at our usual table, one of only three rounds in the entire room.

There are enough chairs to accommodate eight people, but I've opted not to invite anyone to join us today, not even Matt.

This is because Sam and I have serious work. On Monday, the students of Spencer High will nominate candidates for this year's Homecoming court. Principal Frick will post the official ballot by the end of the day, and once she does, the campaigning is *on*. I, of course, am a shoo-in; I've served as class princess every year since I was a freshman. But this year's different.

This year, I'm going to be queen.

I wiggle my fingers in Matt's direction and offer up an appropriately coy-yet-demure smile. My boyfriend grins and, despite being sandwiched between a six-foot-four-inch running back and three-hundred-pound wide receiver, Matt blows me a bona fide kiss. His teammates don't even give him shit about it, because both of them have wanted to bone me for years. I cast my eyes downward, deepen my smile, and coax my cheeks to flush pink. Matt can't take his eyes off me. But neither can Sam, for that matter.

Yes, I am the future Homecoming Queen of Spencer High, and my underwear model–hot boyfriend is both quarterback and captain of our nationally ranked football team. Together, we're not only high school royalty, we're the stuff of legends.

Does this make me a cliché, too?

Maybe. But clichés are the currency of the world. At the end of the day, I'm the one other girls aspire to be, the one every straight boy—and at least one not-so-straight girl—dreams of being with.

I look up and catch Sam frowning in Matt's direction. Her new distaste for him aggravates me. She's been like this since junior prom—the night I granted Matt full passage to my promised land. As though the first eight months of our relationship didn't matter to her, or at least didn't matter as much. Sealing it with sex? *That* apparently mattered.

I thought she understood. But perhaps I shouldn't have given her so much credit.

"Hey," I say softly, snaking my hand over to Sam's to give it a little squeeze. "You okay?"

Her head whips back to my direction and she pulls her hand away. "Yes. Of course. Why?"

"No reason."

Sam sighs and opens her pink plaid notebook to a fresh page.

"We only have four days left," she says. "It's going to be tight."

"Three," I correct.

"Oh, right," she says. "Today's Thursday."

I nod. "Natalie Night."

"Three days," she affirms. "*Very* tight."

Homecoming is a big deal at Spencer High, and winning queen has been a part of the plan for as long as I can remember. There was a story published in the local paper—this was years ago—claiming that every Miss Indiana for the past three decades was a former Homecoming Queen. It's not true. There's no documentation anywhere that proves this. But for whatever reason, the story stuck with my mother. Winning Homecoming Queen is No. 13 on her quite literal (not to mention ridiculously long) list of things I need to do in order to one day become Miss America.

I know there are other ways to get out of this small town. With my grades, extracurriculars, and standardized test scores, I could get a scholarship to just about anywhere in the country. But I don't want something as mundane as college to be what carries me away from Spencer. I was born for bigger things.

Natalie grew up thinking she was born for bigger things, too. But despite her movie-star good looks and hip-switching famous gait, the highest she ever got was second runner-up in Miss Indiana. I already know that I am better than her, but it doesn't stop me from wanting the crowns to prove it.

Sam starts making a list of prime locations to hang my campaign posters so that we'll know how many to make. She's got

this covered, so while she talks herself through the process, I
tune out and survey the room. Our back corner table offers the
best possible vantage point. From this angle I can see Sloane
Fahey sipping on a diet pop and staring lustily in my boyfriend's
direction—as if freckle-faced gingers posed any kind of a threat.
Across the aisle from her, poor Ivy Proctor lunches alone, sur-
rounded by a force field of empty chairs. She does an admirable
job of acting like she doesn't care that her only companion is a
library book.

Then there's Taylor Flynn, the chubby junior who's spent
the last two years pretending that she and the ratchet bunch of
misfits that make up Spencer High's a cappella group are, in
fact, cool—a delusion perpetuated by pop culture portrayals of
show choir. She pops up from her table, wiping tears from her
mascara-streaked eyes, and makes a beeline for the door.

"Taylor!" I call out as she passes by. "What's wrong?"

Taylor stops dead in her tracks. Slowly, she turns to face me.

"Nothing, Alexandra," she says. "I'm fine."

"Are you?" I ask, knitting my eyebrows, feigning concern.
"You don't look fine."

She swallows hard, then says, "Mr. Willis just told the Spattertones that our fall concert's been canceled. Something about a
budgeting snafu. You know how Frick is."

"Oh, no. That's awful."

She nods vigorously in agreement, then bursts into a fresh
round of tears. "I had three solos!" she practically wails, little
lobes of back fat jiggling with each sob. "And Gramma already

booked her flight from South Dakota. She's going to be *so* disappointed!"

It's hard not to feel sorry for Taylor. I mean, I wasn't *trying* to ruin her life when I got Sam to convince her mother, the head of Spencer's Parent Teacher Organization, that the Spattertones concert was scheduled too close to our fall musical. Nor was Taylor an intentional target when I whipped Mrs. Mays, the World's Most Dramatic Drama Club Coordinator, into a frenzy over the idea that *Evita* would suffer if the audience was diverted by the promise of quirky covers of their favorite pop songs.

But this is *my* senior year, and so help me God, I will be Eva Perón in front of a sold-out house. Taylor's just an unfortunate—but necessary—casualty.

"You know," I say, "you could join the chorus of *Evita*. Then your grandmother would still be able to see you perform. It wouldn't give you three solos, but—"

"It's something," she finishes for me. "Yeah, maybe that's a good idea."

"Of course, I'll put in a good word with Mrs. Mays for you." I wink. "You know how she adores me."

"Thank you, Alexandra." Taylor is finally breathing steadily again. "You're so . . . kind."

She says this last word like she's surprised by it. Not an entirely unexpected reaction.

For the record, there are precious few people in this school I genuinely like. And there are even fewer who genuinely like me, although nearly all of them, if asked, would say they did.

This is because the majority of my classmates know that I am someone they're *supposed to* like. I have the ear of every teacher, coach, and administrator here. I make things happen at this school. I am someone they want on their side.

Taylor sniffs back the last of her tears. "I'm going to go talk to her right now. Thank you, Alexandra. Seriously—thank you." She flashes me a grateful smile.

Taylor lumbers away on what I'm certain will prove a fruitless mission. Mays has had her show blocked and choreographed since before school started. No way will she want to work in extra cast members now. But my "willingness to help"? It throws Taylor off my scent.

"One goal accomplished," Sam says in a low voice. "Now can we please focus? We've got a campaign to win."

THREE

Sam

By the time the bell rings, our list is fairly complete. And it is long.

In addition to creating and distributing campaign posters, there are several events for which we'll need to prepare. The nominations go live about a month before the Homecoming dance, which is where the voting takes place. In between there's the pep rally assembly, where each of the candidates is interviewed onstage, and the Homecoming game itself, where the candidates make short, unscripted speeches during halftime, on a prompt pulled randomly from a box.

The Q&As aren't where queens are made, though. That all happens outside of the spotlight. Casual conversations in homeroom. Circulating the tables at lunch. Sucking up to the right people during after-school activities. Harnessing the power of social media.

"Looks like we have our work cut out for us," Lexi says, and by "we" I know she means "you," because—let's face it—*I'm* the one who will be doing 90 percent of the work for her

Homecoming Queen campaign. Just like *I'm* the one who'll be writing her paper on *A Streetcar Named Desire* for AP English tonight, while she's off logging time with Natalie.

Matt insists on walking us to class every day, even though his next one is in the exact opposite direction. Then he lingers so long that he literally has to run the length of the school if he wants to make it to World History before the final bell.

The halls are fairly wide, but so are Matt's shoulders. I imagine he has to take out a few people on his way.

He suctions himself to Lexi's side, wrapping one heavily muscled arm around her and hoisting her Marc by Marc Jacobs backpack onto the other. Together, and despite Lexi's slender frame, the two of them take up a lot of space—so much so that I always end up trailing a few steps behind.

Everyone's so busy waving at Lexi and fist-bumping Matt that no one ever notices me. They're like Power Couple Camo.

But it's fine. I can see more from here. And there is so much to see.

Matt's on the shorter side for a QB, only about five foot ten, but what he lacks in height he makes up for in genetically perfect everything else. Dark caramel hair he keeps military-neat for football, then grows out in the off-season. Big brown eyes framed by lashes almost as long as Lexi's. A pouty poem of a mouth that always seems to be smiling, even when it's not.

Just Google "Channing Tatum high school pictures" and you'll get a pretty decent idea of what I'm talking about.

And then there's Lexi. Lexi, whose legs go on for days, despite the fact that she barely clocks in at five foot six. Whose long, raven mane flows down her back like shiny black water. Whose sapphire eyes look photoshopped even when she's standing a foot in front of you. Whose lollipop pink lips are plump and perfect even when they're naked, without so much as a hint of gloss.

They taste pretty sweet, those lips.

When we reach Mr. Banerjee's class, Matt and Lexi assume their standard position—Lexi leaning against the wall, Matt leaning into Lexi. I duck around them and head inside. I've seen that show too many times to need another encore. Here's how it goes: things will be whispered, giggles will be exchanged, and if there are no teachers in the hallway, spit will be swapped. It happens, exactly this way, every. Single. Day.

What *doesn't* happen every single day is a New Girl sighting. So I'm beyond surprised to see Mr. Banerjee deep in thoughtful conversation with a pint-sized prepster who does not look at all familiar. She has chin-length, strawberry-blond hair and two dimples punctuating the sides of her smile.

They're too far away for me to read their lips, and I don't want to get caught staring, so I pull out my copy of *Streetcar* and pretend to read, sneaking glances whenever I can.

Lexi slides into the desk next to me. "Who the hell is that?" she whispers.

I shrug. "Never seen her before."

"Is she wearing a *skort*?"

I stifle a snicker. "Yeah, I think so."

Lexi never loses her sunny smile, but her eyes have darkened.

She doesn't like surprises, and we've somehow made it all the way to sixth period without hearing a single word about this particular New Girl. That's on me. Lexi's made it very clear; it's my job to keep an ear to the ground at all times. With a mom in the PTO, that's usually pretty easy.

I start to whisper an apology when Lexi lifts her hand to silence me. "She's cute," she says mildly.

"I guess." I shrug. "If you like that sort of thing."

She turns to me, the corners of her lips quirking upward. "Not your type?"

I blink, not sure I want to respond. The bell rings then, ending the uncomfortable exchange.

Mr. Banerjee and the New Girl move to the middle of the room. "Class, I'd like you to meet Erin Hewett. She is a new senior and comes to us by way of San Diego, California. Erin, please introduce yourself."

Erin's cheeks pinken just a smidge. Despite what I said to Lexi, I *do* think she's kind of adorable, skort and all.

"Hi, everyone," Erin says with a little wave. "I, um, just moved here, like Mr. B. said. My mom's family is from Indiana, though, so I used to visit lots when I was younger. Um, I was supposed to start the school year here, but there were some real estate . . . issues? Anyway, I'm happy to be here now. Oh, and I might be cheering for the Spartans! I'm, um, a tumbler."

There's something totally disarming about the way Erin delivers this monologue, and it's immediately apparent that more than one boy takes notice.

Lexi raises her hand, and Mr. Banerjee calls on her. "I just wanted to say welcome. I'm Alexandra, and if there's anything you need, I want to personally offer my assistance."

"That's really sweet," Erin says. "Thank you, Alex."

I flinch. Lexi hates it when people call her that. "Do I *look* like a boy?" she's apt to snark, as soon as they're out of earshot. Of course, *she's* the one who got everyone to call *me* Sam back in second grade.

"Alexandra," Lexi corrects in a friendly tone, never once breaking character.

"Alex*andra*," Erin repeats. "Gotcha."

There's something almost dismissive in the way she does this. Just a whiff of condescension, but I can tell it's there, and, if that diamond edge in her eyes can be believed, so can Lexi.

Erin takes a seat in the middle of the room. Lexi and I exchange glances. I can tell she's thinking the same thing:

We are going to need to keep our eyes on this one.

FOUR

Alexandra

About halfway through eighth period, it hits me how little time I have to prepare for this year's Homecoming race. Between my schoolwork, college applications, play rehearsal, Key Club meetings, and a somewhat needy boyfriend (albeit one of super-hottie proportions), I do not have a ton of free time. And what little free time I do have is claimed by my mother. Or, more accurately, my mother's plans for me.

Becoming Miss America was Natalie's dream. When she stalled out before ever making it to the big show, and then got knocked up with me before she could have a second at-bat, becoming Miss America became her dream for me.

Competing in pageants was never optional. It was just something I did, even before I started to crawl. Natalie was fanatical about my "career," too. She wasn't like those fame-hungry moms on TV, entering their kid in any pageant that offered a crown. No, she was picky. Natalie doesn't believe in glitz pageants, especially not for little girls. I never had a flipper of fake teeth, never wore a wig of someone else's human hair. My talent never focused on something exploitative, like those poor creatures whose mothers stick them into Shirley Temple skirts and teach them how to shake nonexistent tatas.

No, I always sang, always dressed in something respectable. My pageant gowns were more glamorous than sexy. And I have yet to compete in something that had a swimsuit competition, though I have had to do fitness and active wear.

I started working with my pageant coach, Craig, about five years ago. He preps me for almost everything—talent, evening gown, interview, presentation, platform development, modeling, dance, hair and makeup. You name it, Craig covers it.

Except for The Walk. That's Natalie's area of expertise, or so she believes. The Walk, she says, is what made her famous. And it's The Walk that would have carried her all the way to Miss America, had she not been the victim of pageant sabotage.

The way Natalie tells it, on random nights when the magic combination of booze and pills turn her confessional, she was the odds-on favorite for Miss Indiana the year she competed. But then she took a turn too fast during the evening gown competition and landed on the side of her right ankle. She claims that someone put bowling wax on the soles of her shoes, but that was never proven.

Natalie started to recover mid-fall; she landed softly and didn't break anything, but she did end up with a bad sprain. Despite the pain, she kept going. By the time she came out for swimsuit, her ankle had swollen to almost twice its size. She got a standing O during her final lap around the stage—at least, according to Natalie—but it wasn't enough to rescue her score. She was named the second runner-up. Before she could work her way back the following year, my still-legally-married-to-his-second-wife father managed to get her knocked up with me, prohibiting her from competing for (and winning) that ultimate title: Miss America.

By effectively ending her pageant career I involuntarily signed up for mine. She entered me into my first competition when I was just shy of six months old. When I won the 0–12 months division, she knew she'd made the right decision in keeping me.

Thursdays have always been Natalie Nights—the one night each week that she gives me quality face time. The fact that it takes the shape of pageant training doesn't faze me anymore. In fact, I almost wish she'd go back to the time when she'd berate me about my lack of a thigh gap instead of just drunkenly recounting her glory days, which is what our practices often devolve into since my father died two years ago. It's better than nothing.

Señora Gonzalez prattles on about the various idioms used to describe weather *en español* as I begin to run through a mental end-of-day checklist: girls' room for touch-ups, locker for books, pharmacy for drugs. That should do it.

My legs cross, uncross, recross. Class can't end soon enough. If I don't arrive at home by 3:30 on the dot, Natalie will be on edge. She will deliver her umpteenth speech on Professionalism and how I am Not Taking My Career Seriously Enough.

And then our weekly practice session will become a rant-a-thon, stretching four hours past the amount of time Natalie can handle sober. And a sober Natalie is one of the only benefits to our Thursday sessions.

Señora stops in front of my desk and points to my foot. *"No rebote,"* she says. *"Me estás poniendo nervioso."* No bouncing; you're making me nervous.

The few classmates who aren't completely brain-dead titter in response. There are some other things I can think of to do with this foot as it relates to Señora Gonzales, but—

"Lo siento," I say automatically. *I'm sorry.*

Señora offers a curt nod, then goes back to talking about the weather. I'm distracted by the ill-fitting nature of her poly blend skirt, a tea-length, A-line number that's so tight in the ass, it shows the outline of her enormous granny panties. The skirt's a particularly drab shade of olive that casts Señora's marshmallow legs a ghastly green hue. I must remember to tell Natalie about this later. It will give her a good chuckle.

After the final bell, I head for the bathroom. There I retrieve the MAC Naked Liner from my makeup bag. I use it to carefully draw a line just outside my top lip (to make it look fuller) and just *inside* my bottom one (to slim it up). Then I turn the pencil on its side to lightly shade them both in. Next, I draw a lip brush across the top of Myth, my go-to MLBB lipstick (My Lips But Better), and with short, feathery strokes, paint over the liner. I blot on a scratchy paper towel, then add a second coat. As a final touch, I gently dot some clear Lipglass in the very center of my mouth using the pad of my pinkie.

Perfect. Natalie will be pleased. She has always admired a subtle lip.

I quick-walk to my locker, trying my damnedest to look as if I am moving at a normal, everyday pace. Matt is standing there, waiting for me. Odd. He usually heads right to practice.

He's wearing his jersey over his school clothes, which is also odd. His hands are clasped together in front of him, and he keeps shifting his weight from side to side. Almost like a teenage version of the pee-pee dance.

When I'm only a few feet away, Matt lifts one fist and raps it twice against the bank of metal lockers. Then he bellows, "Let's do this!"

A handful of Matt's teammates stream toward him from different directions, all carrying different things. Chick Myers, the widest wide receiver in all of Indiana, pops a fedora off his head and places it on top of Matt's. Then Bobby Jablonski, the super-tall running back, hands him an acoustic guitar. Matt threads himself through the strap and, much to my horror, begins to strum.

There's a crowd forming around us, no doubt curious as to why my boyfriend has picked this moment in time to make a complete ass out of himself. Instead of pouring out the school's doors and into the warm late-September afternoon, they're all just standing there, staring. A few are even whipping out their phones.

It takes me a few blinks to realize that Matt plans on singing to me. Right here, in front of everyone. As he warbles the first few lines of Jason Mraz's "I'm Yours," I force my jaw to drop a little, trying to look appropriately stunned and touched at the same time. Inside, though, I am furious. This little stunt of Matthew's is going to cost me. How much, I'm not sure. It all depends on exactly how late I am getting to Natalie.

The gawking crowd swells, second by cheesy second. I don't tear my eyes off Matt, of course, so I can't make out many distinct faces. Still, I can *hear* the squeals of delight from my female classmates. I almost feel sorry for the boyfriends of Spencer High who, as a result, will now be held to ridiculously high standards of romance.

Matt's voice grows louder and more confident with each verse. He's not a bad singer. And he's definitely easy on the eyes. Is that my Grinch heart growing just a smidge?

As Matt coos, "This is our fate, I'm yours," I realize that there's a very good possibility we will end up on YouTube. In fact, we may even go viral. I cover my face with my hands, careful not to smudge my eyeliner, then look up, partially masking my smile behind my fingertips. A gesture I hope reads as "I'm both amazed and humbled by your outpouring of emotion. How did I ever get so lucky to find someone like you?"

My boyfriend's grin grows even wider, threatening to split his beautiful face in half. I have played my part well.

With one final "I'm yours," Matt finishes strong. The crowd erupts in cheers. He holds up one hand to silence them. "Give me a sec," he says. "There's more."

Two of his teammates unfurl a paper banner, the kind that the cheerleaders make before each game to psych the players up. Only, this one reads, "Happy 1st Anniversary, Alexandra." Another hands me a dozen red roses wrapped in brown paper and tied with a raffia bow.

"I've had a crush on you since kindergarten," Matt says, eliciting a chorus of "aww" from the girls in the audience. "But it wasn't until last year that I finally got up the courage to ask you to Homecoming."

It's a good thing he waited, too. It wasn't until the summer after sophomore year that Matt transformed from awkward-bordering-on-ugly to oh-my-god-hotness.

"You said yes," he continues, "and every day since, I've felt like the luckiest guy in the world. I love you, Alexandra Miles. Someday, I'm going to marry you."

I'd like to see you try, I think, as every girl in earshot has a complete fucking meltdown. I manage to muster up some tears, my eyes brimming with unspilt drops. In a move I perfected when I was ten, I squeeze out exactly one. No one will ever accuse *me* of being an ugly crier.

Matt swaps the guitar for a football. Before I can figure out what it's for, Matt says "Catch" and lobs it toward me.

Without thinking, I drop the roses to reach for the ball. It lands against my chest with a dull thud. *What the shit, Matt?* I think, my inner fury returning. Surely there's a more graceful way he could've done that. And what am I supposed to do with a football, anyway?

"Turn it over," Matt instructs, as if he's read my mind.

On the other side of the ball, spelled out in rhinestones, is one word, followed by a question mark: "HOMECOMING?"

Oh, he's *good*. A few dozen more IQ points and we might have made a formidable team.

Matt kneels down in front of me, and for a heartbeat I fear he's about to actually propose. But then he says, "Alexandra Miles, will you tackle one last Homecoming dance with me?"

"Yes," I say, nodding for the iPhone cameras. "Of course I will!"

More cheers ensue. Matt rises, throws his arms around my waist, and lifts me up, squishing the football between us. I giggle appropriately. When he puts me down, he takes my face in his hands and lays a deep kiss on me. All of that work I did in the girls' room? Ruined.

"What in the Sam Hill is going on out here?" a familiar, cranky voice brays, breaking the mood entirely. It's Principal Constance Frick, the proverbial thorn in my side. Her sheer presence parts the throngs of admirers who surround us. I turn and see her standing there frowning, manly hands planted square on what Natalie calls "birthing hips."

"Alexandra Miles," she says in a voice oozing disapproval. "I should have known you'd be at the center of this little spectacle."

"You can blame *me* for that," Matt says cheerfully. "Sorry, Ms. Frick."

Frick's face softens a bit as she drinks him in. You can practically see the impure thoughts dance across her old-lady brain.

"Let's clear out now," she commands. "School's over." She tips her head in Matt's direction before clomping toward her office.

Matt pulls me closer and whispers in my ear, "You make me so happy, babe."

"You too," I murmur, trying to figure out how quickly I can extricate myself from his grasp without causing drama. Doesn't he realize it's Thursday? And that he's making me inexcusably *late*?

"Sorry to interrupt," I hear Sam say from behind me. "But I need to steal your girlfriend."

Samantha. Here to rescue me, like the loyal little sycophant she is. Thank God.

"What's up, Sam?" Matt asks.

"It's, um . . . well, Alexandra promised me a ride," she says, stumbling over her words. "I have a thing I have to get to. Like, *now.*" She swoops down to pick up the fallen flower bouquet, then thrusts it at me.

"Right," I say. "Matty, I'm so sorry. I have to run. Call you tonight?"

"Sure." His eyes are locked on Sam. He's managed to hide his irritation well, but I can see it simmering under the surface.

I plant a kiss on the corner of his mouth to placate him. "Tonight," I say again.

"I'm counting the minutes," he replies, devoid of any sarcasm.

We head to the senior parking lot. Once out of earshot, Sam says, "You're welcome."

Her tart voice strikes the wrong nerve. "Thank you," I say, a little more sharply than intended.

"You'd think that Matt would know by now that Thursdays are off-limits. I mean, *I* do."

"It's our anniversary," I shoot back. "It's not his fault it fell on a Thursday."

"But it *is* his fault that he waited until after school to surprise you."

Why is she goading me when she already knows I'm running late?

I stop dead in my tracks. Sam stops too, confused.

"I think I like you better when you're less needy," I say icily. "And oh—I hope you don't mind taking the bus tomorrow morning. I have some things I need to take care of before school."

I turn on my heel and walk away, leaving a stunned, speechless Sam in the parking lot as I speed off toward the pharmacy.

FIVE

Sam

"Need a lift?"

It's the New Girl. Erin. My ears burn with embarrassment. Did she hear the way Lexi just blew me off? And if there had to be a witness, why did it have to be *her*?

"No thanks," I say. "But I appreciate the offer, umm . . . Ellen?"

"It's Erin, actually." She smiles as she says this, and there's something about the expression on her face that catches me off guard. Then I realize: her smile is genuine.

It makes me uncomfortable.

Erin pushes a lock of hair behind her right ear and I watch as her slender fingers trail across her jawline to complete the same action on the other side of her face. "You're Sam, right?"

I nod, wondering how she already knows that. Then I blurt out, "Do you always offer rides to strangers?"

She laughs. "Not especially. But you're hardly a *stranger*."

Our eyes meet, and my breath catches in my throat. Is it possible that she's . . . ?

"We're classmates," she finishes. "And to be honest, my offer isn't entirely altruistic. I figured I could pick your brain about the *Streetcar* paper on the way to your house."

Of course. Maybe that smile wasn't so genuine after all.

Normal breathing resumes, and I assess the situation. Cozying up to Erin *could* piss Lexi off even more. Then again, maybe she'd approve of me gathering some inside intel. Better yet, taking Erin up on her offer could accomplish both.

"Okay," I say. "If it's not too much trouble."

"Not at all."

We walk across the lot to Erin's car, a bright white MINI Cooper with a convertible top. It's adorable, and totally suits my new skort-wearing friend. She hits the clicker to unlock the car, but opens the passenger-side door for me anyway. Who *does* that?

I give Erin my address, and she types it into her iPhone. "Might as well give me your number, too," she says, so I do. "You want mine?"

"Okay."

She puts her hand out, and for a second I wonder if she's offering it to me to hold. But before I do something stupid, it registers that she wants me to hand over my cell.

Her thumbs are the fastest I've ever seen, and I'm mesmerized by how quickly they clickety-clack through the info. "Here you go," she says, handing it back. I look down and see that she's used emojis to bookend her name—a pink heart with yellow stars to the left and a blushing smiley face to the right.

Lexi would gag at this girly display, but me? I swallow hard.

As we drive to my house, Erin chats not about the AP English assignment, but about her former life in California. I learn that she's not from San Diego proper, but Poway, a suburb of the city she describes as "idyllic." It's the second SAT-prep word I've heard her use in the past ten minutes, but there's nothing forced about the way she speaks. She was cocaptain of the cheer squad at her old high school, as well as a peer counselor, student council representative, and member of Key Club, for which she served as the fund-raising chair.

It's this last piece of information that catches my attention. Of all of Lexi's extracurriculars, she's most territorial over Key Club. She's been president since sophomore year.

Last fall, when Sloane Fahey decided to join, Lexi was livid for weeks. Her anger only intensified when Sloan ran for—and won—secretary, an upset over Lexi's handpicked candidate, Jen Tyner. Secretly, I was impressed. Sloane's one of the only people at Spencer High with big enough balls to challenge Lexi directly. It's even more impressive considering how Lexi fucked up her life sophomore year.

"You guys have Key Club at Spencer, right?" Erin asks. "Your friend—Alex*andria*—she's the president, isn't she?"

I can practically hear the eye roll in how she says Lexi's name. Dangerous. We were right to think we needed to watch out for this girl.

"Yes," I say. "It's very important to her."

My subtle warning goes completely over Erin's head. "Oh, me too!" she says. "In fact, I was absolutely heartbroken that I didn't get to see my last project through to completion."

"Oh yeah?"

"Yes. I was organizing a Jail and Bail lock-in for this huge project we were working on."

"Jail and Bail?" I ask. "What's that?"

"You've never done one? Oh, it's the best. You get a bunch of people to volunteer to be 'arrested'—teachers, coaches, the principal—and then they have to call people to raise their 'bail' and spring them from the jail cells.

"It's totally a hoot," she continues, "and it raises beaucoup bucks. We should totally do one at Spencer!"

She's right; it does sound fun. And it probably would raise a lot of money, as long as no one incarcerated Frick (because really, who would pay her bail?). But I know that Lexi wouldn't like the New Girl waltzing in and planning a high-profile fund-raising event, especially not on her first day.

"Anyway," Erin prattles on, "we've been raising funds for the past two years to buy a van that could be converted into a bookmobile. A bunch of teachers and our school librarian were involved and everything. My Jail and Bail was projected to bring enough not only to get the van, but also to pay for the conversion."

"Wow," I croak. "That's . . . huge." Much bigger than anything Lexi's ever tackled, and way more impressive than the pancake breakfasts and Lost and Found auctions she organizes each year.

"So who would I talk to about bringing a project like that to

Spencer?" Erin asks. "Alex*andria*?"

"I don't know," I lie. Obviously, nothing gets done without Lexi's approval. "I'm not in Key Club." I steer clear of it, just like I do the half dozen other organizations that Lexi runs. Publicly, that is. I'm usually involved behind the scenes; the work I do is invisible.

"I guess I could just propose it at a meeting," Erin says. "The next one's tomorrow, right?"

We pull up to my house. Erin parks the car and cuts the ignition. "I hate to ask, but do you mind if I come in for a sec? I really need to use the little girls' room."

She is thanking me and getting out the car before I can protest. I show her to the powder room, wondering if I can usher her back out the door before my mom gets wind that I have brought a girl home. I don't need her getting the wrong idea.

But it's too late; Mom has seen us out of the second-floor window. She rushes downstairs to find out who my "new friend" is.

"Just a girl from school," I tell her in a low voice. "She's a transfer. She needed some help with an English assignment."

Turns out that Erin is parent catnip. From the minute she introduces herself, my mother is charmed. I know because she keeps beaming at me, as if befriending Erin is some sort of accomplishment on my part. To be fair, Erin probably scored fifty points just by *not* being Lexi.

My mom can't stand her—like, actively hates her—but she tolerates Lexi because, despite the fact that my mother graduated a quarter of a century ago, she still understands the social hierarchy of a Midwestern high school.

"It's hard enough to be a girl who likes girls," she told me once. "It's even worse when you live in a Bible-thumping town like Spencer."

There are just under six thousand people who reside in Spencer's city limits. There are two elementary schools, two middle schools, and one high school. By the time you hit freshman year there, you pretty much know everyone you're ever going to know. And everybody knows everybody else's business.

So when I accidentally came out in eighth grade, it wasn't long before the whole town was buzzing about it. How does one "accidentally" come out, you ask?

It happened when this girl Meredith Snow wrote me a letter confessing that she had a crush on me. I'd never really thought of Meredith in that way—she was a vanilla sort of girl that always melted into the background—but I knew I liked girls, and Meredith was the first one who'd shown any interest in me.

I carried the letter around in my bra for about a week. I couldn't risk anyone finding it, especially not Lexi or my mother. Neither of them would approve, for different reasons.

It took me forever to figure out if I should write Meredith back, and what I would say if I did. When I finally penned the response, I confessed that I wasn't sure anyone else in our class liked girls except for me. And that even though I didn't know her all that well, I'd like to get to know her better. Would she be interested in going to the movies with me?

I slipped the note into Meredith's locker one morning before homeroom. When I got to third-period English, one of three classes we shared, Meredith was waving my note around and saying loudly, "See? I told you she was a lezzie!"

If it were possible to die of embarrassment, they'd have been holding my funeral at lunch.

Gym class was the worst. Ashley Chamberlain complained to Coach Tate that she wouldn't change into her uniform if I was in the locker room. Why couldn't I go change with the boys?

It was Lexi who stuck up for me. "You're a disgusting homophobe," she told Ashley. "Not to mention a conceited one. Just because someone likes girls doesn't mean they'll like *you*."

What made this all the more shocking is that Ashley was—and still is—one of the hottest girls in our entire class. And at the time, Lexi's rank on the popularity food chain was considerably lower. Taking Ashley to task took guts.

But Lexi stood her ground. She'd deliver verbal spankings to anyone who so much as gave me a weird look. She also went to our then-principal, Mr. O'Connor, and asked for permission to start a Gay-Straight Alliance. He denied her request, so she asked my mom for help. By that time, my mother was well aware of my sexual orientation. She strong-armed the entire PTO into backing Lexi, and by spring, our GSA was seven students strong.

And as for Meredith? When she didn't get expelled for her little stunt, Lexi orchestrated a cheating scandal and, with the help of my brother, Wyatt, and his computer-hacking skills, placed

Meredith at the center of it. She ended up in a super-strict Catholic school two towns over. No one even talks to her anymore.

My association with Lexi—and her surprising loyalty to me—has shielded me from the bad behavior of others ever since, and my mother understands this. After all, she didn't become the president of the PTO of every school I've ever gone to by accident. She knows how to work the system better than anyone.

My mother asks if Erin would like to stay for dinner, but before she can accept the invitation I interject, "She can't. We have a huge assignment due in English tomorrow."

"Not for me," Erin says. "Mr. Banerjee gave me until Monday, since I'm new. But I can see you're stressing over the essay, so I'm going to go. Rain check?"

"Of course," my mom says. "Any time."

As Erin's MINI Cooper rounds the corner, I text Lexi: *Got scoop on NG. Call if interested.*

That should be enough to pique her curiosity. Once I fill Lexi in on Erin's background, and let her know that I have an "in" with the New Girl, she'll forgive me for whatever I did this afternoon to piss her off.

It doesn't occur to me until much later, when I'm fully immersed in writing not one but two versions of the AP English assignment, that Erin didn't ask me a single question about *A Streetcar Named Desire* after all.

SIX

Alexandra

Between Matt's little stunt and an argument with that new incompetent ass of a pharmacist—the one who tried to tell *me* I couldn't fill my mother's Xanax prescription for another six days—I don't make it back to my house until nearly 4:15. I'd made sure to text Natalie from the pharmacy, to let her know I was held up running *her* errand, but she never responded.

She hardly ever responds. I'm not sure why I still try.

As I round the corner onto our street I see a gunmetal-gray Jaguar squealing away from the curb in front of my house. There's only one person that could belong to: my uncle Douglas. I feel a fleeting disappointment that he didn't stick around long enough to say hi, and make a mental note to ask Natalie about his visit.

But I forget all that as I enter the house, which is filled with an acrid smell of chain-smoked Virginia Slims. It's no secret that Natalie likes a smoke every now and then, despite the fact that she warns me frequently about the dangers of cigarettes ("They'll age you quicker than having a child," she's said on more than one occasion). But she hates—absolutely abhors—the smell. In fact, I can't remember the last time I caught her smoking inside.

So that's the first thing I notice. The second? Our house is *dark*. The brown velvet curtains are drawn and every light is off. I wonder if it's been like this all day.

"Natalie?" I call out. "Where are you?"

No answer.

I take a deep breath and almost choke on the smoky stench. The smell is so strong, she has to be on the first floor. I snake my way through the living room, past the formal dining room, and into the kitchen.

Natalie sits at the small round table where I do my homework (alone) and eat most of my meals (also alone). She's staring out a window she hasn't bothered to crack. The saucer of a coffee cup serves as a makeshift ashtray. It overflows with stark white butts ringed by black cherry lipstick.

"You're late," she says out of habit, not because she cares. She's not even bothering to look at me.

"I sent you a text," I say. "There was a . . . problem. But I fixed it." I place the bag of Xanax on the table and push it toward her like a sacrificial offering.

Next to the mock ashtray is a tumbler with just a splash of bourbon left in the bottom. Cigarette dangling from her mouth, Natalie reaches for the nearly empty bottle of Blanton's and refills her glass. There's only about two fingers' worth left, but if Natalie's bleary eyes and sloppy movements are any indication, she's already three sheets to the wind.

"Do I have time to get changed before my lesson?" I ask her.

She ignores the question, opting instead to focus on the bouquet of roses I'm still cradling in one arm. "That a prop? For today's *lesson*?" That last word comes out as a bitter hiss, and a cold dread runs down my spine. Whatever's going on with Natalie can't be the result of my lateness alone. The reaction is too disproportionate.

"They're from Matt," I explain.

"How fancy of him."

Her tone is so contemptuous that I find myself rising to Matt's defense for the second time this afternoon. "It was actually kind of sweet. He staged this whole thing to ask—"

"Someone should tell that boy that red roses are offensive," she interrupts. "A real man should know how to buy his woman flowers. Your father, for instance. He used to bring me freesia. And peonies, when they were in season."

It's been two years since my father died, but the only memories I have of him and flowers are the ones from his funeral.

This reminds me of seeing Doug's Jaguar. I call Doug my uncle but we're not technically related. He was my father's lawyer and best friend, and in the years since my dad's death he's been like a de facto dad to me. Each year at Homecoming, the princesses and queen candidates are escorted onto the field at halftime by their fathers, just before taking part in the traditional Q&A. After my father died, Uncle Doug stepped up and offered me his chic-suited arm.

"Did Douglas stop by?" I ask.

"No."

"Really? I could've sworn I saw his car."

"You saw wrong." Natalie stubs out her cigarette and takes another sloppy sip of bourbon. I almost hope she uses it to wash down a couple of Xannies, because then she'll pass out. Otherwise, she'll wait until the sun has set and then have me drive her to the liquor store so she can restock.

Natalie has become something of a shut-in since my father's untimely passing. At least during the day. She's less reticent about leaving the house at night. Maybe she thinks the darkness makes her invisible.

I look at the clock on our largely dormant stove; it's nearing four thirty. In addition to my date with Natalie, I have a bunch of homework to wrestle through, plus the phone call I promised Matt. And if I don't get to bed at a reasonable hour, I'll wake up with under-eye circles. They won't be as dark as the purple half-moons Natalie sports, but they'll be every bit as ugly.

Time to speed things along. "I was thinking we could work on onstage questions today," I say. "I'm still sounding a bit Pollyanna-ish. Should I go get the flash cards?"

"Do whatever you want," Natalie says flatly. "I'm not feeling well tonight."

"What's wrong?"

"I just told you. I'm not feeling well."

"Yes, but how?" I prod. "Do you have a fever? An upset stomach?"

"I have a daughter who asks too many questions," she spits back. "Please, just leave me alone."

"But, it's *Thursday*," I protest.

"So what? There'll be another one next week."

Natalie rips open the package from the pharmacy. She wrestles with the amber-colored plastic bottle but in her current state of inebriation can't seem to work out the childproof cap.

"Here, let me," I say. I take the bottle from her, open it, and shake a few blue pills into the palm of my hand. "One or two?"

"Three," she replies without hesitation.

"Three?"

"I haven't had any today. And I haven't slept more than a couple hours at a time in a week."

I hand over the pills. Natalie takes them with one last gulp of bourbon, slams the glass down, and stands. It takes her a second to find her balance, a problem she tries to mask by smoothing her pencil skirt. How she's maintained such shapely calves in her current state of decay is beyond me.

She walks over to me and lifts my chin with one hand. "Your mouth is naked," she says. "Very lazy of you."

I knew I should have taken a few extra minutes to fix what Matt's kiss ruined. You never know when Natalie's going to turn back on. "Sorry," I mumble.

"I'm going to bed," she informs me. "Oh, and you may want to rethink your usual Lean Cuisine for dinner. Those things are full of sodium and your face is looking puffy."

And with that, my once-beautiful pageant queen mother saunters off into the night.

SEVEN

Alexandra

I decide to skip dinner altogether. Instead, I head to the basement and run five miles on the treadmill. It takes about fifteen minutes for the endorphins to kick in, but once they do, they set my brain on fire. I've always loved to run; that's one thing my father and I had in common. When I was younger, we used to head over to Banning Park and race each other around the paved trails.

But then the running trend hit Spencer, Indiana, and even Frick, that miserable frump, became a Couch to 5K convert. That's when I took my running indoors. Now I do my miles in the basement instead of out in the open air. It's not nearly as satisfying, but it saves me from having to make small talk with all of the sneakered sheep in this town.

After a cold shower—great for the hair and skin—I settle in at the kitchen table with my laptop and check email. My in-box is clogged with the usual noise, including another request from Sloane Fahey to run lines together this weekend. It's the third time she's asked, and the third time I've hit delete without responding. Ever since Mrs. Mays named her my understudy for *Evita*, Sloane has operated under the delusion that she can make demands of me. Clearly, she's learned nothing since sophomore year.

I put that little wannabe in her place once, and I can do it again. Only this time, I won't be as kind.

There's also a message from Liz Brookover, the director of the Hoffman County Library, looking for a student to take over a story time program in the children's room. I couldn't care less about reading to a bunch of sticky, screaming toddlers. But what *does* interest me is the part about Brookover wanting to expand the program to the branch over on Williams Street—a small, run-down library that doesn't even *have* a children's collection.

Craig and I were recently discussing the possibility of me changing my platform from the dangers of texting while driving to something with a little more heart. And just like that, I know exactly what my new platform will be: providing underprivileged youth with access to books. That shit is pageant *gold*.

I dash off a quick application and send it to Brookover, along with a reminder that after all of the work I did on last winter's book drive—and how I failed to report the accounting inconsistency I uncovered—she owes me one.

If I teach you nothing else, let it be this: Never waste a moment of your effort serving someone else's goals. Always use their machinery to pave the road to your own success.

Next, I head over to YouTube, to see if anyone's uploaded a video of Matt's serenade earlier this afternoon. Nothing yet. I'll have to get Sam on that task tomorrow. If she can track down the footage, we can leak it ourselves. Sam's got a million aliases. Her computer geek brother, Wyatt, sets up fake profiles for us as needed. He even routes the uploads through a complicated system of proxies so the videos can't be traced back to us.

Is it overkill? Maybe. But as my father always said, better safe than snared in a scandal. Wyatt gets a half chub every time I say his name; it's come in handy on more than one occasion. All I have to do is have some faux-confessional late-night chat with him once in a while when I spend the night at Sam's house. It's enough to keep that fish on the line.

Finally, I pick up my phone to call Matt. That's when I see that I've missed a handful of texts from Sam. She claims to have some interesting information about the New Girl. I message her back: *You can tell me about NG on way to school. Pick you up @ 7:45.*

She couldn't have discovered anything too juicy. If she had she would've been on the phone before she and what's-her-face had barely parted ways. Still, I find it useful to reward good behavior. Especially when it comes to Sam.

I roll up to Sam's house at exactly 7:52, knowing full well she's been waiting on the curb since at least 7:40. She's learned to be ready before I arrive, and I've learned that it's good to keep her guessing. I don't enjoy being late to anything—punctuality is a hallmark of a great leader—but in this case, my lateness is strategic. Better to let Sam squirm, wondering if I'm actually going to show up, than to allow her to think I've forgiven her so easily.

Sam slides into the passenger seat and hands me a travel mug full of coffee. "No sugar, extra cream, dash of cinnamon," she says, my eager-to-please puppy.

I offer her a tight smile as a thank-you. Then she reaches into her backpack and retrieves the AP English paper she's written for me.

"What's it about?" I ask.

"The light motif, and how it reflects Blanche's truth."

"And what's yours about?"

"Shadows, and how they symbolize Blanche's descent into madness."

I nod approvingly. This way, it looks like we *talked about* the assignment with each other, but worked on our own papers separately.

"I even printed them on different stock," Sam points out. "Yours is bright white. Mine's recycled."

"Smart," I say. I reach over and give Sam's knee a little squeeze. "I appreciate you helping me out with this."

Sam's eyes cast downward, lasering in on my hand. When I go to remove it, I make sure to let it graze a few inches up her thigh.

It takes so little to keep my pet happy. Just a few strokes here and there.

"So," I say, pulling away from the curb. "You have information?"

"Right. Yes."

After a brief pause, I prompt, "May *I* have this information as well?"

"Of course. Sorry, I was a little distracted."

I bet she was.

Sam gives me the bullet points on Erin Hewett: cheerleader, peer counselor, student government rep. In other words, nothing remarkable.

"She was the fund-raising chair of her school's Key Club," Sam continues. "She's planning on attending today's meeting."

I'm instantly irritated. Isn't it bad enough that I have to deal with Sloane Fahey every Friday afternoon?

Then she says, "Erin was working on this project back home—raising money for a community bookmobile—and she wants to start one like that at Spencer. I think she's going to pitch the idea today."

"How bold of her—planning events before she's finished her first week," I drawl.

Sam nods in agreement.

"And what did you say," I ask her, "when she informed you of this?"

"I played dumb. Pretended I didn't know how things work in Key Club."

"Good."

The way I'd like to handle this situation is vastly different from how I probably should handle it. I'd *like* to give Erin a smackdown—preferably publicly—for daring to think she could walk into *my* school and take over *my* club. But I *probably* should employ a much lighter hand. No, better to find an indirect way of teaching her how things work.

"Track her down before lunch," I instruct Sam. "Make it known that all new Key Club business needs to go through Sloane."

"Does it?"

"Obviously not. But I want her to *think* it does."

Sam smiles. Such a smart little puppy to boot.

EIGHT

Sloane

Heave. Heave again. One final spew. Flush. Brush.

Reapply lipstick.

I perform my anxiety-fueled morning ritual in the small, second-floor girls' bathroom located outside Ms. Hanna's classroom. *Her* morning ritual consists of taking a massive dump in the stall to the far left. She does this before a single student arrives on campus, but the stench lingers until well after third period.

Result: no one ever uses this bathroom before lunch.

Correction: no one *except me* ever uses this bathroom before lunch.

So I am beyond shocked when I exit the far-*right* stall to see one Alexandra Miles touching up her mascara in the mirror over the sink.

"Hi, Sloane," she says, like this is an everyday occurrence. "You feeling okay? Sounds like you're . . . a little sick."

"Just getting over a stomach bug," I lie.

She nods sympathetically. "I'm glad I ran into you. I've been meaning to talk to you about Key Club."

I do not want to have a conversation about Key Club. I want to brush my teeth. But I also do not want to brush my teeth in front of Alexandra. So I say, "What about Key Club?"

"I'd like you to take on more of a leadership role," she says, turning back to the mirror and her mascara.

"In what sense?" I ask, trying to mask my surprise.

"Well," she says, "I feel like we've been a little . . . scattered. The club's doing too much, don't you think? If we cut back on new activities, we could focus our energy on existing projects. Strengthening them. Making them better." She screws the cap back on the tube and swaps it out for a lip gloss that I know for a fact costs more than fifteen dollars a pop. Whereas the "gloss" I use is a mentholated ChapStick knockoff I picked up for fifty cents.

"Do you agree?"

I answer yes, even though I know she wasn't really asking a question. What Alexandra wants, Alexandra gets.

"How can I help?" I say. No sense tiptoeing around the fact that she's about to issue an order.

She pats some lip gloss on with her pinkie finger before replying, "What if you put forth a motion at today's meeting to table all new business until after, I don't know, Homecoming?"

And there we have it. Alexandra's true motive: refocusing her *own* attention on a bid for Homecoming Queen. It's a lot of wasted energy, if you ask me. We all know there won't be any other viable contenders. Especially not after the way Matt Leitch publicly declared his love for her yesterday afternoon.

If I had a boyfriend like Matt, he'd be all I need.

And yet—

"You'll have my full support," Alexandra continues. "*If* you decide to make that motion, that is."

Translation: *do this or incur my wrath.* Since I don't really care either way I shrug. "Sure. I'll do it today."

"Excellent! Maybe then I'll have more time to run lines with you!"

So. She *has* been getting my emails.

"Great," I tell her, because what else is there to say?

Alexandra moves toward the door. *Finally.* There's a sour burn in my mouth I need to get rid of before homeroom. I start to reach in my satchel for my toothbrush when she turns around and says, "You might want to be careful, Sloane. I've heard that 'stomach bugs' can damage your vocal cords over time."

Bitch, I think as she exits stage left.

Thank God there's only eight months until graduation. Then I'll be rid of Alexandra and this podunk town forever.

NINE

Alexandra

There's an undercurrent of energy flowing through the halls of Spencer High.

I don't like it. Or, should I say, I don't like *her*.

Erin Hewett. She's all anyone can seem to talk about today. *Have you met the new girl? She's so incredibly nice! She's from San Diego, can you believe it?* As if growing up in California was some sort of personal accomplishment, and not just a fact of geography.

As the day progresses, more details emerge about Erin. She knows how to surf. She's spent the past two summers as a lifeguard. She once dated a swimmer who won two gold medals in the Junior Olympics.

"Is she an actual person," I seethe, "or will the next thing I hear be that she's really a mermaid who made a deal with an evil octopus for some human legs?"

Sam laughs quietly at my kind of joke.

When she's not submerged in water, Samantha informs me at lunch, Erin is, apparently . . . nice. She's a Nice Girl. People seem to genuinely like her.

"For now," I say. "Once that shiny, New Girl smell wears off, she'll be no different than Taylor Flynn or Alyssa Fields or any of the other wannabes of absolutely no consequence."

"Maybe," Sam says, unpacking her lunch bag in her slow, methodical way. "But then again, maybe not."

There's something she's not telling me. I know this because she's taking an extra-long time to arrange the components of her meal.

Sam does this thing where she assesses her food and places it in order of consumption, eating the things she likes least first and saving the things she likes best for last. Sometimes, when she's torn between where to place two things—in this case, a plastic sandwich bag of baby carrots and a green apple—she'll move them around a few times. The apple emerges ahead of the carrots, but lingers behind a foil pack of Oreos her mother has included as a treat.

I stab a fork into my sad, wilted salad and say, "Spill it, Sam."

She nods. "It's probably nothing. A rumor, maybe."

"Rumors can seem like truths to the less intelligent," I say.

Sam takes a deep, dramatic breath. "Okay. So, the school Erin transferred here from—Poway High—their Homecoming is in the beginning of October, about three weeks earlier than ours. Actually, they do *everything* about three weeks earlier than we do, including going back to school. I confirmed this with Google."

I stare at her, silent.

"Anyway," she continues, "because they're so far ahead of us, they'd already announced the Homecoming court before Erin moved away."

I stop. "And she was on it?"

"This is what I heard from Hayley Langer," Sam says, "whose cousin lives, like, one school district south. Crazy, right? But I can't confirm that part with Google."

Across the room, at a table smack in the center, I see Little Miss Sunshine herself, giggling with Hayley and her gaggle of girly-girls. Even though they aren't technically sitting with any guys, all the hetero boys at the surrounding tables keep sneaking peeks at her.

But that's *all* they do—take a quick, curious look. They're not lingering. She's not hot enough for that. It's a shame, really. A hot chick would be easier to take down, because head-turning hotness would piss off Spencer's female population in a major way.

But nice? Cute? These things aren't threatening to them.

They're threatening to *me*.

"Rumor or not, we need to shut this kind of chatter down," I say. "Now."

Matt and I are lingering outside of Mr. Banerjee's classroom when I see Erin approaching from afar. Instinctively, I pull Matt a little closer. *Mine.*

My boyfriend is whispering something in my ear when Erin reaches the doorway. She stops, turns to the left, and looks straight at us. It's weird.

I'm about to introduce her when she says, "Matt? I thought that was you."

I fight the frown on my face as Matt responds, "Yo, Erin. How's it going?"

"Good," she says. "Everyone here is *so* nice."

There is a clog of students building up behind Erin, but not a single one of them complains about how she's blocking the doorway. What is *happening* around here?

"Oh my gosh!" Erin exclaims. "I'm totally holding up traffic. I'll see you later!"

She disappears inside the classroom without once acknowledging me directly.

When Erin is fully out of earshot, I give Matt an artificially playful poke to the ribs. "How do you know the New Girl?" I ask.

He shrugs. "She's a cheerleader."

"She got here, like, five minutes ago."

"Babe, we practice on the same field," he says, grinning. "But keep talking. Jealousy looks adorable on you."

"Jealousy? You wish."

Matt's expression—a mixture of rom-com mooniness and bald lust—tells me that he either doesn't believe me or he's too busy picturing me naked. He leans in for a kiss. I duck.

"I have to go," I say, peeling myself off the wall and out from under Matt's muscled chest.

He gives me a pouty face. "No kiss?"

"Later," I say. "*If* you're a good boy."

His smile is real, and it is blinding.

Sometimes I wish I actually felt something for Matt. But love requires far more energy than I'm willing to allow.

In addition to English, Erin also has AP Physics with me and Sam. Before the bell rings, I watch her work the room. And make no mistake—that's exactly what she's doing. She even exchanges a few words with Ivy Proctor, who looks nearly cheerful for a change.

Nobody talks to Ivy anymore. Not really.

A little background: Ivy Proctor used to be a minor-league somebody. Granted, this was back in the fourth grade, when popularity required little more than wearing the right clothes, throwing a decent slumber party once in a while, and not being fat. But then something changed, and slowly but surely, Ivy faded into the background.

Until sophomore year, that is, when she went full-on psycho in biology. One minute, we're sitting at our desks, listening to Mr. Barksdale drone on and on about primordial ooze; the next, Ivy leaps up from her desk, lets out a bone-chilling scream, and punches her fist through a window. Everyone was pin-drop silent for about five seconds before all hell broke loose.

It was terrifying. Girls were screaming and crying, boys were cursing and yelling. Barksdale was the worst, though. He didn't go to Ivy. He didn't even call for help. He just stood there, gawping, his jaw practically scraping the floor.

And in the center of it, Ivy stood, still as a statue, staring at her shredded hand. The blood gushed down her arm and formed a dark red pool at her feet. There was blood everywhere, actually, including spatters on Ivy's pale cheeks. An unforgettable spectacle of epic proportions.

The girl didn't shed a tear. Not a single one.

Finally, Wes Fetterolf ran out for help. Barksdale woke up from his temporary coma and ushered all of us out of the classroom and down the hall to the library, leaving Ivy alone until a scared-shitless Mrs. Martindale, the school nurse, was summoned to the scene. We heard the ambulance arrive and crowded around windows trying to catch a glimpse of Ivy being carried out on a stretcher.

And that was the last anyone saw of Ivy Proctor for the next sixth months, even though people didn't stop talking about what happened in all that time. Ivy's mid-year meltdown rocked our entire community; it even made the front page of the *Herald-Gazette*. Things like that just don't happen in the sleepy town of Spencer, Indiana.

Losing her sanity restored Ivy Proctor's popularity, but in the worst possible way: everyone speculated over what happened, why it happened, and where Ivy ended up after it happened.

When she returned to Spencer for the start of junior year, she only made it through two and a half days before withdrawing for the second time. It was too much pressure, I suppose, to withstand that kind of spotlight. She didn't transfer either. Rumor has it her mother homeschooled her.

No one knows why Ivy decided to come back again now—or what in the world possessed her to start dressing like an uglier version of Wednesday Addams. You'd think someone who wanted to blend into the background would sport far less eyeliner and wear a little color.

Regardless, this time people aren't asking her any questions, or even making rude comments. They just steer clear. She may be a psycho, but the sad, haunted look in her oversize watery blue eyes keeps the student population of Spencer High on their best behavior. They're not antagonizing Ivy; they're pretending, as much as possible, that she's not there.

Instead of paying attention to what's going on with parabolas and projectile motion, I spend the period replaying the Erin Hewett Highlights Reel in my head. The only way anyone would've learned about Erin's previous Homecoming court appointment would be from Erin herself. It's not the sort of thing that naturally comes up in conversation, either. Not within twenty-four hours of enrolling in a new school.

No, people heard about that because Erin *wanted* us to. Given that information, I don't care how nice everyone else seems to think she is. I know the truth.

Erin Hewett is making a bid for Homecoming Queen, and she'll do whatever it takes to win it.

I know, because she's using *my* playbook.

I turn to Sam, who of course is watching me watch Erin. "Whatever it takes," I mouth.

She nods. *Message received.*

TEN

Sloane

Key Club meetings start at 3:45 p.m. Fact: Alexandra always, always walks in at 3:44 p.m. on the dot. You could set your watch to it.

Except today. Today is the first time in the history of Key Club (or, at least, the length of time I've been a member) that Her Highness strolls in two minutes late. "Apologies," she says breezily. "I had an important matter to attend to."

Her tone doesn't match the sharpness of her eagle eyes, which scan the room with expert precision. For whatever reason, she isn't liking what she sees. Her resting bitch-face frown deepens slightly. But when her eyes land on me, it's replaced with a smile.

Did everyone forget to tell me it was Opposite Day?

Alexandra calls the meeting to order, even though our advisor, Mr. Vick, hasn't arrived yet. He takes a thirty-minute smoke break at the end of the day that may or may not include illegal substances, depending on whom you ask. It's just as well. He's kind of a letch, and leers at any girl who dares to show leg.

P.S.: the only one of us who wears a skirt on Key Club day is

Alexandra. If anything, being around Mr. Vick causes her hemlines to *shrink*.

After I take attendance, Alexandra asks *me* if *I* want to lead the Key Club pledge. There's an audible gasp of surprise from Hayley Langer.

"Sure," I say, feeling even more confused. I even mess up part of the pledge, saying "to serve one nation under God" instead of "to serve my nation and God."

Hayley giggles. I steel myself for Alexandra's anger, but instead she smiles at me and nods approvingly.

I am both relieved and horrified—and simultaneously ashamed by my relief and horror. Why the hell should I care about Alexandra Miles's opinion of me?

I think it has something to do with her freakishly strong magnetism. She's like the sun. You never really stop wanting to feel that warm, buttery light on your face. Even if you've been burned by it on more than one occasion, as I have.

Alexandra likes to start each meeting with a motivational quote. Today's gem is "You can do anything, but you can't do everything." This, I'm guessing, is to set me up for the motion she wants me to make. I should feel like a puppet on a string, but again: she's the sun.

And I am an idiot.

Mr. Vick wanders in as Alexandra goes over old business from our last meeting. He gives her the up-down, letting his eyes rest on the side of her ass just a little too long. Or, at least, long enough for Alexandra to tug her skirt down half an inch. Then he retires to the corner, where he pretends to read the newspaper—the kind with actual pages—but really keeps stealing glances at all of the underage females in the room.

I take the minutes as the meeting progresses, but keep missing little things since I'm not paying full attention. It doesn't matter; Alexandra edits them every week anyway. I'm trying to work out in my head why her polarity has suddenly flipped in my favor—is it only because she wants me to do this thing, or is there something more?—when she calls for new business.

"I have some," I say, raising my hand. Hayley gasps again. And people say *I'm* the drama queen.

"I've been thinking about the quote Alexandra shared at the beginning of the meeting," I begin. "It's so *true*. If you're trying to do everything, you're not doing any of them very well, because your efforts are diluted. I feel like . . ." Here, I pause for effect, pursing my lips as if I'm searching for the perfect words. "I feel like maybe we—as in, the Key Club—should think about scaling back some of our efforts, so that we're not so . . . scattered."

Alexandra once again nods approvingly, and flashes me a smile. It's like a shot of adrenaline, this her-liking-me thing.

I kind of hate myself for it. Especially after everything that went down sophomore year.

"If we cut back on new activities," I continue, "we could focus our energy on existing projects. Strengthening them. Making them better."

"I couldn't have said it better myself," Alexandra adds.

Maybe that's because I used your exact *words.*

"Is that a motion?" she asks.

"Right," I say. "Yes. I'm putting forth a motion to table all new business until January."

She frowns slightly. I know I've overshot her request, but if I say "until after Homecoming" they'll all know she was the one who put me up to this.

"I second!" Susan Apple rings out. "It'll be a nice breather while I'm working on college apps." The other seniors nod their heads in agreement.

"Okay then," Alexandra says, her voice tight but even. "All in favor?"

It's unanimous. After the meeting is adjourned, Susan comes up to me and says, "Thanks for doing that, Sloane. It really will be a huge help." And then Hayley sidles over and says, "Nice job, Fahey. You got more moxie than I gave you credit for."

I marvel at the irony. By doing exactly what Alexandra wanted me to, people think I've challenged her again.

And they're loving me for it.

Drama Queen: 1, Beauty Queen: 0.

ELEVEN

Alexandra

I watch Sloane Fahey pick up a few popularity points post-meeting and fight the urge to put Little Miss Upchuck back in her place. What good would it do? In the grand scheme of things, she is nothing. She will always be nothing.

Then why does she irk me so fucking much?

And whatever happened to Erin Hewett? It annoys me that I went to so much trouble to shut her down and she didn't even bother to show. Where *is* she? Sam should have been on this. I check my phone. Nothing.

"I think that went well," Sloane says to me, like we're friends now. I offer a tight smile in response.

"What?" she says. "No 'thank you'?"

She's joking—I know this—but I'm not in the mood. "I have to go now."

"You mentioned us running lines . . . ?" Sloane reminds me, her voice almost hopeful.

I tell her I might have some time on Sunday and that I'll text her later if that's the case. Then I gather up my things and go. It's almost 4:15, Matt's picking me up for our anniversary dinner at 6:30, and I still have to track down Sam, who I sincerely hope is digging up some decent dirt on Erin, and scan YouTube to see if Matt's and my video is in circulation yet. If it goes viral it would not only ensure my place as Homecoming Queen, but also set me up nicely for my run at Miss Indiana next year.

My brain is so busy running through my mental to-do list that I almost miss it. Almost.

Principal Constance Frick and Erin motherfucking Hewett. *Hugging* in the faculty parking lot.

I stop dead in my tracks, not even caring if they see me watching.

Frick pulls away, and the two continue chatting. Erin is nodding a lot at whatever it is Frick has to say. I'm not close enough to hear or read their lips, but there's something awfully familiar about the way they interact. Erin turns as if to go, but not before Frick plants a quick kiss on the top of her head, like she was her grandmother or some gross thing like that.

Suddenly, I remember what Erin said on her first day, about having family in Indiana.

Is *Frick* her family? Principal Constance Frick, who's hated me since before she even met me, simply because I had the bad luck to be born to Natalie Miles?

Well, shit.

Things start to make a lot more sense. Like how Erin, who arrived out of nowhere, has shown me a complete lack of respect. If she is connected to Frick—and I can't think of any other reason why a high school principal would be hugging and kissing a brand-new student—then Frick could've hand-fed her any number of lies about me, or talked enough trash that Erin didn't feel the need to kiss my ring.

That's a mistake on her part.

Frick may be the principal, but *I* can make Erin Hewett's life at Spencer High intolerable. And there's no way Frick can protect her from that.

TWELVE

Sam

"I can't just *make* a video go viral," my brother, Wyatt, informs me Friday afternoon. "By the very definition, a video becomes viral because people feel compelled to share it. There's no way to manufacture that, though obviously frat boys and soft drink companies have been trying for years."

Patience, Samantha. Patience.

"Look," I tell him, "I'm not asking you for BuzzFeed-level anything. We just need to get it up and out there. I'm absolutely certain it will find its own audience. I just need you to—" Here I pause, and give him my best "I adore you, O brother of superior intelligence" smile. "I need you to be *you*, Wyatt. I know what you're capable of."

Wyatt frowns. Have I gone too far?

"I guess I don't understand why you even care," he says finally. "You hate that guy."

He's right. I do hate Matt.

"But I don't hate Lexi," I say.

"True." Wyatt snorts. "You're practically in love with her."

Now *he's* the one that's gone too far.

"She's my best friend," I say tightly. "Besides, *you're* the one who wanks off to her bikini pics."

Wyatt's cheeks turn bright red in less than three seconds. "I don't have time for this," he informs me, looking down at his keyboard. "I have to study for my SATs."

"That can wait. Lexi can't."

"And why's that?"

"Because on Monday, the nominations for Homecoming Queen open, and hers should be the only name on that ballot. Or, at least, the only name that matters."

He shakes his head. "But you know she's a solid."

"I *used* to know that. Before Erin Hewett arrived."

"That new girl?"

I nod.

"She's pretty cute."

"My point exactly."

Wyatt still looks unconvinced. It used to be easier to get him working on Lexi's behalf. When he was a freshman, she spent a week teaching him how to French-kiss. That currency lasted quite a while. Early last year, before she started dating Matt, she offered him lessons on how to get game. She even let him practice unhooking her bra a few times—looking, no touching, of course. But the longer she stays with Matt, the less pliable Wyatt becomes.

"They won't last forever, you know," I tell him. "He's not smart enough for her. But I know someone who is."

Wyatt rolls his eyes. Now he knows I'm reaching, but even so, the flattery works. "Fine," he says with a heavy sigh. "I'll do it. But get out of my room. Go make me a sandwich or something."

"Make it yourself, pig."

When I check my cell, I see there's a missed call from Lexi and a new voice mail. I listen to the message immediately.

"Erin Hewett and Frick," Lexi barks at me through the phone. "Find the connection."

Erin and Frick are somehow connected? Interesting.

Since Wyatt's handling the video, I retreat to my own room to investigate. I'm actually a little irritated that I wasn't the one to make this discovery in the first place. I rarely miss something so big.

I need to dig deeper.

At first, Erin Hewett's digital footprint doesn't reveal anything out of the ordinary. Her Facebook profile, which I'd just skimmed through yesterday, isn't locked down. Yet there's nothing remotely incriminating attached to her name. No drunken party pics, no untoward selfies, no shots of her making out with the Junior Olympics swimmer (or anyone else for that matter). Her status updates are kind of dull—"First day at the new school. The kids at Spencer High are awesome!"—but being boring isn't exactly a crime.

I switch off to Frick. Here's what I know about her:

- She's in her late fifties.
- She's spent her whole life in Spencer, Indiana, save for the four years she lived in Fort Wayne, getting her degree at IPFW. In fact, she was Lexi's mom's history teacher back in the day.
- She buys the majority of her clothes in the old-lady department of JCPenney.
- She doesn't have any kids (that we know of).
- She used to be married to Dave Bridgeton of Crazy Dave's Used Cars, but they went through a messy divorce a few years ago after he cheated on her (repeatedly, if rumors are to be believed).
- She can't stand Lexi. Seriously, she doesn't even try to hide it anymore.

I Google various combinations of the above names and locations. Nothing turns up. I find a couple of Yelp reviews from Frick, including one for a dry cleaner in Fort Wayne (who writes Yelp reviews for a *dry cleaner* anyway?), but nothing that ties her to Erin.

After twenty minutes of fruitless searches, I switch gears again. Maybe I'm coming at this from the wrong direction. Maybe I need to start at the end and work backward.

Like: how *could* they be connected? Is Erin Frick's long-lost daughter that she gave up for adoption? Unlikely, seeing as she would've been pregnant while she was in her early forties—something that wouldn't have gone unnoticed in our town.

Could Erin be the daughter of a child Frick gave up for adoption when she was in college? I quickly do the math. If Frick had a kid at, say, eighteen, and that kid had a kid at eighteen, it's possible that yes, Erin could be a grandchild.

Possible, but also unlikely.

What I want to do is call Lexi to see how she knows there's a connection in the first place. Details would be useful here. But if I call her, I'll only piss her off more. No, I need to produce results on my own. And fast.

Could Frick be Erin's *aunt*? Definitely possible. But how could I confirm that? Do I have to re-create the girl's entire family tree?

I'm struck suddenly by the thought that maybe I'm barking up the wrong branch of that tree. Maybe the connection between Erin and Frick comes courtesy of Crazy Dave.

Within minutes, I hit on something big. Crazy Dave's baby sister, Corrine, married a Gerald Hewett nearly nineteen years ago.

Bingo!

Four clicks later, I confirm it: Corrine and Gerald Hewett gave birth to one Erin Louise Hewett in Carlsbad, California, just shy of three years after they said "I do."

I take a breather from my laptop to check on Wyatt. He's playing some nerd game on his computer, the one where he's got to rescue little green spacemen before they blow up or something.

"I thought you were working on the YouTube thing?" I say.

"It's done," he informs me, never removing his eyes from the screen. "We're already up to four hundred views."

"Nice," I say, duly impressed.

"You owe me for this."

"Whatever."

I return to my room to confirm. Lexi's "Homecoming proposal" video is at 473 views and counting. In less than twenty minutes.

I don't know how Wyatt pulled this off. Then again, I don't want to know. Plausible deniability and all.

Lexi's going to be more than pleased. Hell, *I'm* pleased. I text her: *NG is F's niece (by marriage). Oh & you need to check YouTube. Someone uploaded a video of you & Matt this afternoon. Almost 500 views!*

Not bad for a Friday afternoon. Not bad at all.

THIRTEEN

Alexandra

By the time the first bell rings on Monday morning, Matt's and my YouTube video has more than 13,000 views.

I knew that boy was good for something.

Even better, everyone is talking about it. People whom I know for a fact weren't even in school that day are claiming they were there to witness his grand romantic gesture firsthand.

In homeroom, the Homecoming ballots are passed out. Technically, we are all nominating senior class princesses. Five princesses will be selected, and those will become the candidates for Homecoming Queen. The queen vote doesn't take place until the dance. The four runners-up get itty-bitty tiaras as their consolation prize.

I've never been a runner-up, and I don't intend to start now.

Even so, I do not write my name in the box for senior class princess. I never write my own name. In years past, I nominated Sam, and she nominated me, effectively canceling out each other's votes. It's an acceptable loss. There's just something so crass about writing your own name on that dotted line.

But this year's different. There's someone who needs my vote even more.

It took me hours to select the just-right outfit for today: ivory lace minidress over heather-gray tights and worn, reddish-brown boots, all tied together with a soft charcoal cardi and a fluffy, floral infinity scarf. It's a little bit soft, a little bit pretty, and a little bit sexy, without looking like I was trying to be any of those things. Do you have any idea how difficult it is to pull off a combination like that?

Natalie does. She was awake uncharacteristically early this morning, having one of her rare "up" days. As I headed out for school, I found her reorganizing the kitchen and guzzling black coffee out of an antique shaving mug that used to be my dad's. It makes my heart drop into my stomach, seeing her clutch that mug. She's never gotten rid of any of his stuff.

"Good call on wearing your hair down," she said, nodding approvingly. "You look warm. Approachable."

"That's what I was going for."

She set the shaving mug down and walked toward me. For a second, I almost flinched. But then my mother—in a move she hasn't made in more than a year—leaned in and kissed me on the cheek.

"Good luck today, honey," she said. "Not that you'll need it."

I hate how good that made me feel.

The absolute best part of today is this: I don't hear a single person mention Erin Hewett until AP English, when Mr. Banerjee says her name during roll call.

Like I told Sam before: it wouldn't take long for that shiny, New Girl smell to wear off. Matt's Homecoming proposal just helped get rid of it a little faster.

Frick won't post the Homecoming candidates for another forty minutes, so I don't know for certain that my thunder has completely drowned out the Erin Hewett Fan Club. But I'm sure I've silenced it enough to matter.

In Spanish, the clock hands move along at a glacial pace. Tick. Tock. Tick. Tock.

After what feels like an eternity, the final bell rings. Students pour out of the classroom, but I take my time packing up. I can't just run to the bulletin board outside of Frick's office. Better to have Sam do that and report back to me.

I go to my locker. I trade out the books I need for homework. I wait to get a text from Sam.

It doesn't come.

My pulse quickens. I'm not worried about making the ballot—I know my name will be on the list. But will hers? This is what I need to know.

I type a single question mark into iMessage and press send. Sam reads the message.

Still no response.

I'm about to head over to play rehearsal when I feel Matt's thick arms around my waist. He nuzzles my neck and gets a little side boob action with his forearm. "Congratulations, my future queen," he whispers into my ear.

I grin despite myself. "What about you?" I ask over my

shoulder. "Are you my future king?"

He presses closer. "You know it."

Matt spins me around and pins me against the locker, kissing me long and deep, with a hunger that's not entirely familiar. It's kind of hot, actually. *Too* hot. If Matt doesn't cool down soon, we're going to end up getting naked right here in the hallway.

"You might want to slow down," I say. "You've got practice. I've got rehearsal. This—whatever this is—has to wait."

"What if I don't want to wait?" he growls.

I'm tempted to pull him into the janitors' closet, but that directly conflicts with my personal rules of engagement. I'm actually debating whether or not I need to relax those rules when I hear the sharp bray of Frick: "That's enough, Miss Miles."

Matt pulls away a bit, but not entirely. "Sorry Ms. Frick," he says, and gives her one of his patented grins. "Guess I got a little carried away."

"This isn't behavior befitting a Homecoming Queen, now is it, Miss Miles?" she says, ignoring Matt entirely. "It'd be a real shame to have to disqualify you for conduct unbecoming."

I'm sure she'd be heartbroken.

"I have to go to rehearsal," I tell Matt. "We'll pick this up later." I cut my eyes away from his face and let them lock on Frick's. "When we're off school property."

"Hate to tell you, Miss Miles," Frick says, "but those rules of conduct apply off-campus, too." Her thin lips curl upward in what I think is supposed to be an evil smile. "You should ask your mother about that sometime."

She turns on her heel and walks away.

Sloane Fahey is on top of me the minute I enter the theater. "How about Friday?" she suggests. "We can just hang after Key Club."

I'm too irritated by Frick's comment about my mother to think of a valid reason why Friday won't work. "Fine," I say. "Friday. *Whatever.*"

Sloane looks taken aback by the sharpness in my voice. This only proves to irritate me more.

"Damn it, Sloane, I said yes!" I snap at her. "What more do you want from me?"

"Don't do me any favors," she huffs.

Ordinarily I wouldn't care—this is, after all, Sloane Fahey we're talking about. But it's poor form for me to act so bitchy the day the nominations are posted. I decide to toss her a bone.

"It's not you," I say, by way of an apology. "Frick just chewed me out in the hallway. I'm a little on edge."

"What did you do now?"

"Nothing. I was just talking to Matt."

Sloane snorts. "Yeah, I'm sure *that's* what you were doing."

"I'm sorry," I say, "but what I do with my *boyfriend* isn't really any of your concern, is it?"

She looks me straight in the eye and says, "Nothing you do is any of my concern, Alexandra."

So, the kitten has claws. Interesting.

"I'm going to chalk this up to good old-fashioned jealousy," I say in a tight, even tone. "Everyone knows you can't get a boyfriend to save your life. And honestly? I feel bad for you."

Her right eye begins to twitch. I've struck a nerve.

"But I would advise you to watch your tone with me," I continue. "Because we both know what happens when you cross that line."

We stand there, staring at each other, in a game of chicken. Finally, Sloane's gaze breaks away and she shakes her head slightly. "You think you're Teflon, don't you?"

"Excuse me?"

"Nothing ever sticks, right? You can do or say whatever you want, and you always walk away a winner. Well, guess what, Alexandra. You're about due for a takedown."

Where is this coming from? Even after everything that went down sophomore year, Sloane Fahey has kept her nose glued to my ass. This? This is new.

My amusement seems to irritate her even more.

"Someday somebody is going to make you regret how you treat people," she says.

"Oh, really? And who's that going to be? You?"

"Probably not," she says with a shrug. "Doesn't mean it won't happen."

Something about Sloane's words unnerves me. It's not like she wields any sort of social status at Spencer. And she's not someone I'd ever be threatened by, not in a million years.

Honestly, it's not even what she said, but *how* she said it. Like she's been harboring some deep-seated resentment toward me stretching back to the Jonah Dorsey scandal sophomore year. I mean, yes, that situation got really ugly. But Sloane never stopped clinging to my shadow. She never stopped trying to get me to be her friend again.

People like Sloane Fahey—who, let's face it, have little to lose—can become dangerous variables in a heartbeat. They're not easily controlled because their actions are far too erratic. On the other hand, a Sloane vying for my attention, trying to insinuate herself into my social stratosphere, is predictable. Pathetic, but predictable.

I'm going to need to keep my eye on her. There's just too much at stake.

FOURTEEN

Sam

This year's senior class princesses are (in alphabetical order):

- Ashley Chamberlain
- Erin Hewett
- Hayley Langer
- Alexandra Miles
- Ivy Proctor

The printout hangs on the bulletin board outside the main office. I stare at it in disbelief.

Lexi isn't going to like this.

Not one bit.

It's bad enough that Erin made the ballot, though I presume that was Frick's doing. I mean, the girl's been a student here for literally three days. People like her, sure, but Homecoming court? It's a stretch.

The real head-scratcher is *Ivy Proctor*. What is *that* about?

There are 327 kids in the senior class. So it's not like Ivy got that nomination on the basis of a couple of stray votes. At the very least, she had to have gotten a couple dozen. That's not an accident.

Twenty votes is a coordinated effort.

Lexi texts me a question mark. She's dying to know the results. I debate whether or not I should give them to her. If I tell her she's on the ballot, she's going to want to know who the competition is. And if I tell her *that* without having some good intel, all hell will break loose.

Think, Samantha. Think.

What I need is to know the number of votes that went to each candidate. Frick wouldn't have done the count herself, would she? That's what she has peons for.

Peons like Iris Testaverde.

Iris has been Frick's secretary for years, long before we were freshmen. She looks like a character from *Saturday Night Live*, all baby-blue eye shadow, loud floral prints, and augmented boobs bursting out from her blouse, even though she's a long way from the right side of forty. Her husband, Greg, owns this dinky Italian restaurant on the edge of town that's popular with the geriatric crowd. It keeps him pretty busy—or at least busy enough that he hasn't noticed his wife's banging the football coach behind his back.

To be fair, most people don't know about Iris and Coach Dawson. Lexi and I only found out after we convinced Wyatt to rig up a tiny spy camera in the main office. She was looking for some dirt on Frick, I think, but was just as shocked as I was to find some on Iris instead. Let's just say that girlfriend knows how to get her freak on. Wyatt threatened to burn out his own corneas just to try to unsee the footage.

Iris doesn't know about the tape. She doesn't even know that we know about her affair with Coach.

It's a handy card to have, and one we haven't played . . . yet.

I can't think of a better time to pull it out.

My plan is simple: I'll wait until Iris clocks out for the day, and then follow her to her car. There will be fewer witnesses that way. Less chance of someone overhearing.

At four on the dot, Iris exits the main office and heads out the front doors. I shadow her to the faculty lot. She's fumbling for her keys when I call out, "Excuse me, Mrs. Testaverde?"

Iris jumps about ten feet high, then whips around to face me. "Good Lord in heaven, child. You scared me half to death!"

"Oops," I say. "Sorry."

"Well, what do you need, Samantha?" Iris asks. "There's a turkey breast in my Crock-Pot waiting for me to tend to it."

"I'm glad you asked," I say. "I have some . . . questions . . . about the Homecoming ballots."

Iris arches an eyebrow. "What kinds of questions?"

I bite my bottom lip and look down at my feet, like I'm really struggling.

"Well?" she prods. "What is it?"

I let out a slow, measured sigh. "I'm a little . . . *concerned* . . . about the nominees for senior class princess."

She snorts. "You're not the only one."

"Oh?"

Iris looks around the parking lot. There's no one in the immediate vicinity. She steps closer to me and leans in. "That poor Proctor girl. Hasn't she been through enough?"

"My thoughts exactly," I say. "How many votes did she get, anyway?"

"Enough. More than enough, actually."

"More than Erin Hewett?"

Iris purses her lips so tightly together that they form a thin, magenta line. "I've already said too much, Samantha. I really need to be going."

She turns back toward her car, and I blurt out, "Erin didn't have the votes, did she?"

No reply.

"Is it the turkey breast you're running off to, or is it Coach Dawson?"

I cringe even as I say the words.

Iris's cheeks are brick red, and her eyes are burning craters into my face. "She had . . . votes."

"But not enough to get on the ballot."

"Let me repeat: She. Had. Votes."

"Where are the forms? The ones we filled out this morning."

"In the recycling bin."

"Your office?"

Her eyes narrow into thin slits. "If your mother only knew what a snake you were . . ." she says, her voice trailing off.

"She'd be proud," I say quietly.

Iris continues to try to burn holes through me with her angry stare.

"I need those ballots, Mrs. Testaverde. We should probably go get them now. If you hurry, you can still make it back to your turkey breast on time."

There are nearly eight hundred half sheets of copy paper spread across every available surface in my room. I have them divided by grade, which isn't difficult since Iris ran the ballots off on different colors for each class. Freshmen are pink, sophomores are blue, juniors are green, and seniors are goldenrod. Even though I'm really only interested in what's going on with our class, I have meticulously sorted the ballots for each of the grade levels. I don't want to miss a single thing.

I'm sitting on the floor, using my bed as a seat back, with the senior class ballots fanned out around me. It doesn't matter how many times I recount them (six, for the record), the results are always the same:

Ashley Chamberlain: 27

Erin Hewett: 11

Hayley Langer: 31

Alexandra Miles: 89

Ivy Proctor: 23

There are one- and two-off votes for various other seniors, celebrities (JLaw, really?), and rando made-up names like Butterface McGee—a total of twenty-one. That leaves nine classmates' votes unaccounted for. I'd have to get Wyatt to hack into the school's system to verify the number of absences from today, but it's a reasonable enough number that I don't feel like going to the effort.

The good news is that Lexi's ahead by a clean enough margin that she *should* have this Homecoming race locked up.

The bad news is that I am utterly clueless as to who's behind the twenty-three Ivy Proctor votes. The fact that she earned almost as many as Ashley did confirms my initial suspicions: this is a coordinated effort. But who orchestrated it?

And here's an even better question: *Why?*

I've been ignoring texts from Lexi all afternoon, and I can tell she's starting to get pissed. My phone dings again. *I'm coming over.*

Perfect, just . . . perfect.

I don't even bother to tell her not to; I've put her off long enough. All I can do is prepare my mother for Lexi's impending arrival. She won't be happy either.

I stand up, careful not to disturb my piles of paper, and step over them. There's a circle of blank carpet marking where I was sitting. At least she'll see how hard I've been working.

FIFTEEN

Alexandra

Sam's frumpy mother frowns at me from across the room. She is always frowning at me. Even when she smiles at me, it's really a frown wearing a smile's costume.

It's fairly safe to say Jessica Schnitt doesn't like me.

That feeling is mutual.

Even though I'm one of Jessica's least-favorite people in the state of Indiana, if not the entire world, the woman insists on feeding me every time I come over. My guess is that she wants to make all of the thin people she knows fat like her. Natalie would absolutely die if she saw the things I am forced to eat at the Schnitts'. Homemade macaroni and cheese. Deep-fried chicken tenders. Twice-baked potatoes smothered in some sort of creamy sauce. It's enough to make a girl go Sloane Fahey once in a while.

When the torture that is a Schnitt family dinner is over—in addition to the caloric-laden fare, I must also contend with Wyatt's sad attempts to both flirt with and impress me—Sam and I head up to her room. My thus-far pasted-on smile melts away when I see the piles of "evidence" strewn across her beige carpeting.

"What *is* this?" I demand.

She fills me in on her afternoon activities. I manage to control my rage, but only just barely.

"You traded in the sex tape for . . . *this*?" I seethe. "Without even asking me?"

Clearly, this isn't the reaction she was expecting. "Not the tape," she says. "Just the affair part. This Ivy thing—it had to be a coordinated effort, right?"

"So?"

"So I was trying to figure out who. And why."

I shake my head. I cannot remember a time when I have been more disappointed in Sam. I need to tack in a different direction.

"It was me, stupid," I hiss at her. "*I* am behind Ivy's nomination."

Sam stands there, her mouth forming a cartoon O. "But *why*?" she says finally. "Why would you *do* that?"

"Isn't it obvious?"

She doesn't respond.

"She's my insurance policy," I say. "My secret weapon."

Sam shakes her head. "I still don't get it."

"Look," I say, "no one *hates* Ivy. They pity her. And now that she's up for Homecoming Queen, they'll be talking about *her*, not that New Girl."

"Oh. I guess that makes sense."

This is not the entirety of my backup plan, of course. But Sam doesn't need to know about the rest. Not yet, anyway.

"So why didn't you tell me?" Sam asks, a wounded look on her face. "I would've taken care of it."

It's adorable, how sincerely she believes that she alone could have convinced a significant portion of Spencer High's student body to vote a bona fide pariah into Homecoming contention. And do it without arousing anyone's suspicions or generating untoward gossip that could blow back on me.

"I needed to keep your hands clean," I tell her.

She nods, but I can tell she's not buying it. Her job is typically keeping my hands clean, not the other way around.

"Can we focus on what's really important here?" I say. "Erin Hewett and her eleven votes."

"That's a good thing, right? I mean, she barely made the ballot."

I fight the urge to roll my eyes. "She got eleven votes after being in my school for all of *two days*. There's no telling where she'll stand in the polls a week from now."

There's no doubt in my mind that Erin Hewett is a threat that needs to be neutralized. I won't have her waltzing in here at the eleventh hour and stealing Homecoming right out from under me.

"It's time to focus, Samantha. We've got a crown to win."

I decide to take a drive after I leave Sam's. I need to think. Plus, I want to blow off some steam before I head home to Natalie. I could find her at home, still flying around, or she could've crashed . . . hard. I have no idea what I'll be walking into.

I knew there was a possibility that Erin Hewett could end up a candidate for Homecoming Queen. A new student from coastal California is exactly the kind of shiny object that would attract the attention of my classmates. But eleven votes? In *two* days?

Is it possible that some of the ballots were faked? I play out the scenario in my head. Frick is Erin's aunt. Frick hates me. Frick would do anything to take me down.

There is no doubt in my mind that Frick is twisted enough to try to manipulate this election in her niece's favor. Especially if it means delivering a blow to my undefeated record.

As for Erin herself—if she was, as she informed so many of our classmates, a candidate for Homecoming Queen in her old school, it's *possible* that she's hungry enough for the win to do whatever Aunt Fricky tells her.

Winston Churchill said, "Victory at all costs, victory in spite of all terror, victory, however long and hard the road may be; for without victory, there is no survival."

Is that what Erin is doing? Ensuring her social survival at Spencer?

I can't take the chance of being eclipsed by the New Girl. Not when so much is already on the line.

Goddamn that Erin Hewett! Everything had been going according to plan until *she* showed up. Now, suddenly, there are all of these unknown variables.

I don't like it, not one bit.

I feel so agitated that I decide to try the deep breathing

exercise I learned from the headshrinker I saw after my father died. Breathe in through the nose for four seconds, hold for three, exhale slowly through the mouth for five. *Four, three, five. Four, three, five.*

The headshrinker was a waste, but the deep breathing thing actually works. I can literally feel the tension start to drain from my body. Time to go home, take a hot shower, and butter my body with that coconut-scented stuff that makes Matt want to devour me. Maybe I'll call him to see if I can come over. Maybe his hotness is the cure to all that ails me.

That's when I realize where I am.

The corner of Lakeside and Lafayette.

No. No no no no no *no*—

I don't want to be here. It makes me think about *him*. About what happened to him.

I don't want to think about that. Not today. Not ever.

I make the left onto Lafayette, then a sharp right onto Baker Street. Only, I take the turn too fast and end up scraping the curb. There's a loud thunk, followed by a hiss—or maybe the hiss is only in my head. All I know is that thirty seconds later, the check tire gauge comes on, indicating a flat.

"Son of a bitch!" I smack the steering wheel with the palm of my hand and end up banging my wrist too hard. The pain is surprisingly sharp. That's definitely going to leave a bruise.

The breakdown lane is too narrow for my liking, but I don't want to risk further damage. I ease over, throw the hazard lights on, and get out of the car to inspect the tire. It's bad. Not only do I have a full-on flat, but I've also managed to rip the rim to shreds.

This is what happens when you allow for distraction. You crash. You burn. And you don't have anyone to blame but yourself.

I'm going to have to call for help. Who's it going to be? Uncle Douglas or Matt? Doug will tell me to call AAA. Matt will come and change the tire himself.

I choose Matt. I don't love playing a damsel in distress, but I hate breaking a nail even more.

I'm fishing around for my phone when a timid voice addresses me by my full name: "Alexandra Miles?"

I look up, startled to see none other than *Ivy Proctor* standing before me.

Seriously, what are the odds?

But there she is, in the flesh. Everyone's favorite head case and my potential new BFF. She is out and about, walking what appears to be the world's ugliest, slobbery-est dog on the planet. Although, to be honest, the beefy mutt looks more like he's walking her.

"Are you okay?" she asks me.

"What do *you* think?" I say, a little too sharply. My tone causes Ivy to recoil visibly. I shake my head as if to clear the cobwebs. "No. No, I didn't mean . . . I'm so sorry," I say. "I didn't mean to snap at you. I'm just . . . rattled."

Beefy strains at his leash, crying and slobbering all over the sidewalk. "Butcher, settle down," Ivy commands in a stern voice.

It's the most confident she's sounded in years. Remarkably, the mutt listens.

"You should call your mom," she says to me.

I stifle a snort. As if *Natalie* could do anything to help in a crisis. And if I told her why I'd swerved off the road, she would have had to go back to bed for three days. She never talks about my father's accident. Ever.

"I can wait with you until she comes," she adds. "If you want."

"Actually," I say, "I was going to call my boyfriend. But, uh, my phone is dead. Can I borrow yours?"

She shakes her head. "I left it at home."

I cannot believe the incredible luck of this chance encounter. It's like I scripted it myself.

"Is your house nearby?"

"Yeah. About a block and a half from here."

"Let me grab my purse. Then I can follow you over. If that's okay."

"Um . . . sure?" she says, sounding anything but.

Ivy walks briskly, probably to keep "Butcher" from choking himself to death.

"Cute dog," I murmur. "What kind is he?"

"A mutt," she says. "Rescue from the pound."

"That's amazing. I really admire people who save animals."

Am I laying it on too thick? Ivy's walking slightly faster than I am and it's too dark for me to register her facial expressions.

"It's just one dog," she says dismissively.

"How long have you had him?"

"A little over two years."

It doesn't take a genius to do the math, but even so, Ivy spells it out for me.

"He was part of my therapy," she explains. "After my breakdown."

"Oh," I say.

"The psychologist I was seeing—the one I still see, actually—she thought it would give me perspective if I had to care for someone outside of myself. So my parents took me to the pound to pick out a dog. Butcher was, like, the biggest, ugliest, most pathetic one there. So, you know, I totally had to take him home with me."

She adds, "I don't know why I'm telling you all this."

I don't either, but I'm not complaining.

"It's okay," I say, touching her elbow. "We were all really . . . worried . . . when that happened. A lot of people care about you, Ivy. Myself included."

Ivy snorts. She actually *snorts*.

"If they do, they have a funny way of showing it," she says. The bitterness in her voice startles me. "People can't even look at me, let alone talk to me."

"I'm talking to you," I point out.

"Because you need my phone," she says.

I stop short. It takes Ivy a few beats to realize I've stopped walking. When she does, she turns to face me.

"Everything okay?" she asks.

"No," I say in an artificially quiet voice. "It . . . it hurts me that you feel like that. I think—and honestly, I can only speak for myself here—but I think a lot of kids just weren't sure what to say to you. It was scary, you know? But it never meant that we didn't *care*."

Ivy looks at me—like, really looks at me, like she's trying to drill down into my soul—and for a second I think she doesn't buy a word of what I said. Her grip on Butcher's leash tightens as he strains to move forward.

Finally, after an extended, uncomfortable silence, Ivy says, "I never thought of it like that. I'm sorry if I hurt your feelings."

I have to hide my smirk. I have her, hook, line, and sinker.

The students of Spencer High have spent the past two and a half years treating Ivy Proctor like a total pariah, as if they might catch the crazies just by talking to her. And here she is, apologizing to *me*, for hurting *my* feelings.

I am fucking brilliant.

For a split second, I question whether or not I should go through with my backup plan. After all, I do have compassion, and poor Ivy has already struggled with so much for so long.

Then again, I'm not the one who made Ivy crazy in the first place. What responsibility do I have to her, really?

I have a Homecoming race to win. And in the fight between Erin Hewett and me, I must—I *will*—prevail. Ivy has a part to play, and if she does it perfectly, I'll find a way to reward her later.

After I get my crown.

SIXTEEN

Sloane

In the 2004 teen movie *Mean Girls*, a voluptuous redhead schemes to take down the bitchy leader of the Plastics, a group of popular girls that terrorize their classmates. That redhead's name is Cady Heron, and she is played with exquisite perfection by Lindsay Lohan (you know, before she became a total trainwreck). Cady is systematic in how she dismantles Regina George, the lead Plastic, by making her fat, turning her friends against her, and stealing her super-hot boyfriend. Eventually, Cady becomes the new Regina and wins Spring Fling Queen, while Regina just gets hit by a bus.

Alexandra Miles is the Regina George of Spencer High School, but a thousand times worse. Because at least Regina was unapologetically, unabashedly bitchy. She didn't try to camouflage her evil under a veneer of sweet or nice, unlike *some* people I know.

So now I am rewatching *Mean Girls* for, like, the fortieth time. Only this time, I am taking notes.

My goal: to destroy Alexandra Miles.

It's true; I'm about to go full-Cady on her skinny little pageant ass. And I don't feel the least bit guilty about it, either.

Because fact: Alexandra Miles thinks she can get away with anything. Lying to people. Manipulating them into doing things for her own personal gain. Crushing anyone who gets in her way.

I should know. She's done it to me on more than one occasion.

But Sloane, you may ask, weren't you *just* comparing her to the freaking sun? Why, yes. Yes, I was.

That is her superpower, you see. It doesn't matter how mean this particular mean girl gets; you never stop wanting her to like you.

My mother says that everyone has had at least one Alexandra Miles in their life. Hers, she confessed, was named Angela Wayne. Angela wasn't the prettiest girl in her class, or the smartest, or even the most popular. She was bossy, and prickly, and could turn on you in an instant—and often did.

"But when she didn't," my mother told me, "you felt like the most important person in the world. Making her laugh was an *achievement*. Earning an invite to sleep over at her house was akin to winning a major award."

My mom says her friendship with Angela Wayne ended in an epic fashion, at a school dance.

"Angela kept telling me I should dance with her ex-boyfriend," she said. "He was a cutie—I can't remember his name to save my life, but I remember that face like it was yesterday. Anyway, I didn't want to, because I knew she'd be mad. Only, she kept goading me about it.

"So, finally, I agreed to dance with him. And then we danced some more. And then, out of nowhere, he leaned in and kissed me. Angela saw—Jesus, she was angry! She started screaming at me, saying friends didn't try to hook up with their friends' exes. It was awful. All of our mutual friends took her side, too, even though I didn't do anything wrong. I just did what she told me to do. Like I always did."

Before you start thinking my mom is some total loser, think. Really think. Who's your Angela? Your Alexandra? Because I know you have one.

There was a time, if you can believe it, that Alexandra and I were sort of friends. This was in middle school, before she was the Alexandra Miles that we all know today. Before she sprouted the rack that would catapult her into the upper echelon of our class.

And okay: her boobs, while admirable, aren't the true source of her power. I know this.

She's a schemer, Alexandra. She schemes her way into getting *everything*.

She even snagged the volunteer gig I wanted at Hoffman County Library. When I called to follow up on it, Mrs. Brook-over told me that the position had gone to someone else. But, she said, she hoped that things were getting better at home, and that I could find some peace. I had no idea what she was talking about . . . until I asked her who did get the job.

So now *she's* the one running a kids' story time program. I would've been great at that. I would've picked really cool books and done voices and everything. Whereas Alexandra probably just wants to steal the souls from their innocent little bodies. Or, you know, pad her already overstuffed résumé.

Here's the other thing: even though I can't prove that Alexandra's the one who spread all of those rumors about me and Jonah Dorsey sophomore year, she's the most likely suspect.

I will not dwell on the past, though. I need to focus on the future.

In *Mean Girls*, Cady enlists the help of her friends Janis and Damian. Well, actually, Janis and Damian are the ones who convince Cady to take Regina down in the first place. But then they help her execute her plans. I don't have friends, really (oh, shut up). But I have something better—potential allies.

Like that new girl, who could possibly be the only person to ever truly threaten Alexandra in a Homecoming race.

Or maybe Samantha Schnitt, who's spent the majority of her life trailing A. with her mouth hanging open, hoping for a pat on the head?

I am going to make Erin Hewett be my Janis. Or is she the Cady and I'm the Janis? Maybe Sam is Damian? It doesn't matter.

Alexandra has taken everything I've ever wanted. Now I'm finally going to take a few choice things from her—like that smug-ass look on her face, for one. And maybe that muscle-y boyfriend, too, just for symmetry's sake.

I don't know exactly how I'm going to achieve this.

All I know is that Alexandra Miles is going down.

SEVENTEEN

Alexandra

It's only been a day since nominations were announced, and the buzz on Erin is already building serious momentum. This, despite the surprising inclusion of Ivy Proctor on this year's ballot. Keep in mind that most people aren't privy to the exact number of votes each of us got. No, to the students of Spencer High, the five of us are starting on equal footing.

I don't need a flash poll to tell me what I already know: it's quite possible that Erin Hewett will threaten everything. I was smart to build in a backup plan; now it's time to put it into action.

Tuesday, after final bell, I slip out of the side entrance and cut across to the student lot. Sam is stationed outside of the front of the building so that she can alert me when Ivy has left. I have a very small window in which to intercept Ivy before she boards her bus, so the choreography here is crucial.

I've just started the car when I get Sam's text: *GO TIME*. I peel out of the lot and squeal around the corner. Sam is saying something to Ivy. At least she had the good sense to stall her.

I beep the horn twice as I pull up to the curb. Both Sam and Ivy turn in my direction and I offer up a friendly wave. Ivy just blinks at me. I realize almost too late that she probably thinks I'm waving at Sam.

I roll down the passenger-side window and call out Ivy's name. She pokes a finger at her own chest—the sitcom equivalent of "Who, *me*?"

Smiling, I nod my head profusely and wave her over.

Ivy is half frowning as she walks down to meet me. She bends so that her face is framed in the open window. "Hey," she says. Such a conversationalist, this one.

"I just wanted to thank you again for last night," I say. "You really helped me out. I was hoping I could offer you a ride home."

"You don't have to do that."

"I know I don't *have* to," I say. "Hop in. It'll give us a chance to talk."

Ivy hesitates. It takes a lot of effort to mask my annoyance. I had to skip an *Evita* rehearsal just to take her home, which meant lying to Mrs. Mays about having an appointment to get my flu shot. The longer I stay here, the greater the possibility one of my castmates will spot me and say something to Mays. Like Sloane.

"Come on," I say. "If nothing else it'll get you home a little quicker."

She climbs in, almost reluctantly. Sam takes this as her cue to head toward the car. I peel away from the curb before she can claim the backseat. I can't risk spooking an already skittish Ivy.

Sam will just have to understand.

"I've been thinking a lot about our conversation last night," I tell Ivy as I make a right out of the parking lot. She doesn't respond.

"I mean, I'd like to think I'm a good person," I continue, "but you were right. I should have been there for you after your . . . incident."

"I never said *that*."

"No, not in those exact words."

"Not in any words," she shoots back.

I need to disarm her somehow. After a pause, I say, "I guess what I'm trying to tell you is that I feel guilty, Ivy. I feel like I failed you at a time when you needed people the most."

More silence. Jesus, no wonder Ivy Proctor doesn't have any friends.

Finally, I say, "Can you forgive me?"

"There's nothing to forgive."

"But—"

"Can we *not* talk about this?" Ivy asks. "I do not want to talk about this."

"Of course."

We drive, not speaking, for a few minutes. Then she says, "You're being really nice. I still don't think there's anything that you need to be forgiven for, but it means a lot to me that you said that. So, yeah. Thank you. And sorry."

I smile my warmest smile. "You're good people, Ivy Proctor."

"You are too, Alexandra Miles."

For the next few minutes, I make light chatter—asking Ivy

about what kind of music she listens to (femme country, though I was totally expecting her to name some emo head case), what TV shows she likes to watch (mostly sci-fi—not surprising), and what she likes to do in her spare time (play video games and read comics). For a second, I think that she's actually kind of the ideal girl for Wyatt. You know, if he wasn't wet dreaming about me 24/7.

Then, at the next stoplight, I pop the big question:

"Have you picked out your dress for Homecoming?"

Ivy gives me a look that I can only describe as disturbed mixed with perplexed. "Uh, no."

"Oh! Neither have I. We should go dress shopping together."

This makes her chuckle. "I'm not going to Homecoming."

I feign surprise. "Really? Why not? It's your senior year!"

"First of all, I don't have a date." *Yeah*, I think, *no shit.* "But even if I did, I mean, it's not really my . . . thing."

"What, are you too good for high school dances?" I tease.

She shakes her head at me like a semi-amused, semi-annoyed younger sister.

"How about this," I say. "You go dress shopping with me, and if we find you something fabulous, you agree to go to Homecoming. And if you don't end up with a date, I know Matt can wrangle you one. We can even split a limo!

"Trust me, Ivy," I continue. "I can make Homecoming the most memorable night of your high school life."

If only she knew just *how* memorable it will be.

EIGHTEEN

Alexandra

"Walk me through it one more time."

I sigh heavily. I hate it when Sam acts dense. I'm starting to wonder if it even is acting.

"You get to school early tomorrow. Start taking down some of our Homecoming posters. Not all of them—but a few in high-profile locations. Definitely the one outside of Frick's office, preferably when Frick can see you."

"And what do you want me to do with them?"

"Place them gently in the recycling bins. Sticking up so people can see what they are—see my face. This will get people talking."

"I don't know, Lexi," Sam says. "I'm just not sure they'll buy you dropping out of the race."

"It's our job to make them buy it," I say in a tight voice. "But if you're not up to the task, I'll just deploy Sloane or one of the other drama queens."

Sam snorts. "Right. Like *that's* ever going to happen."

"I need that rumor going strong before lunch," I say. "I know you can do this, Samantha. I'm counting on you." I say this last bit in an almost-purr. Sam goes crazy when I use her full name, especially in a soft voice.

"I've got this," she says. "Good luck with Corporal Crazy."

I pick Ivy up before school the next day. Instantly I register some changes. She's wearing a pale purple top under her black cardigan—some of the first color I've seen on her this year. And her eyes aren't rimmed in black, either. Just a little kohl on the lash line, and a pale, shimmery shadow on the lids.

It's working. And faster than I expected.

On the ride over, I ask, "What are you doing tonight?"

Ivy shrugs. "Homework. The usual."

"Let's skip the usual," I say. "I have rehearsal until five, but after that—let's go to the mall. We can grab some dinner, look at some dresses. It'll be fun."

"I can't do that."

"Why not?"

"I don't have any money with me."

I wave her off. "It's fine. I can cover dinner. And we wouldn't be *buying* any dresses tonight anyway. Just trying them on and taking pics. I mean, it's not like you marry the first guy you date, right?"

"Actually," Ivy says, "my parents are middle school sweethearts."

No wonder she's so messed up. I ignore this comment and press on.

"I'm not going to take no for an answer," I inform Ivy. "If you say yes now, it'll save us both a lot of time and energy."

She gives in.

They always do.

And now I start to lay the foundation for the next stage of my plan. The one Sam is simultaneously carrying out on campus at this very moment.

"Can I confess something to you?" I say.

"Sure."

"I'm kind of thinking about dropping out of the Homecoming race."

I swear, the girl's jaw literally drops three inches. "What? Why?"

"It just doesn't seem fair. I mean, I've been class princess three years running. Isn't it someone else's turn to shine?"

"You're kidding me with this, right?"

"No," I say. "I'm dead serious. Besides, I have a couple of big pageants coming up. How many crowns does one girl need?"

All of the crowns, I think. *ALL OF THEM.*

"But you're a shoo-in to win," Ivy tells me. "You know that, right?"

Now it's my turn to shrug. "Maybe. The New Girl seems to have some fans."

"No," she says firmly. "Not like you do."

I don't respond, letting silence do the work for me.

"Look," Ivy says after a bit. "You could be *Homecoming Queen*. It's, like, almost every little girl's fantasy."

"Exactly," I say. "And I just think it's time to let some other little girl's dream come true."

I sound so earnest that I wonder if there's some tiny part of me that actually believes the shit I am spewing.

Ivy says, "You're crazy, you know that? And this is coming from someone who's *actually* crazy."

I've got to give the girl credit. She takes herself a lot less seriously than I'd imagined.

"You shouldn't talk about yourself that way," I say. "You know, you're up for Homecoming Queen, too."

And there it is. The elephant in the car.

"That's just somebody's idea of a sick joke," she says. "It's not real."

"Maybe," I concede, because it would be foolish *not* to acknowledge the truth in what she's saying. "But it could be."

We don't say anything else until we pull into the school parking lot a few minutes later. I cut the engine and turn to Ivy. But before I can utter another word, she blurts out, "I don't know why you'd voluntarily give up the chance to be Homecoming Queen, but that's totally your decision. Just . . . leave me out of it. I don't need to be humiliated any more than I already have been, okay?"

She starts to get out of the car.

"Wait," I say, touching her shoulder.

"What?"

"I just want to be your friend," I tell her, in the most sincere voice I can muster.

"But why?" It comes out in an almost-whine.

"Because you need a friend. A good one. And because I genuinely like you, Ivy Proctor."

This, perhaps, is the biggest lie of all.

Ivy sighs. I can tell I'm wearing her down, and it's taken a lot less time and energy than I had imagined.

"Have lunch with us today," I say. "Me and Sam. We can talk more about tonight. Okay?"

She nods. It's a grim gesture, but I'll take it.

"Great," I say. "See you then."

If Sam has done her part as well as I've done mine, in a few short hours I will no longer be the front-runner for Spencer High School Homecoming Queen.

Ivy Proctor will be.

NINETEEN

Alexandra

The rumor mill churns overtime; by the start of third period, everyone is whispering about me and whether or not I'm officially dropping out of the Homecoming race. Sam has played her part very well. When I see people sneaking glances in my direction, I offer them a Mona Lisa smile. You know, with just enough mystery to keep them talking.

My plan is to make the announcement near the end of my lunch period. This is assuming that Ivy takes me up on my invite. I need people to see us together, enjoying each other's company. That way I don't have to officially endorse Ivy Proctor when I step down. They'll just know. Or, at the very least, they'll speculate that my new BFF is a factor in the decision.

I run to the girls' room for a quick touch-up before lunch— "quick" being the operative word. Typically I show up to the caf right before the bell rings. But not today. Today I need to beat Ivy there so I can make sure she lands at our table.

And then *she* shows up. Principal Constance Frick. Standing in front of me like the tall tank of ugly she always has been and always will be.

"Miss Miles," she says in a loud, flat voice. "I need to speak with you for a moment."

I nod, artificially wide-eyed and agreeable. "Sure. I don't have a free period today but I can come by your office after—"

"Now," Frick says sharply. Her lips curl upward like a Disney villain's just before something bad happens to the princess. "It should only take a moment or two."

Fighting Frick could extend this interlude further, so I give in. Thankfully, she doesn't want to drag me all the way back to her office—just to the other side of the hallway.

"Alexandra."

"Yes, Ms. Frick?"

"I just . . . I wanted to know how you were doing. How *are* you, Alexandra?"

I'm not buying the syrupy tone in her voice. "Fine," I say. "Why do you ask?"

"Mrs. Mays and I were chatting earlier, and she mentioned that you missed rehearsal yesterday. Something about a doctor's appointment? I couldn't help but wonder if it had something to do with . . . Well, you know."

"My mother?" I finish for her. "Yeah, no. I told Mrs. Mays that I had to get my flu shot. That's all."

"It's just so *unlike* you to skip a rehearsal. I think that's why Mrs. Mays was concerned. I told her I'd look into it."

Bile rises to the back of my throat. Does Frick think she's

actually fooling me with this caring principal bit? She's counting down the days until I graduate; we both know she can't get rid of me a day too soon. Time to shut this down.

"Thank you for your concern," I say, "but I assure you that I am absolutely fine."

I'm about to bolt when Frick reaches out and puts her hand on my shoulder. Instantly I stiffen. Why is she *touching* me? Isn't that illegal these days?

"You have a lot on your plate, Alexandra," Frick says, her hand still connected to my arm.

I stare at the hand like it's an evil, icky thing, but Frick doesn't move it. Instead, she says, "I am concerned that you may have overextended yourself this semester. Especially with your mother's current state of health."

That's twice now that she's dragged Natalie into the conversation. Not okay.

With a swift move, I lift Frick's hand from my shoulder and push it back in her direction. "I don't have any idea what you're talking about," I say coldly.

I start to walk away before Frick can say another word, but then think better of it. I turn around again so that I'm facing her and say, "But you know what, Ms. Frick? I do feel a little overextended right now, what with college applications and preparing for fall pageant season. I already put some plans in place to cut back. I think you'll be pleased."

Frick's eyes narrow. If there was closed captioning for her thoughts, the words would likely read something along the lines of, "Just what exactly are you scheming, little girl?"

"Thanks again for your concern," I say. Then I turn and walk toward the cafeteria, letting my hips switch as I sashay away.

You may be wondering about my mother's complicated history with Frick. It's actually not that complicated. Frick was her teacher. She was married to Crazy Dave back then. My mom had an after-school job as a receptionist at Crazy Dave's dealership. Crazy Dave liked hot young blondes wearing tight little skirts.

You do the math.

So now Frick's got it in for me, even though my mom wasn't Crazy Dave's first or last. She was just the only one Frick had to deal with on a near-daily basis.

Fuck Frick and her vendetta bullshit.

I've got an election to throw.

TWENTY

Sam

Lexi is late. Worse, Lexi is late when she's supposed to be *early*.
I'm not the one who's been working Ivy Proctor. If she checks out
of the lunch line before Lexi arrives, there's no way she's going
to come sit with me. I mean, if our awkward chat the other day
is any indication, I make Ivy twitchy—and not in a good way.

My eyes dart from the cafeteria's double doors to Ivy, who
is progressing through the line at a decent clip. *Come on, Lexi.*
Where are *you?*

Ivy's swiping her card at the register when Lexi finally walks
through the door. She nods in my direction before heading
toward the line all casual-like. Lexi says something to Ivy, then
points in my direction. I lift my hand in a not-quite-wave. Ivy
just stands there as Lexi hits the lunch line. What the hell is she
buying? She doesn't eat cafeteria food.

After what feels like an eternity, Ivy slowly makes her way
over to where I'm sitting.

"Hey," she says. She sets her tray down but remains standing,
almost like she expects me to shoo her away.

"Hi," I say back. "Um, have a seat."

"Yeah?"

Oh, god. This is going to be so painful.

"Yeah," I say. "We're going to be friends. Lexi says so."

The words surprise me even as they're leaving my mouth. Ivy's eyes catch mine and we both chuckle. Okay, maybe this won't be so bad after all.

Ivy slides into her chair and says, "She gets what she wants, doesn't she?"

"Always."

And that's where our conversation dies. It remains suspended in silence until Lexi appears several minutes later.

"So what are we talking about, girls?" she says in a mock-breezy voice that only I, the only person who really knows her, would identify as fake.

"Goals," Ivy says. "We were talking about goals."

"Like field hockey?"

This makes Ivy and me chuckle again. And *that* makes Lexi frown. She hates not being in on the joke.

"Ivy was just saying how much she admires your determination," I explain. It's not entirely a lie.

"Yes," Ivy agrees, totally deadpan. "You're so determined. It's very admirable."

Ha. If she wasn't such a complete psychopath, I might actually *like* Ivy Proctor. Too bad Lexi's got her in the crosshairs. No sense growing attached to a bunny that's slated for slaughter.

Lexi's smile is tight; she's not buying it. I try to deflect.

"So, are you still thinking about doing that thing we were talking about earlier?" I ask, per Lexi's pre-written script.

"Not now," she says softly, cutting her eyes in Ivy's direction.

"Do you guys need some privacy?" Ivy says. "I can go."

"No," Lexi says. "Stay. It's just . . . Sam's asking about . . . well, what you and I talked about this morning. About me and Homecoming? But I know that makes you uncomfortable, so . . ."

Ivy looks down at her tray. "Oh."

"The answer's yes," Lexi stage-whispers in my direction. "But we'll talk about it later."

"You can talk about it now," Ivy says. "You dropping out of Homecoming Queen doesn't bother me."

I fight a grin. Ivy's not a soft-spoken girl, and she said that last thing loud enough that the table of sophomore girls beside us has heard her. Their overly mascaraed eyes fly open. The buzz begins: *It's true then? She's really quitting?* It makes its way around the cafeteria like a brush fire.

Lexi blushes bright red. How she can control her coloring is beyond me.

The news finally reaches Sloane Fahey, whose freckled face lights up like she's just hit the jackpot on a Hoosier lottery scratch-off. Lexi continues to feign embarrassment. She's talking, presumably to both me and Ivy, but I'm not paying attention. I'm watching Sloane, who looks like she's ready to leap up at any second.

And then she does.

And then she walks over to our table.

"Is it true?" Sloane asks Lexi. Just like that.

"Is what true?"

"You," Sloane says. "You're really giving up the Homecoming crown?"

Lexi doesn't respond, not at first. She looks down at the chocolate chip cookie she bought in the lunch line. The one she hasn't been eating, because she'd rather fart in the middle of a school assembly than get caught eating carbs in public.

"Well?" Sloane prompts. "Are you quitting or what?"

"Yes," Lexi says, her voice barely a whisper. "I think I am."

Sloane's mouth drops open. "You're shitting me. This is a joke, right?"

"Nice language, Sloane," Lexi says. "And no. It's not a joke."

Sloane crosses her arms across her chest. "I don't believe it."

"You don't have to," Lexi retorts. "*I* know the truth."

"Then prove it. Make it official."

I can only begin to imagine how elated Lexi is at this turn of events. Sloane has set her up perfectly.

"Fine," Lexi says. "You want some big, dramatic announcement? I'll give you one."

She rises, pulls her chair away from the table, and then climbs up on it. "Excuse me!" she calls out. "Hello! Can I please have your attention? I'll make it quick."

It doesn't take long for Lexi to get every eye trained on her. The volume in the room goes to zero; the only sound is the pinging of the registers as kids check out of the line.

"I didn't want to make a big deal out of this, but Sloane here is insisting that I do." Lexi looks down at Sloane, her mouth twisting like she's tasted something sour. "Anyway," she says, "while I am so honored and flattered to be nominated for this year's Homecoming Queen, I have decided to drop out of the race."

Her dramatic pause was meant to allow for chatter, but the room remains pin-drop silent. Even the stoners are too surprised to toss out a single "Who cares?"

"There are so many amazing girls on the ballot," Lexi continues. Here, she smiles warmly in Ivy's direction. Without breaking her gaze she finishes, "I think it's time we recognize one of them instead."

A slow clap starts from the other side of the caf. Matt, of course. He pops up, kicking his chair back, and shouts out, "Yeah! That's my girl!"

Suddenly, everyone is clapping, cheering for Lexi. She clasps her hands over her heart, like she's so touched by their support. Before the clapping wanes, Lexi carefully steps down from the chair. Then, to Sloane, she says, "Happy?"

But Sloane is *not* happy, which is crystal clear to just about everyone in the room. She skulks back to her own table, muttering to herself.

"That feels like such a burden off my back!" Lexi declares dramatically. "Now, what were we talking about?"

Ivy looks dumbstruck. Her face screams WTF, but she's smart enough not to say it.

"Goals," Ivy says finally. "We were talking about goals."

Lexi nods. "Oh, that's right. So here's my goal for the day: to find *you* the most gorgeous Homecoming dress in the entire Tall Oaks Mall."

Her eyes sparkle; her beautiful face shines. Lexi is such a star. She always has been, always will be.

As she and Ivy chitchatter on, I feel Lexi's hand under the table, landing on my knee. She squeezes it lightly, then runs her hand up my thigh as she pulls away. For a second, I lose the ability to breathe.

Goals, I think, beating back a familiar ache. *I have a few of my own.*

TWENTY-ONE

Sloane

On a normal day, my sixth-period musical theater elective is my absolute favorite class. For one thing, Alexandra Miles isn't in it. This is the first year we haven't had some sort of performing-arts class together and can I just say how much I love not being eclipsed by her? I am the star of that class. Me. Not her. *Me.*

The funny thing is, she was *supposed* to be in the class. Of course she was. But then, by some magic twist of fate, it got scheduled opposite the only section of AP English offered for seniors.

Here's an Alexandra story for you: when she found out that she had to choose between musical theater and AP English, she actually petitioned the school to get musical theater moved to a different time slot. Even more amazing: *it almost happened.* So why didn't it? Because the only other period that Mrs. Mays could move it to was third. Mays was ready to pull the trigger, too, but then Alexandra told her not to. Third period conflicted with her AP History class, so why even bother?

On the one hand, you almost have to admire a girl who has

no problem asking a teacher to rearrange her entire schedule—a schedule that then affects dozens of other students as well. On the other, it kind of makes you want to scream, "Self-involved much? Who the hell do you think you are, anyway?"

At least, that's what *I* want to yell at her. But I never would, because she'd be all, "I'm Alexandra Miles, that's who." And, like, in a weird way, that answer would make perfect *sense*.

This is one of the reasons why I've decided it's time to take her down. It's like, *enough already*. But Step 1 of my original plan was figuring out how to get Erin Hewett to defeat Alexandra for Homecoming Queen. And now she's gone and dropped out of the race all on her own.

This is the thing that doesn't make *any* sense whatsoever. Fact: Without intervention from me or some other interested party at Spencer High, Alexandra would've been a lock for queen. Hands down. They probably could've gone ahead and handed her the crown for prom, too, just to save us all a little time.

Anyway, here I am, 1,000 percent miserable in what is typically the happiest forty-seven minutes of my school day. Not only because Alexandra just embarrassed me in front of the entire cafeteria (even though that was pretty awful, too). No, I'm miserable because I can't figure out *why* she's dropping out. And I know Alexandra well enough to know that there has to be a reason.

There's always a reason.

Time to regroup. When I first started formulating Operation End Alexandra, I debated which allies I was going to target first—Erin (the competitor) or Sam (the confidante). I'd been leaning toward Erin, but now I know it has to be Sam. She's the only one who might possibly have intel on Alexandra's intentions.

I pull out my Moleskine notebook and open to a fresh page. At the top, in capital letters, I write "SAMANTHA SCHNITT."

It's almost better that Sam's first on the hit list, because at least I know how to get close to her. She's one of three confirmed lesbians at Spencer, and the other two are high-school married. Our Indiana town is too conservative for her to have a lot of opportunities for hookups, if any.

I've never kissed a girl before, but I *am* an actress, and I have no problem playing the part of someone who has. I mean, Meryl Streep did it, right?

The problem is that I only really see Sam on school grounds, and when I do, she's almost always glued to Alexandra's side. That's a challenge.

My first bullet point: ISOLATE SAM.

My second: FLIRT WITH HER.

My third: MAKE OUT WITH HER UNTIL SHE TELLS ME WHAT I NEED TO KNOW.

It looks so simple on paper.

TWENTY-TWO

Ivy

It is 7:42 on a school night and I am eating dinner at Panda Express with *Alexandra Miles* in the food court of the Tall Oaks Mall. We have spent the past two-plus hours trying on potential Homecoming dresses. Or, rather, Alexandra has tried on dresses as I have watched. I do not need a dress for Homecoming. I do not plan on going to the dance. I have tried to tell Alexandra this several times, but she does not believe me. Or if she does, she is convinced that she can change my mind.

She is very persuasive, that is for sure.

I have known Alexandra since we were little kids, and I think we were probably friends at some point. Not real friends but like the fake kind that exchanged grocery store valentines and invited each other to our birthday parties because that is just how it was. But we have not even been fake friends now for many, many years.

I push my Sweetfire Chicken around the plastic bowl while Alexandra explains to me about how she trains for a pageant. She did not volunteer this information; I asked her to tell me about it. I have asked her a lot of questions tonight, because each question means that she keeps talking and I do not have to. She prattles on about cabbage salad and practicing her walk but I am only half listening to what she is saying. The other half of my brain is trying to figure out why Alexandra Miles has taken such a sudden interest in me. The easy answer would be that it is because I am inexplicably one of the nominees for this year's Homecoming Queen, but I do not buy it.

She is being nice. *Very* nice. Nice in a way that I do not remember Alexandra ever being. It is strange in that she is one of the most popular girls in the whole school—she always was, even in grade school—but she does not have a lot of friends. In fact, her only real friend is Samantha, and even with her I am not sure if what they have is friendship or fealty. Her boyfriend, Matt, adores her. But I have seen them together since the start of the school year and she does not look like she adores him. She kind of wears him like a human accessory.

There is something about this entire situation that does not feel right to me. I am pretty sure that my nomination for Homecoming Queen is a sick joke—that I was put on the ballot so some twisted high school bullies could reenact the pig's blood scene from *Carrie*. This is why I am refusing to go to the dance. Well, one of the reasons, anyway.

Alexandra talks with her hands, but in a weird way, like a game show hostess pointing out prizes. I nod along as she talks, but really I am just trying to figure her out.

See, if this is truly part of a plot to humiliate me at the dance, then Alexandra *must* be in on it. Correct? This would explain why she is trying so hard to be my friend. Why she herself has dropped out of the race. Why she is spending all of this time to help me find the perfect dress—she has even offered to help me find a *date*.

I am Ivy Proctor. I am the crazy girl. The one who had a public breakdown in the middle of biology class. Who bled all over Mr. Barksdale's linoleum floor without shedding a single tear.

Nobody wants to be my friend. And I cannot blame them.

Then again, none of this feels like Alexandra's style. Hayley Langer—this is something that she would do. But Alexandra is a good girl. She is a straight-A student. President of the Key Club. A pretty, perfect pageant queen.

Dr. Sanders would say that I am catastrophizing or one of the other many cognitive distortions she tells me I exhibit every time I see her. The frequency of my visits has increased to twice a week now that I am back at Spencer. This is due more to my mother's anxiety than my own. I have spent the past eighteen months making myself numb to the high school thing. I am focusing on college now. College means getting away from everyone and everything in Spencer, including my cloying parents.

College means having a chance of truly starting over fresh. Going somewhere where no one knows who I am or what I have done.

Another reason for avoiding the dance: if some horrible

prank were to take place, it would surely be captured on multi-ple phones and uploaded to the internet where it would live on, a stain on my face and my name ad infinitum. It is a miracle that it did not happen the first time around. I guess everyone was too freaked out to remember to press record.

I will not let myself be a target.

"Target?" Alexandra says. "What do you mean?"

Did I say that last part aloud? I must have, or else why would Alexandra be asking me about it? It's not like she can read minds.

"Target *girl*," I say on the fly. "Like, wearing a dress from Target. I can't let myself be *that* girl."

"Never," she says back. Alexandra's face is full of horror. It almost makes me giggle. She puts her hand across her chest like she is about to recite the Pledge of Allegiance and says, "I solemnly swear that I will never allow you or any of my friends to purchase a dress for a semiformal from any store that also sells laundry detergent and baby wipes."

She says the words so fluidly—"you or any of my friends"—that I cannot help but wonder if maybe she is for real. It is impossible to know for sure until something bad actually happens. Or is it?

"What's your angle?" I blurt, before I can puss out.

"Angle?" she echoes.

"Yes, *angle*. Before I got nominated for Homecoming, you didn't so much as look my way. Now this? It doesn't make any sense."

Alexandra's dark-blue eyes drop to the table, and her perfectly manicured hands twist in her lap. "You're right," she says quietly. "It probably doesn't make any sense . . . to you."

"But it does to you?"

"You don't have to believe me," she says.

I do not respond. This is a trick I learned from Dr. Sanders. Silence makes most people uncomfortable. If you do not say anything, they will, just to avoid the dead air.

Alexandra does not disappoint. "What you don't get, Ivy, is that I *was* you. Before I learned to channel my energy into pageants, I was so . . . angry that it could've been me in that biology classroom. I came so close, so many times, to completely losing it. . . ."

Tears start to fall, making delicate tracks down her smooth, unblemished cheeks. It is like art, watching her cry like that. Like her crying face should be in a museum.

"Pageants gave me something to focus on," she says through the tears. "Something that would make my mom proud. And then, after my dad . . . you know . . . *died*, and my mom turned into a Tennessee Williams cliché . . . I had to focus even harder, to get her to see me. I'd already lost my dad—I couldn't lose my mom, too."

Whoa. Alexandra never talks about her mother. Never. Once upon a time, Mrs. Miles was this glamazon of a woman—tall, flawlessly gorgeous, and reeking of big-city style, even though she had never lived a day of her life outside of Spencer. She was awesome, in the truest sense of the word.

But after the horrible car wreck that claimed Mr. Miles's life, Alexandra's mom came completely unglued. On the rare occasion that she picked Alexandra up from school, she would be half in the bag, and do completely bizarre things like show up wearing one of her fur coats over a silk peignoir and a pair of tennis shoes. You could tell how mortified Alexandra was, but she never said a word, and no one else ever said a word about it either—at least not to her face. It was this unspoken rule in the Spencer community: you could gossip about Natalie Miles all you wanted, but doing it in front of her kid was 100 percent off-limits.

I cannot believe Alexandra is talking about this with me.

"I used to see a therapist," she continues, catching me by surprise. I am sure there are tons of kids in Spencer who see shrinks but like my meltdown and Alexandra's cracked-out mom, no one ever talks about it. "It was after I lost my dad. He was kind of a quack—the therapist, not my dad—but he really encouraged me to stay active in pageants, even when I wanted to quit. He'd say, 'You can't let other people dictate how you feel about yourself, but sometimes it takes a little external validation to help generate the internal kind.'"

Alexandra reaches across the table and squeezes my hand. "I want that for you, Ivy. I want you to know how amazing it feels to have the spotlight on you for all of the right reasons. Not because your dad died or you lost your shit in a very public way. But because you were *chosen*. Because you're the one they picked to wear that crown."

For a split second, I can see it. Me, on that stage, wearing a deep purple strapless gown and a pair of scary-high stilettos. Principal Frick placing that rhinestone tiara on top of my head. Walking down the steps for the ceremonial slow dance with this year's king. I have never slow danced with a boy. I have never gone to a high school dance, period. Everything I know about them comes from TV and movies. But boy, would it be nice to have that movie moment—the one without the pig's blood pouring on my head.

"And just think what you running could do for the others—the outsiders who feel like they could never fit in," she says. "Imagine, Ivy, what it would be like for one of their own to be honored that way."

I chuckle. "Even the outsiders wouldn't have me."

Alexandra sighs. "Look," she says, pulling her hand away. "I'm not going to make you run. Not if it makes you that miserable—"

"It doesn't," I say. "Honestly. It's scary more than anything else."

"Of course," she says. "You're putting yourself out there for public judgment. I still throw up before every pageant—and not because I'm trying to fit into my dress, either."

This makes me chuckle. Alexandra wipes the last of the tears from her cheeks and smiles brightly.

"It can be so much fun, Ivy. I can make it fun. I'll be, like, your campaign manager!"

She instantly starts rattling off ideas: when I will get my hair cut, what I should be wearing to school, how I should be doing my makeup, who I need to be seen with. She even pulls out her iPhone and starts making an official list.

I have no idea what I have just gotten myself into, but for whatever reason, I am not interested in finding a way out.

TWENTY-THREE

Alexandra

With Ivy on board, my top priority is making sure that Erin Hewett knows what's going on—not only that I've dropped out of the race, but that I'm throwing my full support behind Ivy. If I'm lucky, she'll take the news back to Frick and I'll kill two birds with one well-played stone.

Ivy. It's almost pathetic how quickly she caved. All I had to do was drop a few tears and spew some rah-rah bullshit about how if she ran, she wouldn't be doing it for me or even herself but for all of the outcasts everywhere. *And she ate it up!*

Now that I've made her want it, she'll do just about anything I tell her to. It's almost like having a second Sam, only this one doesn't want to jam her tongue down my throat.

Speaking of: I should give Original Sam a call. I'll need her help if I'm going to turn Ivy into someone worthy of a crown.

Our training starts tomorrow.

I don't get home until almost nine thirty; Natalie has already gone to bed. At least, I assume she's gone to bed. Her door is locked and the blue light from a perpetually-on television set seeps out into the hallway. I knock softly, as I always do, to let her know I'm home. Sometimes I get a grunt in response. Mostly I get silence.

I prefer the grunt. At least then I know she's still alive.

Things weren't always this way with Natalie. While I've never really loved her—at least, not in the way you're supposed to love your mother—there was a time, years ago, that I admired the hell out of her. For one thing, Natalie was preternaturally gorgeous. She looked like a movie star marooned in the Midwest. Plus, her body was banging; years of pageant training left her with legs so cut they would make a grown man cry. And even though the gossipy moms in Spencer were convinced she'd gotten her boobs enlarged and her butt lifted, I can assure you that everything about Natalie is 100 percent au naturel.

But beyond her looks, Natalie had an absolutely brilliant mind. You wouldn't know it if you met her today, or even if you'd had a casual conversation with her back then. Most people pegged her as this vapid trophy wife, but it was all an act. My mother could walk into a room full of strangers and size them up in five minutes flat. She'd know in an instant not only whom she should be talking to but also *how* she should be talking to them. She knew exactly what to do to get whatever it was she wanted, whether it was information, attention, or things. In the peak of our training, right before my father died, I felt like I was finally starting to measure up. Like she had looked at me with that appraising look and liked what she'd seen.

That version of Natalie died with my father, though I don't understand why things got so dire. She was only thirty-four when he was killed in the collision, and she was still the most stunning creature ever to walk the streets of Spencer, Indiana. Natalie could've landed herself any one of a dozen eligible bachelors, men who had even more money and power than my dad. She must have really loved him. Or whatever version of love her iced-out heart could manage.

But instead of getting back out there, she crawled into the bottom of a bottle of bourbon and rotted into the erratic, pill-popping wretch she is today.

I knock again. The sound on the TV gets louder—Natalie's way of telling me to fuck off.

Why do I even bother?

I retreat to my own room and instinctively check my reflection in the full-length mirror. My makeup has held up remarkably well for such a long day, but my lips definitely need to be refreshed. I switch out the MLBB shade for MAC's Russian Red—Matt's favorite. Then I Snapchat him a kissy-face shot with the caption "Miss me? I miss you." I shift positions slightly and take a second selfie, only this one I send to Sam.

Within thirty seconds she texts me a question mark. I reply: *OMG that was meant for Matt!!! Sorry!*

She waits two full minutes before texting me back: *I figured*

I let another two minutes go by before asking her if she has time for a quick chat. This time, she responds immediately: *Of course*

It's late and I have a ton of homework I need to bang out before bed. I probably could've skipped the photoplay, but where's the fun in that?

On the phone, though, I'm all business. I give Sam a quick overview of the evening—high-level detail, nothing too specific. She asks a lot of questions, about where we went and what shops we hit and why we stayed out so long. Typically I'd have a higher threshold for Sam's neediness, but not tonight. Tonight I'm exhausted from the sheer effort I've expended pretending to like Ivy Proctor.

It's going to be a long three and a half weeks.

"Can't you pick me up on the way to Ivy's?" Sam whines when I tell her I can't give her a ride to school in the morning.

"No. I told you. I have to get there really early. I can't let the girl dress herself, now can I?"

"But I can help," Sam says. "You know I'm great with the straightening iron."

It's true. She's a whiz with them. But the last thing I want is Sam stepping in too soon, metaphorically peeing on the poor girl just to mark her territory.

"No," I say more firmly. "I have to establish trust first. You'd just scare Ivy off."

"How?" she demands.

"Why are you arguing with me?"

"Because I don't understand why you need to keep me and Ivy separated. I'm still a part of this plan, aren't I?"

"Samantha," I say, "you're part of *every* plan. You know that.

Or, at least, you should know that by now."

This, I think, will shut her up. Me reminding her of the over-arching goal: to get us the hell out of Spencer. So what if I don't *actually* intend to take her with me? Or hell—maybe I'll want to, when the time comes. Maybe there's a usefulness to Samantha Schnitt that extends past graduation day.

"Please," Sam says. "Don't shut me out."

And with that, I've reached my limit.

"I'm hanging up now," I say.

"Why?"

"Because you're acting like a jealous girlfriend!" I snap. "And I don't have time for that."

I hang up before she can protest. When she calls me back, I silence the phone. It goes to voice mail but she doesn't leave a message.

I turn my phone off before plugging it in to charge. Then I dive into the pile of homework I need to plow through before I can turn in for the night.

The next day, I arrive at Ivy's house a full forty-five minutes before we have to leave for school. When I informed her that I would be doing this, she told me that she wasn't much of a morning person.

"Too bad," I said. "We have less than a month until the election. Every day counts."

Ivy lives in a flat, oatmeal-colored rancher that has about as much personality as her dull, doughy mother. It is freakishly clean, despite the large, slobbering dog that typically has free rein, but, at my request, is currently incarcerated in the kitchen. No dust, no tacky clutter. And every wall is painted the same boring beige, which mirrors the color of the carpet.

Except Ivy's room. Her small, boxy space looks like an eggplant threw up all over it. There is dark, moody purple *everywhere*. A weirdly shiny bedspread. A shaggy area rug. Even her *dresser* has been purple-ized.

Purple is clearly Ivy's signature color.

The one exception to all of this aubergine is the curtains, which are a black velveteen and seemingly hung for the sole purpose of blocking out all natural light.

Maybe this is why Ivy dresses so poorly. It's too dark to see what she's putting on her body.

I look around the space trying to locate a light switch. There's a purple crystal chandelier that should theoretically throw off some light.

"Does that thing work?" I ask, pointing up at the fixture.

"Sure," she says. "You might want to close your eyes for a sec while I turn it on."

I don't heed Ivy's warning, but really wish I had. The minute she flips the switch, the room is positively flooded with bright light. Instinctively, I shield my eyes with my right arm.

"Told you," she says, and I can practically hear her grinning. "That's why I never turn it on."

I resist the urge to roll my eyes. Instead, I say, "Closet. Where is it?"

She reaches toward the black-and-white poster of a big head—some sad-looking musician from decades before we were born—that is apparently masking the closet's door. She swings it open to reveal a double layer of clothes, almost all of which are black, with a few purple pieces thrown in for good measure.

"What. The. *Fuck*," I say before I can stop myself. Ivy turns to face me, her eyes wide, as if she's never heard anyone drop the f-bomb before. How am I ever going to turn this hopeless case into Homecoming Queen material?

Then I remind myself: *You are Alexandra Miles. If anyone can turn Ivy Proctor into a star, it's you.*

"Ivy Proctor," I say. "What are you doing? You are a reasonably attractive teenage girl. You're a little on the short side, but at least your body has the right proportions for your frame. And even though you try to hide them, I can tell you've got some decent boobage underneath those baggy tops you're always wearing."

Ivy's pale face flames red. She crosses her arms over her chest as if to shield them from my sight.

I circle around her, examining Ivy from every possible angle. "Your hair—it's dyed, correct?"

"Yes."

"It needs to be lightened. More of a golden brown than black. We can take care of that after school. And no more black eyeliner. At least, not so much you look like you're heading out on a hunting trip."

She winces at that last bit. I take a deep breath and do my best to dial it down a few notches.

"Look," I say in a soft, soothing voice. "I know you probably think all of this stuff is really shallow. And it is. Of course it is.

"But how you look—how you present yourself to the world—makes a statement. I'm judged all the time based on my choice of clothes or shoes or hair or makeup. And I'm not talking about the pageant world, either."

"I know all this," Ivy says. "I'm not *oblivious*."

"Then *act* like it. I want to help you win, but I can't do it without a little help from you in return."

I've spoon-fed Ivy a fair amount of bullshit this morning, but that last part—it's not entirely false. I mean, no one will actually get a chance to judge Ivy—but if they aren't rooting for her, she's got nowhere to fall.

"I'm in," she says, her voice barely above a whisper.

"That's all I needed to hear."

TWENTY-FOUR

Sam

"Hey there, stranger."

I turn to see her standing there. Erin Hewett. Clutching a stack of books to her chest like TV characters often do but real people never seem to. She is not wearing a skort. She is wearing a plaid miniskirt that is at least two inches shorter than our dress code dictates.

I guess you can get away with not following the dress code when you're the principal's niece.

We are standing just outside the main doors. I am waiting for Lexi to arrive with her new project (aka Ivy Proctor). I'm not entirely sure why Erin's here, though.

"Hi," I say, because I don't know what else to say. Her bare legs are still California tan. She radiates sunshine, this girl, down to her strawberry-blond hair with little wisps bleached by many, many hours spent on the beach.

At least, this is what I imagine. I guess it's possible that she had it done in a salon.

I don't like thinking about Erin Hewett's legs, or her hair, or any part about her, really.

"I feel like we haven't talked in for*ever*," Erin says. "And there's been so much going on."

"Like what?" I ask.

"Oh, you know," she says. "I heard about Alex*andra*'s big announcement yesterday. That's, like, really cool of her to do."

I nod. "Yeah. Cool."

I'm not great at making conversation. Especially not around super-cute girls that I'm not supposed to think are super-cute, or kind, or soft, or . . .

"Do you need something, Erin?" I blurt out.

"Nope," she says. "Just thought I'd say hello."

I keep thinking she's going to walk away but she doesn't. She's smiling at me. Is that part of her niceness, or is it something else?

Or do I just want it to be "something else"?

Behind her, about thirty feet away, Sloane Fahey is looking in our direction, skulking. Almost like she's watching us. That's the second time I've caught Sloane doing that in two days. Why?

I'm so consumed by what's happening in my immediate vicinity that I totally miss Lexi pulling into the parking lot. In fact, she and Ivy are already climbing the steps before I even register their presence.

Now there are four of us on the landing, a strange square of awkward.

"Hi, Ivy," Erin says with an unnecessary wave. "Congrats on your nomination! You too, Alexandra—even though you've decided not to run."

"It's true," Lexi says. She links her arm through Ivy's. "I think there are much worthier candidates this year."

Ivy looks horrified, both by her words and the whole arm-linking thing. I know it's just for show, but it irks me anyway.

"Agreed," I say, only I cut a sidelong glance at Erin. The corners of Lexi's mouth turn down just enough for me to notice.

"I know it sounds corny," Erin says, "but honestly? I don't care who actually wins. I just think it's amazing to be nominated! I was on Homecoming court at my old school, before we moved—"

"So we've heard," Lexi interjects. "Such a shame you had to miss out on that."

This doesn't faze Erin in the least. "Oh, it's fine. It's all a lot of phony pageantry anyway, isn't it?"

I suck in a sharp breath. "Phony pageantry"—that had to be directed at Lexi. Frick thinks pageants are frivolous; she's used that exact word with Lexi when Lexi's needed time off from school to compete. "Frivolous competitions don't warrant excused absences," Frick once said. "Not even if they award small 'scholarships' as incentive." She even made the air quotes around "scholarships." I can confirm this; I was there when it happened.

"Well, I see being voted Spencer High's Homecoming Queen as a huge honor," Lexi says. "It means your peers have voted you the embodiment of school spirit."

"Really?" Erin volleys back. "Because I kind of thought it was more about craving validation from your peers."

"If you truly feel that way, Erin," Lexi says, in a voice full of venom, "maybe you should consider dropping out, too."

Erin blinks in rapid succession. She's overstepped and she knows it. "I . . . I'm so sorry, Alexandra. I didn't mean to offend you. You either, Ivy." Her green eyes well up. I can't get a read on whether she's being genuine or if, like Lexi, she's mastered the art of the fake crying.

I still can't get a read on her, period.

"Please excuse me," Erin says, clutching her books even tighter. "I need to use the ladies'." With that, she rushes off— but not toward the girls' bathroom. No, she heads straight into Frick's office.

Lexi withdraws her arm from Ivy's and turns to face the girl. "And that is what I mean by always being 'on.' You can't say things like that without consequence. Now the whole school will know exactly how Erin feels about Homecoming."

"How will the whole school know?" Ivy asks. "She only said it to us."

"Because we'll let them know," Lexi says. "They have a *right* to know. Spencer students take Homecoming seriously. I meant what I said—we see it as a real honor."

This is fairly accurate. Even so, I can't help but say, "You didn't need to be so hard on her, Lexi."

"Oh, please," she says with a dismissive wave. "You can't possibly buy into that nice-girl act, can you?"

"She's been nothing but nice to me," Ivy adds. "Even *before* my nomination."

Lexi's eyes narrow in response. "Then maybe you should ask

Erin to be your coach. Oh, wait, you can't. *Because she's your direct competition.*"

Ivy nods and murmurs an apology. She is such a docile puppy. No wonder Lexi has taken to her so quickly.

"If you want to be a winner," Lexi says, "then stick with me. I promise I won't steer you wrong. Isn't that right, Sam?"

"Yes," I say, because that is what I'm expected to say. I'm a docile puppy, too. Or at least, that's how Lexi thinks of me. And I let her, too.

I may not have much of a bark, but I have the bite.

That's *my* secret weapon.

TWENTY-FIVE

Sloane

Here is what I know:

- Alexandra Miles has unofficially dropped out of the Homecoming race. I refuse to call it "official" until I get a ballot that doesn't have her name on it. Plus, I'm not entirely convinced she isn't up to something. (But that's not what I *know*; that's what I am speculating.)
- Alexandra is apparently putting her support behind Ivy Proctor. Or at least pretending to. Or at the very least taking the poor girl under her wing. (I guess that's more speculation, on all counts.)
- Ivy Proctor actually wants to *win*. I mean, she's hanging out with Alexandra. Or is she doing that because, up until Alexandra took an interest in her, Ivy didn't have any friends? (Damn it. More speculation!)

So I guess I don't actually know *anything*. Except that yesterday, during lunch, Alexandra made a big, flashy announcement about not running for queen. Which, bee-tee-dubs, I'm not sure I completely buy. This is, after all, *Alexandra* we're talking about. Girlfriend always gets what she wants, no matter who's standing in her way.

Just ask Taylor Flynn.

Or Hayley Langer.

Or me. Just ask *me*, because I know firsthand to what lengths Alexandra will go. To which she has already gone. And all because there was a boy who dared to pick *me* over *her*.

Can we pause for a second and talk about that? About how *I* was the one Jonah Dorsey asked to be his girlfriend, even though Alexandra made it abundantly clear that she was also applying for the position?

I almost blew it, too. I couldn't understand why I was the one Jonah wanted to be with, so I asked him outright: "Are you only dating me because you think I'll put out? I'm a virgin, you know."

He laughed. "Uh, no on both counts. But thanks for the heads-up."

"It's not funny, Jonah," I said. "I'm being serious."

"You're being seriously adorable," he replied, tucking a lock of my hair behind an ear.

I pushed his hand away. "But what about Alexandra?"

"What about her?"

"She likes you, you know."

He shrugged. "So? I don't like her."

"But why?"

Jonah's head tilted to one side, and he eyed me thoughtfully.

"She kind of scares me," he said finally. "And not in the good way, like you do."

"I scare you?"

"It scares me how much I like you," Jonah said. "Does that count?"

When Alexandra realized that Jonah wasn't going to trade me in for her, she was beyond irritated. She never said this, of course. She just started making jokes about how Jonah and I should get a room already, or could we show a little respect for our fellow classmates and cut back on the PDA? And we weren't even the school's worst offenders.

So that went on for about a month, and then the rumors started. She told everyone that we were sleeping together, me and Jonah. That I gave him an STD. That I got it from some dude I boinked at drama camp the summer prior. Or maybe it was one of the four guys I'd been with before him.

None of it was true, of course, but that didn't matter. What's that they say? Rumors have a habit of festering into facts.

Jonah didn't dump me, not right away. He wasn't a dick like that. But what happened was this: The rumors got into his head. Made him question everything. Was I really a virgin? Did I have some sort of STD? Why were people telling him he better keep it wrapped?

It almost would've been better if he had broken up with me immediately. Instead, I had to endure the long, slow decline of our relationship, until one day he finally said, "I need some time to think."

That was right before Christmas. I spent the whole break crying and dreading the post–New Year's return to school. But guess what? Jonah never came back to Spencer High. Apparently his dad got transferred to some suburb of Illinois—I still don't know if Jonah knew or if it was an unexpected, last-minute thing.

Either way, I never saw him again. Except when I stalked his Facebook page, that is.

This is the kind of crap that Alexandra pulls, though. Breaking up a perfectly happy couple just because she didn't get what she wanted.

How she remains one of the most popular girls in school is something I will never understand. And why *she* gets to keep her perfect boyfriend while I'm over here descending into spinsterdom is beyond me.

Le sigh. *Soon enough.*

Okay, here's something else I know:

If I want to take Alexandra down, I'm going to have to get a peek behind the curtain. Expose the skeletons in her closet. Which is why Samantha Schnitt is still at the top of my hit list. I have got to find a way to get close to her. I thought I had my chance this morning, before homeroom, but then Erin Hewett beat me to it. And what's up with that girl, anyway? She's always *smiling*. She's been here a week, and already she has more friends than I do. Is that *because* of the smiling?

Note to self: smile more often.

I am getting *nowhere*.

Fact: I suck at this scheming stuff.

But maybe what I need to do is try playing it both ways. Apologize to Alexandra for my outburst the other day. Compliment her on dropping out of the race. Ask her about Ivy. If she *is* backing her, offer my support to help Ivy get the crown.

Maybe, instead of trying to get with Samantha Schnitt, I simply need to *be* her.

TWENTY-SIX

Ivy

After school, we drive to Alexandra's house, because she has something she has to take care of with her mom. Then Alexandra hands Sam the keys to her car and instructs her to drive me to the Beauty Bar, a posh hair salon off Main Street. "Olivieri is expecting her," she tells Sam, like I am not even standing there. "And he already has my credit card. Here's a twenty for the tip." She peels off a crisp bill, folds it cleanly in half, and hands that over to Sam, too.

The stylist looks more like a Mike than an Olivieri. He's Indiana normal, all denim and flannel and scruffy beard. Lumberjack chic. And he doesn't look at all gay, which is what you'd expect from someone who calls himself Olivieri.

He doesn't ask me any questions, just sits me in a yellow plastic chair and drapes a silver cape thing over me. Then he disappears into a small room.

If my mother knew that this was happening, she would be both thrilled and horrified. Thrilled that I suddenly have not one but two new friends. Horrified that I was letting one of them give me a makeover without any sort of consultation.

But I am here, am I not? That is implied consent.

Olivieri returns with a plastic bowl full of strong-smelling goop. He begins painting it on my hair, not even bothering to explain what he is doing. Some girl thrusts a *People* magazine into my hands. Princess Kate is on the cover; she's expecting again. The reporter speculates it is another girl by the location of her baby bump.

When he is finished with the goop, Olivieri walks away. Roughly twenty minutes later, he returns. He rubs a small section of my hair with a towel, grunts approvingly, and—still not saying a word—directs me toward a sink. After that, I go under a dryer. Then back to the plastic chair, where squares of foil are wrapped around bits of my hair. More strong-smelling goop is added; I spend another stint under the dryer and one more at the sink before finally landing in front of a mirror. I only get a glimpse of my streaky wet hair before squinching my eyes shut tight.

"Good," Olivieri says—the first thing he's said to me since "Come," which is how he waved me back in the first place. "Keep 'em closed."

I do as I am told.

He combs and snips and twists and razors my hair. I can feel everything as it is happening, even if I cannot see it. I know the back of my neck is bare, because there is a breeze that tickles it. I really hope my mother doesn't freak out. "My friend made me do it," I will tell her. *My friend*. That should get me a pardon.

Product is applied and there is more hair drying, more twisting, more everything. It is almost dark outside. How long have we been here, anyway?

"Done," Olivieri pronounces. "Open 'em."

I am speechless.

My dyed-black hair is now the golden brown of a waffle just off the iron. There are wisps of blond running through it; they look sun-bleached, and not something that came from a bottle. It is what I think of as artfully messy—like I just got out of bed, only I'm now the kind of girl who looks like a supermodel first thing in the morning.

Suddenly, Sam has joined us. "Whoa," she says approvingly. "You look . . . *hot*."

"Uh . . . thanks?"

Olivieri snorts. "Thank *me*," he says. "I gave you the hotness."

Sam slips him the twenty and we head to check out, where I am given a pink bag full of product. "I need all of this?" I ask.

The lady behind the register nods. "Olivieri's instructions are in the bag. You look good, doll."

It is almost five thirty by the time we get back into the car. Sam texts something to someone—Alexandra, I assume. "We're running a little late," she informs me.

"Yeah," I say. "I told my mom I'd be home before dinner."

"We're not going home. We're picking up Alexandra and then heading back to school."

"Oh?"

"It's training time."

The stage looks like something out of a nineties' movie montage. *Clueless: The Ivy Proctor Edition*. There are dresses hanging from every available surface. Half-opened boxes of shoes are all over the floor. There is a table littered with costume jewelry and—hand to God—an actual *boa* draped over a full-length mirror.

I am wearing one of Alexandra's old pageant gowns. It is a fluffy cupcake of a frock. "Tea-length," she calls it. "I wore it for talent, not evening gown. Killed with the judges, though."

I am also wearing panty hose. I *never* wear panty hose. Not to mention the fact that my legs are unshaven. I hardly ever shave them; I don't have a ton of leg hair and what I do have is thin and baby-soft. But it is also dark, and that does not escape Alexandra's notice.

"Shaving isn't optional," she tells me. "Pits, legs, privates. No exceptions." To Sam she says, "Make her a waxing appointment. With Olga. Be sure she knows we don't want a Brazilian." Alexandra turns back to me. "You should be neat, not bald."

I want to ask her who in the world she thinks is going to see my neatness, but I fight the urge.

She hands me a pair of sky-high heels that are two sizes too big. Sam stuffs the toes with crumpled-up paper towel stolen from the girls' restroom. It takes a lot of paper towel to make my feet fit, but we get there. The real challenge is trying to walk in them.

"You can't put your weight on the heel," Alexandra instructs. "Step lightly, on the ball of your foot. Not your sole, the *ball*. Do you know what the ball of your foot is?"

"I know it doesn't look like it," I say, "but I *am* trying."

"Try harder," she shoots back.

I am given speeches about the three Ps of pageant success: posture, poise, and presentation. According to Alexandra, my posture is for shit, I lack poise, and my presentation leaves a lot to be desired.

"No more denim!" she barks. "You walk like you've spent your whole life wearing jeans. Skirts only until after the election. Nothing too short, either. Despite what Hayley Langer and her crew think, if a skirt doesn't hit your knee, it is most definitely too short."

I always figured that being pretty took a lot of work. That is what women always say in the magazines, what actresses say in interviews. But honestly? I had no idea just how much work it could be.

My stomach starts grumbling around seven. Thirty minutes later, Alexandra declares us done for the day. Or so I think.

"Which do you want to tackle tonight—clothes or makeup?" she asks me. "I'm thinking makeup, since it will have the biggest impact with the hair. But your clothes . . . you need new clothes, Ivy."

"I need to go *home*," I say. "I need to eat dinner."

"Dinner is for losers," she retorts. "Are you a loser, Ivy?"

Sam cuts in, "You know, I could eat, too. Maybe we break for dinner, then regroup?"

It is the most she has said since we were alone in the car.

Alexandra checks her wristwatch, a slender silver one with diamonds crusted around the face. It looks old, like it was handed down to her from a grandparent.

"We don't have time for a break," she says.

"Then maybe a snack," Sam suggests.

Alexandra sighs heavily. "Fine. Something quick. Let's move."

While I change back into my own clothes, they huddle in a corner to go over details. I hear Alexandra ticking off a list of cosmetics I will need to purchase. I wonder if she plans to pay for them, too. I don't have her kind of money, that is for sure.

In the car, Alexandra continues to give us orders. "No purple anything," she declares. "Teal is your new color. You'll look good in teal. Not eye shadow—just clothes. And limit the black. We can't have you looking like you're headed to a funeral."

Apparently, we are doing both clothes and makeup this evening.

I had thought shopping might be more relaxed than my three Ps practice, but I was dead wrong. Sam and Alexandra book it across the food court with me ten steps behind, practically running to keep up. "Dinner" turns out to be a protein-boosted acai smoothie from Jamba Juice so that we do not have to bother with a table or even utensils. Then we suck them down as we speed-walk to Forever 21.

Sam pulls garments off the rack with a freakish kind of precision. She can take one look at a shirt and know in an instant whether it has a "generous cut" or "unforgiving lines." I point out an ankle-length, floral print skirt that looks great with a baggy sweater, or at least it does on the mannequin. Alexandra shakes her head no.

"Why not?" I say. I am thinking that long skirts equal less-frequent leg shaving. But what I say is "It's girly, right?"

"It's shapeless," Alexandra says. "Our school is forty-seven percent male. Boys vote for boobs. You hide those and you can kiss the crown good-bye."

"Oh."

I point out a few other things that catch my eye but make Alexandra roll hers. She hates everything I like. Sam offers no opinions whatsoever.

After I try on several configurations of garments, we land on a combination that pleases Alexandra: a high-waisted maroon pencil skirt paired with a slim-fit black turtleneck sweater tucked in.

"This. Yes," Alexandra says. "Retro is the way to go."

"Sure," I say. "Retro. Got it."

But I do not "got it." Everything about this day feels completely surreal. When I go into the dressing room with the striped sweater dress that Alexandra insists I try on, I see some strange girl in the mirror . . . and then realize that *I am that strange girl*. I have new hair. I have new clothes. And, as long as we hit the makeup counter in time, I will have a new face, too.

By the time we leave, I am the new owner of four pencil skirts in various colors and fabrics, plus matching tops, two sweater dresses, a couple of pairs of tights, some earrings, and a boxy purse. All Alexandra-approved, all Alexandra-purchased.

"I hope she doesn't expect me to put out," I joke to Sam as we head to meet Alexandra, who apparently does not like waiting in checkout lines, at the MAC store.

Sam's head whips around so fast I could hear a cartoon swoosh. "Why would you say something like that?"

"Because she's buying me all of this stuff," I say. "It was a joke. I'm joking."

She squinches her eyes at me, not saying anything. Finally, after what feels like an eternity of judgy silence: "Nothing about this is funny."

Then she strides away from me, like we didn't even come here together. I have to double-time it just to keep up.

At MAC, Alexandra shows a lady with scary eyebrows pictures of the outfits we purchased and says something to her about a new "neutral retro" look. I have no idea what that even means, but I sit, not saying a word, as she paints a bunch of things on my face. Alexandra nods approvingly, giving Scary Eyebrows feedback as she works.

I am not allowed to see until she has finished. The makeup lady hands me a black plastic mirror. Her face is blank. I raise the mirror up, not sure what to expect, and let out a short gasp.

I was right: I have a brand-new face.

Cheekbones, to start. I have them now. They are an optical illusion, but so is everything about this version of me. My eyes look bigger, my lips look fuller, and I can't help but think, *So this is what it feels like to be pretty.*

"Take it all off," Alexandra tells Scary Eyebrows. "Start from the beginning, only this time, show her how to do everything."

Scary Eyebrows obliges; my guess is that she works on some sort of commission. Or maybe she gets a bonus based on how much product she pushes. It is a lot of makeup. The total ends up in the hundreds. No joke.

Alexandra moves on to another store while Sam handles checkout. She tells us to meet her at the car.

"What's wrong?" Sam asks as we head to the parking lot. "You're white as a ghost."

"I can't afford all of this," I say. "I'm never going to be able to pay her back."

"You won't have to."

"But how can I not?"

"Listen," Sam says. "They have money. They had it when her dad was alive and they have more of it now that he's dead. A lot more. Don't worry about it, okay?"

But I am worried. Of course I am worried. Alexandra has invested a lot in me. Time. Money. What if I fail her? What if I lose this race she so badly wants me to win?

What did I do to deserve all of this? *Any* of this?

How did I, crazy Ivy Proctor, ever get so incredibly lucky?

TWENTY-SEVEN

Alexandra

When I get home, post-mall excursion, it is to an empty house. I don't mean that metaphorically speaking, either. I mean that no one is here. Natalie isn't at home. She was here when I left, after our pageant practice. So where is she now?

I wander through the living room and into the kitchen. There's no note there. None in my bedroom either. There aren't any text or voice mail messages—I didn't even miss a call.

It occurs to me that I should be worried. After all, my mother doesn't own a car anymore. I mean, technically my car is her car—*was* her car—but she pretty much stopped driving not long after my father's accident. Her decline in driving was proportional to her escalated boozing, so this turned out to be a good thing.

I could play Nancy Drew and try to figure out where she is and what she's doing, but I don't have it in me. Besides, I can't remember the last time I had the house to myself. It is deliciously quiet. I need to take advantage of it while I can. Surely Natalie will be home in the next hour or so. It's nearing ten o'clock.

Within the next hour, I've breezed through my homework *and* cleared out my email. Matt's and my YouTube video now has more than 27,000 views; it's more than doubled in the last two days. You can't buy that kind of PR.

Eleven thirty comes and goes; still no Natalie. I'm going to pay for staying up so late anyway, so I decide to sneak in a quick run before bed. I can feel the steel in my muscles, the blood pumping through my heart. With each mile, my head grows clearer.

Natalie *still* hasn't returned by the time I hit the shower. I send my mother a text letting her know that I am worried about her. She doesn't answer. By the time I slide into bed, quarter past midnight, I am honestly a little scared. I call Natalie's cell; it goes direct to voice mail.

"It's me," I say. "And it's really late. I hope you're okay. Call me if you need anything."

As tired as I am, I can't fall asleep. I head down to the kitchen for some warm milk and a Benadryl when I hear the key fumbling in the lock. I run to answer the door. Natalie is standing on the stoop, illuminated only by the full moon. Her hair has been pulled into an impeccable chignon and her makeup is magazine-perfect.

"Where have you been?" I ask her, and not in a disappointed parent kind of way. I am genuinely curious.

She gives me a long, long look. Then she steps over the threshold, pushes past me, and walks straight upstairs without so much as a simple explanation.

What the fuck *ever*.

～

"I don't know what happened. I swear I followed the instructions."

A tearful Ivy Proctor stands before me, looking like a drunk sorority girl who just burned herself trying to light a cigarette backward. Her newly dyed hair is both limp and frizzy at the same time. Her makeup is cartoonish; I have to wonder if she applied it in the dark. And she's wearing that dreadful black hoodie of hers, the one that has thumbholes in the cuffs so that they always cover half the hands, over the new teal sweater dress my credit card purchased last night.

In other words, she is the hottest of hot messes.

"Take it off," I say.

"The hoodie?" Ivy asks.

I shake my head. "All of it."

"You want me to . . . strip?"

"God, no," I say. "I want you to get back in the shower. Wash your face. Put on your old clothes. Now."

More tears spill down Ivy's cheeks, making black tracks through rouge-red circles. To Sam I say, "Didn't I tell them we wanted waterproof everything?"

"I'll return it," Sam says, not missing a beat.

Ivy stands there, her narrow shoulders shaking as she cries. She's a quiet crier, and for whatever reason this infuriates me even more.

"Get in the shower!" I snap. "Now!"

She runs off without another word.

I am seething. Only Ivy Proctor could fuck up a thousand-dollar makeover.

"You could've warned me," I say to Sam. She doesn't respond.

After a minute, Sam sets about straightening the messy room. There are bags, tags, and clothes all over the floor. She is very Sam about the whole thing. Slow. Deliberate. Methodical.

Also infuriating.

"Any new dirt on Erin?" I ask as Sam folds clothes neatly on the foot of Ivy's bed.

"Nope," Sam says. Her tone is clipped. She can't possibly be angry at me. Can she?

There are only three weeks until the election. Three weeks in which to turn Ivy into a viable candidate before I posit myself as the front-runner once more.

Have you figured it out yet? My plan? I'm building Ivy up, placing her on a sky-high pedestal, only to push her off it at the eleventh hour. And in the wake of her destruction, I will arise, a phoenix forming from her ashes.

It's a brilliant plan, and one Erin Hewett would never see coming. Hell, you didn't see it coming, did you?

I would understand it if you are struggling to keep up. There are sophisticated machinations at work. The only thing you really need to know, right now, anyway, is that this whole process is going to be a *bitch*.

"Three weeks isn't enough," I say, more to myself than anything. "We need more time."

"Or less," Sam offers. "Is Matt hosting this year's Puritan Party?"

"Of course. The captain always hosts."

The Puritan Party is a tradition that stretches back to before Natalie was a student at Spencer High. After several years of the Spartans not winning a Homecoming game played on their own turf, the then-coach issued an edict: For two weeks immediately prior to the game, no player was allowed to indulge in drinking, drugging, smoking, or screwing. Anyone caught violating those rules would be kicked off the team. The party-hardy boys decided to have one last blowout the Saturday before restrictions went into effect—which by all accounts was a bacchanalia of epic proportions. Afterward, the team followed their coach's instructions to a T, and two weeks later, they slaughtered the Spirit Lake Lions, our long-term rivals. Prior to the game, the Lions had been having an undefeated season, so this was an extra-big coup.

A second Puritan Party was held the following year; again the Spartans were victorious. By year three, it had become a Spencer High tradition. The Puritan Parties continued, the players cooperated, and our high school hasn't lost a single Homecoming game in the past twenty-four years. If we win this year, we'll even break some sort of Indiana record.

"Why are you asking me about a social event?" I say. "We're in crisis mode."

"The guest list for the Puritan is pretty elite," Sam replies. "As a cheerleader, Erin will automatically be on the list. But Ivy won't."

"So?"

"So you should bring Ivy."

Just like that, I get what she's trying to say.

"You're fucking brilliant," I tell her. "I could kiss you right now, that's how brilliant you are."

Ivy reenters the room wrapped in a beige towel, with a second one turbaned on her head. So I don't know if Sam's turning red because of what I said or because she's in such close proximity to a semi-naked girl.

"I don't know what I'm supposed to be wearing," Ivy says sheepishly.

"Change of plans," I tell her. "We're going to wait a week before unveiling your new look. So for now, do everything like you normally do. Or like you did before I came along."

Ivy looks stricken. "You said we didn't have a single day to waste. You said—"

"I know what I said. Now I'm saying something different."

"What about my hair?"

Sam answers for me. "You need a hat. What about that old brown one you wear sometimes?"

Ivy roots around a pile of clothes that Sam hasn't folded and fishes out a knit skullcap. She takes off her turban and tucks her wet hair inside of the hat. "Like this?"

"Jesus," I say. "You look like a marshmallow wearing a woolly condom."

A quick glance at my watch tells me that if Sam and I leave now, I'll have at least fifteen minutes to make the rounds before first bell.

"Another change of plans," I announce. "We're going to head

out now and meet up with you later."

"But I already missed the bus."

"So get your mom to take you. I'll bring you home after school. Late, of course. We have a *lot* of work to do."

"But—"

I grab Sam's hand and pull her toward the door before Ivy can continue her protest. We need as much time as possible before homeroom. There are seeds to be planted, and I know exactly where to start.

TWENTY-EIGHT

Sloane

I am stationed near the school's entrance, partially hidden by a tall carton of cast-off shoes people have donated to the homeless. I am lying in waiting for one Alexandra Miles. Or, if I can't find her, lying in wait for Samantha Schnitt. But if they're together, then it's Alexandra, definitely.

And together is how I first spot them, whispering conspiratorially as they walk through the double doors. My plan is to wait until they pass, then slip out from my hiding place and call out Alexandra's name. Only, for whatever reason, Samantha is looking over my way. I panic and dip down into the box, trying to hide my face.

It doesn't work.

"Making a deposit or a withdrawal?" Alexandra says. I can practically hear the smirk in her voice.

I pop up and flash Alexandra a smile. Sam is nowhere to be seen.

"Oh, hey," I say brightly. "Good morning. How are you? There's something I wanted to—"

"I need you to run the meeting for me today," she says, cutting me off.

"Key Club?"

"No, our mutual AA meeting. Yes, Key Club. I have things I have to take care of after school."

"But . . . But you always run the meeting," I say. "You never miss."

"There's a first time for everything."

Typically, this would be when Alexandra would turn on her heel and walk away. In addition to running meetings, ruining relationships, stealing volunteer opportunities, and not answering emails, Alexandra really likes to have the last word.

But today she doesn't do this. Instead, she says, "You wanted something?"

"I did? Oh yeah, I did."

"So what is it?"

I swallow hard. "I wanted to apologize. For what I said the other day. I was just—"

"Hurt," she finishes for me. "I know. And I'm sorry."

My shock must register on my face, because the next thing I know she's laughing and saying, "Don't be so surprised. I know how to apologize."

"It's just—"

"Listen," Alexandra says, taking a step closer to me. "I've been thinking. It makes sense that you and I clash from time to time. For one thing, we have a lot of the same . . . interests. Like the acting thing, and Key Club, and you know, lots of stuff."

This list of things we have in common is starting to sound like an offshoot of a humblebrag. Because, hi, everything she's naming is stuff she's beat me at.

"What's your point?" I say.

"I don't want there to be bad feelings between us. High school's too short for that." Alexandra reaches out and squeezes my hand with hers. There's an earnestness in the way that she's looking at me that makes me wonder if she's actually being sincere.

"Give me a call this weekend," she says. "Maybe we can make plans to get together. I'm working with my pageant coach on Saturday, but I can always make time for a friend." She offers a final warm smile and a little wave before turning and heading off down the hallway.

Fact: I am 100 percent dumbfounded. I stand there, speechless, watching her disappear in the distance.

What just *happened*?

Or, the bigger question: Why did that just happen?

I almost—almost—believed that little performance of hers. Right up until she called me her friend.

We have never been friends. Not really.

And more than that: we will never be friends. Ever.

So why is Alexandra Miles suddenly trying to make nice with me? Is it because of what I said the other day? Does she suddenly see me as some sort of threat?

Maybe I don't suck at this scheming thing after all.

TWENTY-NINE

Sam

Ivy eats lunch with Lexi and me now. This is a thing. A temporary thing, but a thing nonetheless. I know this is happening, and when Ivy sits down at the table with an apologetic smile—it's the only way she knows how to smile, I think—it feels almost normal.

What doesn't feel the least bit normal is who else decides to invade our lunch table today.

"Hey, friends!" Sloane Fahey says in her breathless, over-the-top way of hers. "Mind if I join you?"

She doesn't wait for an answer. She sits, puts her pink plastic Hello Kitty bento box down, and lifts off the lid.

I brace myself for Lexi to blow, but she doesn't. Not even when Sloane starts eating some sort of tofu-and-vegetable concoction with a pair of flowered chopsticks. Instead, she says, "Sloane, you know Ivy, right?"

"Of course," Sloane says. "Everybody knows Ivy."

Ivy's face turns red in an instant.

"She means because you're up for Homecoming Queen,"

Lexi says, rescuing her least-favorite redhead.

"Yes!" Sloane chimes in, sounding one step down from frantic. "That's exactly what I meant!"

"Oh" is all Ivy can say in return.

We pick at our food in awkward silence. What is happening here? Everything about this scene feels wrong.

Then Matt approaches, almost as if on cue, and breaks the tension. "Hey, babe," he says, nuzzling Lexi's cheek from behind. "Can I steal you for a sec?"

"Of course," she says. "What's up?"

"Can't a guy just miss his girl?"

Gag.

I hate it when they act like this.

"Come sit with us for a few," Matt says. "You too, Ivy. I want you to meet my friend Bobby."

"Um," Ivy says. "Sure?"

She says it just like that, too. Like it's a question. But, ever the puppy, she follows the golden couple over to Matt's table of football players. It's one of the long ones with the built-in bench seating. The guys squeeze together to make room for Ivy, who slips neatly in between Bobby Jablonski and Chick Myers. She's so tiny that Chick's body looks like it might swallow her up.

This must have been preplanned. Part of Lexi's scheme to get Ivy ready for her debut at the Puritan Party. Or maybe she's trying to get Bobby to take Ivy to the dance.

I don't know because she didn't tell me.

There are a lot of things she hasn't been telling me lately. This is not like Lexi. I am her closest confidante. I am the one who knows her better than anyone else on the planet. Me, not Matt. *Me.*

For instance, I know for a fact that she has never talked to Matt about losing her father. Whereas I was there, at his funeral, holding her hand when her mother wouldn't. I was the one she cried in front of—real tears, not the fake ones she can summon on command. I was the one who listened to her stories about him, and how he spoiled her. "Not with money," she said, "though clearly there was plenty of that. It's his attention I miss the most."

Natalie has always treated Lexi as an extension of herself. A baby doll she crafted in her own image. But her dad truly adored Lexi. You could see it in the way his face lit up whenever she walked into a room. They'd go on these long runs together, and afterward, while they were protein-loading, they'd talk about, well, everything.

I wasn't there for these conversations. So maybe Lexi is rewriting the past. Lord knows Natalie does enough of that.

But I knew Mr. Miles, and I don't think she's making anything up. I think when he died, she lost the only real parent she ever had.

When I turn back to my lunch I catch Sloane staring at me. She's been doing that a lot lately. Just looking at me. If I didn't know any better I'd think that she was suddenly into me or something, but everyone at Spencer knows she's . . . uh . . . *super* into guys. Well, according to Lexi's rumors, that is.

So why would she be looking at *me*?

"I never realized how pretty she was," Sloane says, apropos of nothing.

"Who, Lexi?"

"No, Ivy," Sloane says. "I guess I never paid that much attention to her. It's amazing how one day you can look at someone and see something that wasn't there before."

When she says this, her eyes lock onto mine, and she runs her tongue over her bottom lip. I think, *Holy shit, she's trying to flirt with me!*

I stifle a laugh. Oh, man, if only Lexi were here to see this. I decide it's too good an opportunity to pass up.

"I know what you mean," I say to Sloane, casting my eyes downward. "You can think you have a person all figured out, but then one day, they say or do something different, and you just . . . see them in a whole new light."

I slowly raise my eyes to meet hers, and a shy smile forms on my lips. At least, I hope that's what it looks like.

"So," Sloane says, "do you have a date to Homecoming yet?"

"No," I say, which is the truth. "You?"

"Not yet," she says. "There's someone I'm thinking of asking, though."

"Oh, yeah?"

"Yeah," Sloane says. "Trying to figure out if this person is interested."

Time to bring this thing home.

"You should just ask," I say. "You might be surprised by who'd say yes."

I spend the rest of the day thinking up ways to toy with Sloane Fahey. I don't have a problem with her, per se, but I do find it kind of amusing that she's suddenly so into me. It would be one thing if her interest were genuine, but it comes off as just another example of Sloane trying to be more like Lexi—and failing miserably.

"Can you believe the nerve?" I hear Hayley Langer say behind me. I turn to see her toss her bottle-blond hair over one shoulder. "Who does she think she is, anyway?"

"She shouldn't be allowed to run," says Carissa, her top minion.

Carissa's cousin and fellow minion Steph chimes in, "You're so right. She only got here, like, five minutes ago. There should be a rule or something."

They are talking about Erin. And only a few feet away from me.

"It's not about how long she has or hasn't been here," Hayley says. "It's about what she said. About our school. About what it means to be the Homecoming Queen."

I frown. When did Lexi leak this? And why didn't she have me do the leaking to begin with?

"Where did you hear that?" I say.

"Excuse me?" Carissa says. "We're talking here."

"You're talking about Erin Hewett, right? Sorry, didn't mean to eavesdrop."

"Why do you care?" Hayley asks.

"No reason," I say with a shrug. "You might want to keep your voices down, though. You definitely don't want Frick to overhear you."

"Why not?" Hayley says, jutting out her Reese Witherspoonian chin. "She'd probably be as outraged as we are. She might even disqualify her."

"I wouldn't bet on it." I pretend to turn my attention to the contents of my locker. Then, as casually as I can, I add, "Considering their connection and all." I swap out books until I have what I need for this weekend's homework. When I turn to face the girls I see that they're giving me the same irritated-but-still-puzzled look.

"You *do* know about Erin's connection to Frick, don't you?"

"Sure," Hayley replies, looking anything but.

Carissa echoes, "Everybody knows that. Duh."

"Oh, okay. Just wanted to make sure."

I shut my locker and start to walk away when I hear Steph whine, "What is she talking about, anyway?"

Hayley shushes her and says, "Wait until she's out of earshot."

"Too late," I feel like calling out to them, but don't.

When I reach the gymnatorium, I see Lexi and Ivy embroiled in some sort of drama. From the distance, it looks like Ivy is crying into her forearm. Lexi keeps trying to reach out and touch her, but each time Ivy bats her away. I cheat to the right a bit and sidle up as quietly as I can.

"I can't do this anymore!" Ivy wails. "It's all too much!"

"Ivy, please," Lexi says, her voice saccharine-sweet. "Calm down. Let's talk about this."

"There's nothing to talk about! It's over. We'll return the clothes and the makeup and hair products, and I'll pay you back for the cut and color."

"I don't want your two hundred dollars," Lexi says, causing Ivy to gasp audibly.

She starts to cry even harder. "Oh, god, oh, god, how did I let this *happen*?" Ivy buries her face in her hands, sobbing so intensely she starts to hiccup.

Now I'm close enough to see Lexi's jawline harden. She doesn't have the patience for Ivy's particular brand of weakness. I half expect her to slap the girl across the face, just to snap her out of it. Instead, she opts for a different approach: the hug.

Lexi steps forward and wraps her arms around Ivy, squeezing her close. "Go ahead and cry," she says soothingly. "Let it out, Ivy. Let it all out."

I'm so confused by this act of kindness that I just stand there in the shadows, completely transfixed.

After a few minutes, Ivy's sobs subside. She lifts her head and takes a few steps away from Lexi. "I'm sorry," she says. "I shouldn't—"

"Please don't apologize," Lexi tells her. "I get it. I'm sure all of this attention makes you uncomfortable."

Ivy nods, wiping her nose on the sleeve of her gross black hoodie.

"Look," Lexi says, her voice soft as butter, "I don't know why you had that breakdown, and I'm not asking you to tell me. But whatever the reason, it's clearly left scars beyond the ones on your wrists."

Ivy's eyes widen. Instinctively, she pulls the cuffs of her hoodie even farther down her hands.

"You may be able to hide them from everyone else," Lexi says, "but I know they're there. And I don't care. I mean, I care about *you*, Ivy. *This* you. The girl you are now. That other girl—the one who sliced herself just so she could feel something? That girl is gone now."

Ivy doesn't look convinced. I debate whether now is the time to make my presence known—if me entering will defuse the tension. But then I catch Lexi's hand, hanging at her side. She flicks it backward as if to tell me to stop. How did she—

The mirror. Of course. She's known I was here the whole time.

"You may not see it yet, but we do," Lexi says. "Me. Sam. Bobby. I think he likes you, Ivy. But even if it turns out that he doesn't, you have to know that *I do*. I believe in you. The way you've turned your life around? You're an *inspiration*, Ivy. That's why I'm fighting so hard to make you queen.

"I just hope that when they put that crown on your head, maybe, just maybe, you'll start to see yourself the way that I do."

She's sold it. She's sold it so well, I am starting to think she means the things that she's saying.

"Go wash your face," Lexi instructs. "And then we'll get started."

Ivy smiles, and nods, and obediently trots off to the girls' locker room. When the gym door slams, Lexi says, "You can come out now, Sam."

"Sorry," I say. "I didn't want to interrupt. You and Ivy . . . you were having a moment."

She rolls her eyes at me. "Please. You can't possibly be jealous, Sam. Not of *Ivy*."

"I'm not," I say. "I was just commenting on the fact that you two seem to be getting . . . closer."

"Because that's what it's supposed to seem like," she says with a sneer. "I thought you were smarter than that."

The words have a surprising sting. It must register on my face, because then Lexi says, "Jesus, are you going to start crying now, too? Toughen up, Schnitt. You know the first step to escaping Spencer is nailing this competition. And we've got some serious work to do."

THIRTY

Alexandra

It's after nine thirty when I pull into our driveway, ending what has been a long, draining day. For every success I've achieved—like sharing Erin's "phony pageantry" gaffe with a few key gossips, or making it seem normal to invite Ivy fucking Proctor into Matt's circle of bros—there have been double the setbacks. Ivy's botched makeover and subsequent afternoon meltdown. Sam's annoying jealousy and unnecessarily possessive attitude. And don't even get me started on Sloane Fahey's brazenly bullshit attempt to join my lunch table without invitation. The indignity of having to endure her presence—even briefly—was almost more than I could bear.

Before I get out of the car, my phone rings. Matt. It's about damned time. Earlier today he mentioned the two of us getting together tonight, for some "quality time." Translation: he needs to get laid.

"Baby," Matt slurs in a voice thick with beer. "Baby, I miss you."

"Aww," I say. "You're so sweet." Wasted is more like it. But I can't blame him. Most of the Spartan guys get like this the week before the Puritan Party. It's all about the booze and the banging, like they can stockpile sin for the two weeks they promised to abstain.

"I fucking love you," Matt says. "I love you so much. You know that, right?"

"Of course. Me too."

It sounds like he's at a party. But no one we know was having a party tonight. At least, not that I am aware of. Then, in the background, I hear a girl say, "Matty, who are you talking to?"

That doesn't sound like just any girl, though.

It sounds like Erin Hewett.

"So where are you?" I ask.

"The girls decided to have a thing at the last minute. I'm there."

By "girls" he means the Spartan pep squad. They don't like me much, because in their limited worldview I have committed the unpardonable act of dating one of "their" boys. The feeling is mutual.

I don't know what Erin's up to, but I don't like the idea of my very drunk boyfriend being at a party full of indiscriminate cheerleaders. "I'll come get you."

"You don't have to do that."

"I know I don't have to," I say. "But all night, the only thing I've wanted was for us to be, you know, *together*." I swallow my distaste and add, "And that can't happen if you're there and I'm here."

I know Matt. For him to sound this destroyed, he must've been slamming boilermakers all night long. Which means that any attempts I make to bed him will be fraught with the frustration of his inability to get and/or maintain an erection. (Thanks, alcohol.)

Even so, I can't leave him there. Not with *her*.

Thankfully, my words have their desired effect.

"Lemme text you the address," Matt says huskily. "And *hurry*."

Within twenty minutes, I'm making the right onto Poplar Drive. I don't recognize the street, which all but confirms it: my boyfriend must be at Erin Hewett's house. Not only is he at her house, he is drunk off his ass at her house. And I'd bet money that she's been the one plying him with drinks. Trying to get him loaded enough that he might actually cheat on me. As if he'd ever do that, especially with someone like *her*.

Erin's neighborhood is a nice one. Not as nice as mine, of course, but about three or four steps up from Ivy's. There are a lot of cars parked outside. This isn't some impromptu hangout. It's a party. I'd been planning on texting Matt from the car, having him come to me, but now I feel compelled to go inside. It would be slightly humiliating to start dry-humping my boyfriend in public, but doing it in front of Erin—showing her that her sophomoric plan didn't work—might make it worth my while.

I ring the doorbell to the pale blue Colonial, expecting Erin to answer it. Expecting her face to fall when she sees I've crashed her little gathering. But she is not the one who invites me in. Instead, it's Ingrid Bell, cocaptain of the squad.

"Alexandra, you made it!" she says, throwing her arms around me in a girl hug. She stinks of whiskey. I was right: boilermakers.

Ingrid leads me inside. It's not a party-party; the lights are all on and there's not even any music playing. I scan the room and see Erin sitting on a football player's lap. Not just any football player, either—she's cozying up to Bobby Jablonski. The very guy I earmarked for Ivy.

Bobby is whispering something into her ear. Erin is smiling. But she's not looking at him.

She's looking at me.

Does she really think she can beat me at my own game?

"Baby!" Matt bellows, coming up behind me. "You're here!" He buries his face in my neck, doing this weird thing with his tongue that for some unknown reason he thinks I like. I smile and lean into him, assuming the role of rapturous girlfriend. Matt spins me to face him, and lays one on me, bending me backward as he grinds up against me. There are some whoops from the studio audience.

Matt is grinning a sloppy, boozy grin. His eyes look sleepy. He keeps pulling me closer, grabbing at my ass with one hand and my boob with the other.

"Okay, Mr. Handsy," I say, moving both to more respectable places. "Let's get out of here."

"Or," he says in a low voice, "we can go upstairs. I've already scouted it out—there are two spare bedrooms and only one of them is occupied."

When Matt says things like this, I know that I shouldn't be dating a high school boy. Or, at the very least, one who'd suggest having sex in some random guest room one floor up from a party.

"Uh-uh," I say. "You know the rules."

Yes, I have rules. Any responsible teenager who chooses to be sexually active should have them. Mine are:

- Condoms aren't optional, even though I'm on the pill.
- No sex in cars, on school property, at parties, or in other public locations. One, it's gross. Two, sex should be private. And three, I can't control the environment in any of those places. Nothing will ruin my chances of becoming Miss America faster than an unauthorized sex tape.
- There won't be any photographs or recordings made for private use, either.
- I reserve the right to say no at any time, even mid-act.
- No butt stuff. Ever.

"You're no fun," Matt says, pouting.

"And you're really drunk," I say through my smile.

"This," he says, "is very true."

Matt is so drunk, in fact, that the only reason he agrees to leave is because he's about to hurl. He makes it as far as the front landing before projectile vomiting into some boxwood. Then he continues to heave, getting the puke all over his shoes, his shirt, and the decorative stone path that winds up to the door.

A few partygoers look on from the foyer.

"Dude," I hear Chick Myers bellow. "You're so trashed."

"Jesus," I say. "How much have you had?"

Matt doesn't answer me. Instead, he keeps apologizing. "Oh, god, I'm so sorry. Tell Erin I'm so sorry. I'm really, really sorry."

As if on cue, Erin appears with a bottle of water and a wet washcloth. "Here, Matty," she says, handing him the items. "Please, don't apologize."

"Lemme clean it up."

"I'll just hose it down later. Really, it's no big deal."

If the situation had been reversed, and it was Erin's boyfriend who'd just horked up all over my ornamental greenery, I would not be so calm and understanding. I would be *pissed*. And rightfully so.

But now that she's made such a big show of being such a calm, understanding girl, I have to be one, too. Only better.

I rub circles into Matt's back and use Erin's washcloth to wipe the puke from his shirt and face. I pour some of the water on his sneakers to wash off the chunky bits. Like magic, another bottle appears out of nowhere. "Matty needs to hydrate," Erin explains.

"Actually," I say, "water is the worst thing you can give someone who's already vomiting. Ice chips are better."

"Wow," Erin says. "How did you learn that?"

It's not an innocent question. I can see that by the fire in her eyes.

"You should ask your aunt," I shoot back, taking a grim satisfaction at watching the smirk slide from her dainty little lips. "But I'm sure she's filled you in already. Come on, Matt. Let me get you showered up."

As I walk Matt back to my car, I am beyond irritated with myself. Before tonight, Erin didn't know I knew about Frick's and her connection. Neither did Frick. But now it's out there, and for what? A wasted moment. My fault. Fuck me.

"You still wanna do it tonight?" Matt asks as he fumbles with his seat belt.

I don't even dignify his question with a response.

THIRTY-ONE

Sloane

Saturday, 8:16 a.m. I am stationed at a corner high-top table in the Starbucks on Main Street. From my vantage point I can see who's approaching from both directions, but the tinted windows and the angle at which the table is situated keep me hidden from them.

It is the perfect place to "run into" Alexandra Miles.

This is what I know: every Saturday morning, at the butt crack of dawn, Alexandra meets up with her pageant coach at the studio next door. Their three-hour session wraps up around eight thirty, which is when the overeager dance moms start herding in their offspring for ballet lessons. Afterward, she comes in here and orders a skinny latte and a scone, then cancels the scone before they ring her up.

One of these days, she's going to buckle and actually eat the damned scone.

Confession: This is not the first time I've staked out this Starbucks, or Alexandra. Sophomore year, I'd often be doing homework here when she'd come in after her coaching session.

We'd even hung out a few times, especially after we both got cast in *You're a Good Man, Charlie Brown* (she was Lucy, of course; I was Snoopy's understudy and part of the chorus). For a while, the most powerful girl in school was actually my friend, sort of.

Then, after I started dating Jonah Dorsey, she turned on me. Because of her, I spent the second half of sophomore year and the first third of junior year in near exile.

Today's stakeout isn't about any of that, though. For me, anyway. It's a recon mission. Another step in my plan to take Alexandra Miles down for good.

My plan is this: When I see Alexandra approach, I'm going to bury my nose in a book, like I'm just here hanging out, reading. As she stands in line, I'll look up and wave, NBD, and then start packing up my things. I will time this so that as she's handing over her credit card, I'm getting ready to walk, and we will leave together. This is when I will strike up a casual conversation, we'll get to talking, and so on and so forth.

Another confession: I'm not 100 percent sure what I think will come of this conversation, or even what I want to come of it. I just know that I don't know enough to actually *do* anything. And here's the thing about Alexandra: if you flatter her enough, and in just the right way, she'll start talking. She'll tell you things that leave her vulnerable.

Case in point: Sophomore year, before she started all the shit between me and Jonah, we were chatting after play rehearsal. Alexandra's mom almost always forgot to pick her up. She would refuse rides from everyone, stubbornly waiting for her mom until Mrs. Mays had to lock up the building. Then Alexandra would break down and call her uncle, this hot older dude who always showed up in a three-piece suit and shoes polished to a military shine, and he'd come rescue her in his Jag.

On this particular day, my mom was running crazy late. She works as a paralegal for a total douche canoe who doesn't seem to understand the plight of the single mother. Anyway, it was just the two of us, sitting on the curb outside of Spencer, and Alexandra was being uncharacteristically chatty. She'd just won the Miss Hoosier High pageant and was all jazzed about taking home her third Grand Supreme title in a row. I didn't know what that was, but I figured it must be a good thing, since she kept going on and on about it.

"You're too good for Spencer," I said, and I meant it.

"You think?"

I rolled my eyes. "Obvi. You should, like, be on TV."

She wrinkled her nose in that way she does when she's pretending to be humble. "I don't know about all that."

"Come on," I said. "It's only a matter of time before you're out of here. Bigger and better, right?"

The mood shifted almost instantaneously. Her face darkened a bit, and she looked off into the distance—at what, I don't know.

"There are things I need to do first," she told me.

"Such as?"

"Such as crowns that need to be won. Boxes that need to be checked off. I can't leave Indiana until I accomplish certain things. Not even for college. But once that list is complete . . ."

"Then what?"

"Then I am never coming back. Not for her. Not for anyone."

Her blue eyes flashed as she said this, and the intensity of her words spooked me. I felt like she was sharing something with me that she didn't say to a lot of people. I liked that feeling, so I pressed for more.

"This list that you're talking about—is it like an actual list?"

"Typed and hanging on the side of our fridge."

"Wow. How old were you when you wrote it?"

She laughed a short, barking laugh. "I didn't," she said. "But it's charming that you would even think that."

Then she turned to me and said, "You're lucky, Sloane. I've seen you with your mom. She adores you. You don't even have to do anything to make her adore you. She just *does*.

"Not all of us are that lucky," she finished.

And then, as if realizing how much of herself she'd just exposed, she popped up off the curb. "I need to call my uncle," she said. "I forgot that he was supposed to pick me up today."

I offered her a ride, as I always did, and she refused, as she always did. Then she walked a few steps away, and dialed the old dude. He got to her before the douche canoe let my mom leave, but she didn't ask if I wanted a lift. She didn't so much as wave good-bye when she climbed into his fancy-pants car.

Being on a stakeout is kind of boring. To pass the time, I pick up the book I brought—it's this funny little novel about a teenage movie star who goes undercover in nearby Fort Wayne—and read. I'm careful to keep tabs on everyone who comes in and out, and who passes by, but the book's so good that I'm not really paying attention to the time—just reading and lifting my head every time I hear the whoosh of an opening door. When I remember to check my phone, it's already 8:46.

Alexandra should have been here by now. I couldn't have missed her. So where is she?

The minutes tick by. A trio of chubby girls run into the studio. Their even chubbier moms follow close behind. 8:59. 9:07. 9:23.

She's not coming.

She always comes.

What a wasted morning.

I shove the book back into my satchel, toss my paper cup, and hit the ladies' before I head home. When I emerge a few minutes later, I am momentarily blinded by the sun's brightness. It makes my eyes water. I root around my satchel for my sunnies, put them on, and look up.

Across the street I see her. At least, I think it's her. Not Alexandra—her *mother*.

She's walking unsteadily in a pair of stilettos—stilettos! On a Saturday morning!—but I can tell from the way her hips switch back and forth that it's Mrs. Miles. As she makes her way down the sidewalk, she looks around nervously, pulling a shimmery black wrap tightly around her shoulders. A minute later, a cab pulls up and she climbs inside.

Holy shit—did I just witness Natalie Miles doing a walk of

shame? I mean, why else would she be dressed for a cocktail party at nine thirty in the morning?

Then again, Alexandra's mom always has been kind of . . . odd. At least, she has been since Alexandra's father bit it in that accident. Fact: Mrs. Miles has become such a shut-in that she hasn't been spotted at a school event in at least eighteen months. She didn't even show for last year's spring musical. She's rarely been seen, period.

If I book it to my car, I might be fast enough to tail the cab. I can't find out where Mrs. Miles has been, but I can at least see where she's going.

Maybe today wasn't such a waste after all.

THIRTY-TWO

Ivy

My days no longer belong to me. They belong to *her*. Alexandra. My benefactor. My coach. My . . . friend?

When school ends, my training continues. She teaches me how to walk, how to dress, how to act. We have practice conversations in which I am me and she is everyone from Principal Frick to Bobby Jablonski. When I cracked a joke the other day about Pygmalion, she frowned at me and said, "Cut it with the nerd humor. You have to be just smart enough, and not a single IQ point more."

I do not know what she means by that. But I do not question the things she tells me. I figure that you do not get to be in her position without knowing a few tricks.

The schedule is insane, but that is not the most difficult part of the process. No, that would be my mother.

My plain, sweet, simple mother. I have put that woman through hell. This is what her sister, my aunt Gladie, tells me every time she sees me. Even when it is paired with a sort of compliment. "You're looking well, Ivy," she will say. "Thank God, after all that hell you put your poor mother through."

We do not talk about *why* I did what I did. The events that led to my breakdown. We do not have to, now that Gladie's "perfect" little Sean has gone off to college. With him away, my nightmares have stopped. It helps that he does not come home very often. In fact, I have not so much as seen him since last Christmas.

It is better this way. Even my mom says so.

She is not happy about my new hair. Where did I get the money, she wanted to know. I lied and said that Sam's cousin's friend did it for free. The made-up cousin's friend is in cosmetology school. She is just far enough removed from the situation that my mother cannot confirm this fact.

The makeup, I hide. Each night before I go to bed I practice the techniques that the lady at the MAC counter and Alexandra have taught me. I wait until my mother is asleep to do this. Then I wipe it all off, right there in my bedroom, before lights-out. When it comes time for me to wear it to school, I will put everything into a makeup case and pack it all in my school bag. She might be able to see it on my face but she will not know which brands I am using or how much each item costs.

The clothes are a different story. Those I have hidden in various places around my room. I have cut the tags off and washed the pieces a few times. This is so I can convince my mother that they are lightly used hand-me-downs or thrift store finds. That was Sam's idea—a way for me to explain why I suddenly have a whole new wardrobe. I got some money from my dad to cover the thrift store part. I tried to give this to Alexandra, to pay her back, but she waved me off.

"Keep it," she said. "You need it way more than I do."

I did not know whether I should be grateful or offended.

I chose to be grateful.

Even though my big debut is not until Saturday, at the Puritan Party, I am already starting to get a small taste of what it is like to be popular. Or, at least, what my version of popular is. I no longer eat lunch alone. I have plans after school. I get text messages from people other than my mom and dad and Aunt Gladie. When I walk down the hall at school, I look at where I'm going, instead of at my feet.

Is this what normal feels like?

I am nervous about the party. The last one I went to that did not involve members of my extended family was Liza Humphrey's fifteenth birthday, spring of freshman year. She had it at a bowling alley. There was pizza and soda and Liza pretended like the only reason she invited me was because her mom made her and not because we were friends. We were, though. Friends. But even then—even before my breakdown—people had already started to distance themselves. I already reeked of loser. Another gift from Sean, perhaps.

Now they look at me differently. It is not with admiration— yet. Alexandra says this is only a matter of time. I have not been around that long, she says. No one knows what to make of me. The last time I was on the radar was for something bad.

Now it is for something good.

"You need to show them that you're worthy of the crown," she says, at least once a day.

Crowns are a big thing to Alexandra. I do not know exactly how big until the day of the Puritan Party. This is the first time she has invited me over to her house. Her bedroom is a huge palace of pink. Pale pink, like a flower petal. There are about six floating shelves along one wall. They hold nothing but trophies and sashes and crowns, so many crowns. The rhinestones are blinding.

"You won all of these?" I ask.

Sam smirks at me. "No, she stole them. Of course she won them!"

"Those are just the pretty ones," Alexandra says. "The rest are boxed up in the guest room closet."

"How many are there?"

She shrugs. "A lot. Natalie entered me in my first pageant before I knew how to crawl."

We are here to "pre-game." I do not know what pre-gaming is, but I do not tell Alexandra this. I assume it means getting ready for the party. After the party, we will come back here, and Sam and I will spend the night. This is because my mother does not know about me going to the Puritan Party. She would not approve. There is no parental supervision at Alexandra's house; her mother gives her free rein to come and go as she pleases.

Alexandra is an only child, like me. I cannot imagine being an only in a house this big with one parent who barely pays attention to you. It seems like a really lonely way to live.

Sam is using the flat iron on my hair but Alexandra does not like what she sees. She sends me off to take a shower in her personal bathroom so we can "start over."

This is not a burden. Her tub is really wide, like the kind you think only exists in the movies. A glamour tub. Alexandra tells me which shampoo and conditioner to use, hands me a couple of cloud-soft towels and a robe, and leaves me to it.

What I really want to do is take a bubble bath. It is definitely a bubble bath kind of tub. But there is too much to do before the party. The hair, the clothes, the makeup. Plus, Alexandra wants me to practice making conversation at parties. "We need to help them see the real you," she says.

What I think but do not say is this: Why must I do so much work to show them who I "really" am?

THIRTY-THREE

Alexandra

"Think she's ready?" Sam asks me when I return from shuttling Ivy into the shower.

"Not entirely," I say. "But she will be."

"Oh? Is there a plan?"

There is, but it's another one I won't be sharing with Sam. There are some lengths to which I go that would appall even my loyal Samantha. This, I fear, may be one of them.

"Right now, I plan to go downstairs and raid the liquor cabinet," I say. "Back in a few."

I'm practically giddy as I run down the steps. Tonight will be Ivy's coming-out party. No one will expect to see her there. Or even if they do, no one would ever expect her to show up looking so hot.

In the living room, I kneel down next to the once overflowing liquor cabinet. It hasn't had a proper restocking since my father died, and I've been slowly chipping away at its contents. Natalie never goes in there; the only thing she drinks is her Blanton's.

There are two things I need for tonight: a decent rum and

a syrupy sweet liqueur. I score half a bottle of Captain Morgan and an almost-full one of butterscotch schnapps. It's not until after I've closed the cabinet door and am standing up, one bottle in each hand, that I realize Natalie is lying on the sofa, staring at me. She doesn't say a word.

"Sam's driving," I say, my voice steady.

Natalie blinks. Her eyes look so dead they send a shiver up my spine. She rolls over onto her side, facing the back of the couch. Thanks for the conversation, Mom.

There's a strange part of me that wants to scream, "Wake up, Natalie! Your underage daughter is stealing booze so she can party with a bunch of wasted football players. Shouldn't you care just a little?"

But I already know the answer. Yes, she *should* care. But she doesn't.

The only thing she really cares about is me winning my next crown.

My next stop is the kitchen, where I retrieve two of Natalie's Xannies. There are enough in there that she won't miss them. I take the pill crusher left over from when I was too afraid to swallow pills of my own and pulverize them into a pale blue dust. There's a small silver flask that was my father's; I use the funnel it came with to carefully pour the powdered pills into it. This I top off with the butterscotch schnapps. It's got a little burn but mostly tastes like sugar. Definitely sweet enough to cover the bitter taste of the pills.

The flask is my insurance policy. I need buttoned-up Ivy to

get a little wild tonight, and I don't know how many Captain and Diet Cokes it will take to get her there. A few nips off my special flask should do the trick.

My arms are full as I head back to my room—I've got the rum, the schnapps, the flask, a two-liter of Diet Coke, three glasses. I knock on the closed door with one elbow. Sam opens it and immediately relieves me of the bottles. I place everything else down on my dresser and Sam gets to work. I'm not exaggerating when I say that Samantha is an exceptional bartender. She's so precise and deliberate. Just another reason why I keep her around.

I am taking my first sip as Ivy reenters my bedroom, her pale cheeks flushed pink from the hot shower. I hand her a drink. She takes a sip and almost instantly spits it out.

"I don't drink," she says.

Sam tells her, "Don't worry. You'll get used to the taste."

"No," Ivy says. "It's not just that I don't drink. I *can't* drink."

I know what she means without saying it: she's on medication you aren't supposed to mix with alcohol. So's Natalie, but it's never stopped her.

"Drug companies have to put that on the labels," I say, "because most people are too stupid to know how to handle both. But you can mix them. You just need to down a glass of water in between each drink."

Ivy does not look convinced.

"They'll notice," I say, "if you're the only one there sober."

"What about Sam?" Ivy points out.

Without flinching, Sam says, "I'll have exactly two drinks while we're at the party, but they'll be weak and I'll stop a minimum of ninety minutes before we leave."

"Oh."

Now Ivy looks terrified. What did she think happened at the Puritan Party? We've been talking to her about it for more than a week now.

I'm irritated, but don't let it show. Instead, I say, "You know, Ivy, I think it's really cool that you're straight edge like that. We could use this to our advantage."

"We can?" she asks, suddenly hopeful.

"Sure," I say. "But you'll have to work extra hard to show everyone how fun you can be. Oh, and I almost forgot—I got you something."

I hand her a bag from Victoria's Secret. Inside is a black satin strapless bra and a fitted long-sleeved shirt that bares both shoulders and a little bit of cleavage to boot.

"It's a sexy shirt," I say, "even with the really long sleeves." I say this last bit to her rather pointedly. I see the lightbulb go on over her head. *Really long sleeves hide really noticeable wrist scars.*

"Thank you," she says in her whisper voice.

Touches like this—picking out a shirt to keep her secrets hidden—buy me Ivy's loyalty. I can see it in her eyes. She still fears me a little, as well she should, but there is love mixed in with that fear. Gratitude. Hell, at this rate I could probably ask her to throw the election and she'd do it.

If Sam and I play our parts perfectly, I may be able to get out of this completely unscathed.

Am I that good? We'll just have to wait and see.

Sam and I get to work, she on hair and me on makeup. Sam trades the flat iron for a round brush and manages to give Ivy's caramel tresses some serious wave. Like a starlet from the 1940s, or a blond version of Dita Von Teese. I enhance the retro glam look Ivy's features are made for with a teensy bit of liquid eyeliner on her lash line, a hint of blush, and deep red lips.

"Holy shit," I say. "You don't even look like you anymore."

Ivy frowns.

"You look like the movie version of yourself," I clarify. "You, but the best possible version of you."

"Totally," Sam agrees. "Complete hotness. They aren't going to know what hit them."

Ivy's body relaxes visibly. The frown is replaced with a hint of a smile.

"Okay," she says with what feels like grim determination. "Let's do this."

Ivy's bravado lasts about as long as the walk from my bedroom to my car. Before she climbs into the backseat, she clutches my arm with her hand and says, "I think I'm going to be sick."

"You aren't," I say. "You're going to be *fine*. Trust me."

Sam and I have outdone ourselves. Truly. Even though she's more skittish than a class hamster in a room full of kindergartners, she looks stunning. She's wearing a high-waisted teal-blue skirt that puffs out like the bottom of a party dress. This coupled with the form-fitting black shirt shows off a tiny waist that makes even me a little bit envious. Ivy's legs are lengthened by a pair of three-inch heels, and our after-school lessons have paid off—she's walking in them like a champ.

Even Sam has made an effort tonight. She's wearing her nice jeans, the ones that give her a little bit of booty, and a green V-neck sweater that makes her eyes pop a bit. She did some complicated braid thing I've never seen on her before, and it looks almost pretty. When she swipes on a little lip gloss, I start to wonder if there's someone she's making an effort for. Someone other than me, I mean.

In the car, I pretend to take a hit off my flask, then offer some to Ivy. She shakes her head. A polite refusal. I hope Matt picked up something I can mix the butterscotch schnapps into. What would that even be? Ginger ale? Root beer? Root beer would work. I could call it Butterbeer and sell it to her as a mocktail.

There is a sound track to our drive, lots of girl power pop mixed with a little hip-hop for good measure. Ivy nibbles at a cuticle.

"Don't," I tell her as I turn to face her. "You'll ruin your manicure."

"Sorry."

"Just relax," I say. "You're walking in with us. You're walking in Spencer High's front-runner for Homecoming Queen. You're going to make this party your bitch. Just do what we talked about, okay?"

She nods grimly.

I wiggle the flask at her. "You're sure you don't want a drink? Even a little sip? It'll take the edge off."

This time, Ivy doesn't say no. She doesn't shake her head. She just looks at the flask. I can see the gears turning. Finally, she says, "Maybe. Not yet. Let me see how it goes first."

"Sure. Just let me know."

We arrive fashionably late, but not as late as I'd arrive if it wasn't my boyfriend throwing the party. Things are already in high gear though. The music thumps from Matt's parents' state-of-the-art sound system. They're not here, of course. Officially, they can't condone the Puritan Party and what goes on there. But Matt's dad's a big football booster and former state champion. Hell, he probably bought all the booze himself.

Ivy is at my heels with Sam trailing a comfortable margin behind, holding on to our liquor. As luck would have it, the first red-blooded guy we walk into is none other than Bobby Jablonski himself.

"Holy sheets," he says. "You ladies are looking *fine*." He leans toward me and whispers in my ear, "Who's your hot friend?"

I am not making this up. He actually said that. I couldn't write this scene any better myself.

"Bobby!" I say with a playful poke to the chest. "It's Ivy. Ivy Proctor."

His jaw drops like he's in a cartoon. "Fuck me," he says, under his breath but loud enough that I can hear it. I place a hand on his shoulder, stand on my tippy toes, and say into his ear, "She has a crush on you, you know? Play your cards right and she could be your date to Homecoming."

Bobby shakes his head. "Already have one," he says.

"Who?" I demand, already knowing the answer.

As if on cue, Erin Hewett sidles up to Bobby, lacing her little-girl fingers through his beefy digits. "Hi, Alexandra," she says in a saccharine-sweet voice. "Great to see you."

"I didn't know you two were a thing," I say.

"We're not," Bobby answers. If the look on her face is any indication, this comes as a surprise to Erin. "We're just friends."

"Good friends," Erin says, a hint of bitterness in her words.

"Yeah," he says. "But we're not, like, going out." He says this last thing while looking at Ivy, who's looking at the floor again. There's hope, I think, to get him and Ivy matched.

I mean, it's not like Bobby's the only eligible player on the team, or even the only single hot guy at Spencer. It's more the principle of the thing. I had him earmarked for Ivy; Erin snatching him wasn't part of my plan. So now the plan has changed. It'll take a little more work, but it will be totally worth it. Stealing Erin's date out from under her? That's the cherry on top.

"Have you been eating spinach?" I ask Erin.

"No. Why?"

I tap my pointer finger to my mouth. "You've got something green stuck up in there. You should go check it out in the bathroom."

Okay, I'll admit it: that was not my smoothest moment. But it did the trick. She scuttles away, picking at her teeth with an acrylic nail.

"Now, Bobby," I say. "Why would you get yourself a date for Homecoming without giving me a chance to set you up?"

He shrugged. "She just asked. No biggie."

"She asked you? To Homecoming?"

Bobby nods.

"Then it's not a real date," I say. "And you're still available."

For the record: I have absolutely no problems with a girl asking a guy out on a date.

Ivy is still standing behind me, still staring at the floor. I reach out and grab her hand, pulling her in closer.

"Bobby, I desperately need to use the ladies' room. Can you be a sweetie and show Ivy around the house for me?" In one deft move, I place her hand in his, and exit stage left. Sam follows me without any prompting.

Before I can say a word, she tells me she's on it. I take the bottles from her, and she heads off to find Erin. Then I make my way into the kitchen so I can whip up my special cocktail for Ivy. She's going to need the assist. I'll have to be careful, though. I want to get her loose enough that she can shine, but not so loose that Bobby gets the wrong idea. Sluts don't win Homecoming Queen. Nice girls do. Nice girls who boys wish they could fuck, but aren't given the chance to, because the only one they'd dream of giving it up to is their long-term boyfriends.

Suddenly, I have another idea. Maybe I shouldn't be slipping Ivy my special cocktail.

Maybe I should be giving it to Erin Hewett instead.

THIRTY-FOUR

Sloane

Fact: until tonight, I was a Puritan Party virgin.

Also a fact: until this year, I never wanted to attend.

Okay, that's a lie. Of course I wanted to attend. Everybody wants to get invited to the social event of the fall season, but only the coolest, prettiest, most popular girls get to go.

I'm not one of those girls. I know this. My nose is too big, my freckles too dark, my skin too bluish white. My boobs are too small and my butt is too big, yet the only real jelly I have is on my thick, thick thighs.

But.

I have red hair. Real red hair. And guess who's got a thing for natural redheads?

James Leitch.

James is Matt's little brother. He's a freshman and way too pip-squeaky to play an organized sport, so he went the musician route. He's a percussionist in marching band and plays drums in the orchestra for *Evita*. James is cute in an "I-could-have-been-your-babysitter" kind of way, but he's also this disgusting horndog always trying to cop a feel before, during, and after play rehearsal.

I'll admit: I've been milking his crush on me. Only when we're in private, though. Two weeks ago I let him squeeze my boobs for a couple of minutes in exchange for inviting me to this party.

Apparently, I have no shame.

The problem is that now James thinks I'm his *date*. He actually told his friends he was taking this "fine-ass senior girl" to the Puritan Party. When I first overheard him saying this, I got really heated. Who exactly was he taking, I wanted to know. "You," he told me, looking confused. No one had ever referred to me as "fine-ass" before. As a reward, I let him slip me the tongue.

So now I'm at this party, *in Matt Leitch's house*. It's a prime opportunity for me to spy on Alexandra, get closer to Sam, and find out what their deal with Ivy is. Only I can't because, fact: James Leitch is on me like the other kind of leech. A total parasite determined to claim what's his.

I drag him into what I think is a closet but turns out to be a pantry. It's a lit walk-in and the shelves are lined with man-friendly food, like cans of Beefaroni and boxes of Hamburger Helper. He slams his body up against mine and I can feel that he's already hard.

"Whoa," I say, pushing him away. "Not gonna happen."

"You're such a tease," he says. "Why'd you bring me in here if you didn't want to hook up?"

"I need space," I tell him. "You can't be on top of me tonight."

"That's what she said," he quips.

Well, what did I expect from a fourteen-year-old boy?

Answer: probably more than I should have.

"Listen, James. I know you like me. And I . . . am getting used to you. But right now, I can't have people thinking I'm your girlfriend. Or your date. Or your friend with benefits."

"Why not?" he says. Is he pouting at me?

"Because I'm a senior."

"I know," he says. "You're making me a legend."

I can't help but laugh. He's so serious about it, too. He looks at me with eyes not unlike Matt's. Only difference: these eyes want me. They undress me. He's not a bad kisser, if I'm going to be honest. A little too eager, but he'll grow out of that. Two years from now, James Leitch is going to be breaking girls' hearts all across Spencer High. But right now, he's social poison, at least to me.

"Tell you what," I say. "You back off tonight—you don't even talk to me the rest of the party—and Monday, after rehearsal, I'll let you take me for a milk shake."

"By milk shake, you mean I get to touch your boobs, right?"

"No! I mean you get to take me for an actual milk shake."

"Oh. Then can I touch your boobs?"

"Maybe," I say. "If you're a good boy."

"You make me want to be a bad boy," he says, and it's such a cheesy line that I should laugh in his face. But this kid *wants* me. Like, *badly*. Technically there's only a two-and-a-half-year age difference between us. I'm young for my grade; I don't even turn seventeen until next month.

Oh, fuck it. I grab James by the T-shirt and pull him in close. We kiss, with tongue, for a breathless minute or two. His hands are everywhere, but I don't mind so much until they land on my ass.

"Okay," I say. "That's enough. You leave first. I'll come out in a few."

I pull the string to turn the light off. James exits. I check the time on my phone. Three minutes later, I crack the door open. Seeing no one, I start to slip out.

"You naughty thing," says Alexandra Miles. She's standing by the kitchen island, mixing some drinks. "You were totally in there with Matt's little brother, weren't you?"

"He has a little thing for me," I say, then instantly regret the words.

"I bet it's little."

"Grow up."

"Hey," she says. "I'm not the one scamming on a freshman."

"I'm not— He's not— We're not—"

She gives me a look that tells me she's clearly not buying what I'm selling. You know the look: lips pursed, head tilted to one side, eyes boring into you, exposing you for the fraud that you are.

"Whatever," I say. "Why do you even care?"

"*I* don't," she informs me. An evil little smile twitches on her lips. "But the rest of the senior class might find it amusing. Matt's baby brother, getting nasty with the infamous Sloane Fahey."

I ball my fists tightly at my side. "You wouldn't."

She considers this, then says, "Probably not. After all, we're friends, right?"

There's that word again. *Friends.*

I don't buy it for a single second.

"We both know we're not friends," I say flatly. "And I know you're up to something. I don't know what it is, but I know—I just know—it's no good."

The twitchy smile disappears and is replaced by a frown. She steps out from behind the island and walks over to me.

"We could be friends," she says, "if you knew how to play the game. But you're always overstepping. Even though you know exactly what I'm capable of."

Alexandra Miles can be mean. But never have I seen her do it so blatantly.

I say nothing, because I can't even think of how to respond.

Alexandra reaches up and tucks a lock of my hair behind one ear. The move sends chills down my spine.

"You have an unusual face," Alexandra says. "But if you learned how to put makeup on the right way, you might actually be pretty. Play your cards right, and I can do for you what I've done for Ivy. You know how much I like charity work."

She smiles her standard, good-girl smile. It makes my stomach churn.

A couple of younger girls stumble in, sophomores, I think, looking for more alcohol. They see the drinks Alexandra was mixing and squeal.

"Don't!" she says, her voice surprisingly sharp. "Bar's in the den. This is private stock."

"Stock?" one of the girls echoes.

"You. Don't. Touch," Alexandra says. "Get it?"

"Ew," says the other girl. "You don't have to be, like, such a beyotch. We don't want your stupid drink anyway."

They toddle off, and Alexandra resumes her place behind the island. "There's something so trashy about a girl who doesn't know how to hold her liquor," she says to no one in particular— or maybe to me, I don't know. "Here, try one of my special cocktails. I think you'll like it."

She proffers the red Solo cup in my direction, but I shake my head. "No thanks," I say. "I don't drink anything I didn't mix myself."

"Your loss."

I smooth my skirt and head out the other side of the kitchen, which leads to a formal dining room. It's dark and it's empty— or almost empty, that is.

Because who do I find sitting in a ball in the corner, burying her head in her knees?

True story: it's Ivy Proctor.

THIRTY-FIVE

Ivy

"Are you okay?"

Sloane Fahey stands six feet away from me. The room is mostly dark but she has very distinct hair, long and red and wavy, like she just stepped off the pages of a Marvel comic. In other words, she is hard to miss.

"I'm fine," I say. "Just needed a breather."

This is not entirely a lie. I did need to breathe. This party—it is beyond overwhelming.

Everyone is looking at me. Not through me. *At* me. Their eyes are like hungry fish mouths nipping at my skin. It makes me itch.

Before some jokester decided to make me a candidate for Homecoming Queen, I had perfected the art of invisibility. I blended into the background. This was by choice. By design.

I became less invisible after the nomination, of course, when Alexandra decided to take me under her wing. But even then, I was able to hide in her shadow. Hell, I could even hide in Sam's shadow.

But tonight, with my new hair and my new makeup and my clothes and my new shoes, one thing has been made abundantly clear.

I do not have a new personality.

I am still me.

I am still the same, fucked-up little girl who smashed her hand through that window two years ago. The one who wants to puke when a boy looks at her a certain way, because her older cousin took advantage of her in ways he never should have. The one who used to slice the insides of her arms to let his poison out.

What I want to do right now is cry. It hurts, being me. I do not know why I thought I could handle all of this newness, all of this attention.

Walking around this massive house, Bobby Jablonski's hand on the small of my back, I felt like an impostor. A fraud. Like at any second, they were all going to start laughing at me.

But no one laughed. No one pointed. No one called me out.

They smiled at me. They talked to me. And when Bobby Jablonski leaned in close to me, my back against a living-room wall, and whispered in a beer-heavy breath that he was really glad I came tonight, I actually believed him, even though my instinct was to recoil from his touch. (Thanks again, Sean.)

Bobby scared me so much that I had to run away. I told him I needed to use the bathroom. Then I ran in here, crumpled to the floor, and tried not to lose my shit.

Sloane sits down next to me. I wish she would go away. I need to be alone. How can she not see that?

"These people are the worst," Sloane says, apropos of nothing. "They are beautiful and popular, but they're also shallow and self-absorbed. Some are even mean. *Really* mean."

I do not respond. Sloane does not seem to mind.

"But even though I hate them, I want them to like me," she says. "I want them to want to be my friend. When they're nice to me—which, believe it or not, happens on occasion—I feel better about myself."

"Why are you telling me these things?" I ask.

"Because I think we're a lot alike," she says quietly. "I think you hate yourself for wanting them to like you, but hate yourself even more when they don't. Like me."

It is Alexandra's voice I hear in my head: *Don't listen to her. She's a loser. She's just jealous of you. Walk away. Now.*

"Thank you for your concern," I say, scrambling to my feet. "But like I said, I'm fine. I just need to get something to eat."

But I do not leave her to look for food. I make a beeline for the bar. Liquid courage, Alexandra called it. That is all I need right now. Just a little, just to loosen me up.

"There you are!" Alexandra says brightly. She is holding three plastic cups, each bearing one of our names written in Sharpie marker.

"What's in it?" I ask as she hands me mine.

"Butterbeer," she says. "Like from Harry Potter."

"Does it have alcohol?"

"A little," she admits.

"I think I need more than a little."

A slow grin spreads across Alexandra's flawless face. "I've got just the thing." She sets the other two cups down on a shelf and pulls her flask from her purse. "I'll just top it off."

I drink the entire thing in one long gulp. It burns, but in a good way.

"More," I say.

"You sure?"

I nod.

She pours the contents of her own cup into my now empty one and adds another splash from the flask.

"Pace yourself," she says. "You don't want to be the girl puking on the front lawn. And make sure you get some snacks before you drink this one. It'll slow down the absorption in your bloodstream—keep you from getting sick."

But I am not really listening. Instead, I am scanning the room for Bobby. He is talking to some other guys from the team. Erin Hewett is standing a few feet away, in a group of cheerleaders, watching him like a hawk.

"I want him," I tell Alexandra. I am surprised by my own bluntness. "Do you think he could like me?"

"I think he already does," she says. "But pace yourself there, too. You want to flirt, but you don't want to come off as easy. See how Erin's party-stalking him?"

I nod.

"That's a turnoff. He knows he can have her. She's making it too easy."

"So what should I do?"

"Look at everyone but him," Alexandra instructs. "Talk to everyone but him. Dance your ass off. He's already noticed you, right? So have a lot of fun tonight. He'll be drawn to you like a moth to a flame."

I slam the second cup of spiked Butterbeer almost as quickly as I did the first.

"Snacks," Alexandra says. "You have to eat *something*."

"Or do I?"

Without another word, I join a group of senior girls who've turned the middle of the den into a makeshift dance floor. My skirt is perfect; it puffs out with every twirl.

I am electric. I am on fire.

I am the girl I was always meant to be.

Within minutes—or at least what feels like minutes—Bobby Jablonski has joined our little group. He is dancing close to me. I give him what I think is a flirty smile. He shoots one back.

We dance for the duration of a techno remix. Then, heeding Alexandra's earlier words, I dance away from him. He follows shortly after.

I am feeling warm and tingly from the drinks, and also kind of sleepy. I need another drink. And maybe some chips. Maybe.

Bobby follows me to the snack area. "Are you party-stalking me?" I ask, using Alexandra's earlier phrase.

"Could you blame me if I was? You're the hottest girl here tonight."

"I might be the hungriest girl," I say. "But not the hottest."

"Trust me," he says. "I'm not the only one thinking it, either."

For the first time tonight, I do not mind being visible. Not if it means having Bobby Jablonski look at me like he wants to devour me. His attention feels good. Normal. Nothing like Sean's.

"We should hang out," he says.

"Isn't that what we're doing?"

"Naw," he says. "I mean like the kind of hanging out where I pick you up, we grab some dinner, maybe catch a movie."

"That sounds an awful lot like a date."

"Would you like that? Going on a date with me?"

"I don't know," I say. "I might, if you weren't already dating someone."

"I'm not," Bobby insists. "Hewett and I are just friends. She's new, you know? I was being nice. But you . . ."

"What about me?"

"I don't want to be 'nice' with you."

The rational part of my brain recognizes the absurdity of his pickup line. But the irrational part is tickled just to have a boy use a pickup line on me in the first place.

I tell Bobby that I need to find my friends.

"That's cool," he says. "See you around?"

I respond with a smile. This playing-hard-to-get stuff seems to be working. So does the Butterbeer.

Time to find Alexandra to mix me another.

THIRTY-SIX

Sam

Erin Hewett is a little drunk. No, she's more than a little drunk. She's practically *wasted*.

I followed her into the basement, holding a drink that Lexi mixed for her. There's something in it, but I don't know what. Lexi said, "Don't drink the one marked for Erin. Trust me on this."

At first I thought she just spit in it or laced it with a laxative or something. But after Erin had a few sips, her cheeks got really red, and she started to slur her words a bit. By the time she finished the thing, she was wobbling when she walked.

"We should sit," I tell her.

"What?"

"Sit," I say more loudly. There's different music in the basement, louder music. It's dark down here but with neon party lights flashing. I half expect someone to have a seizure.

It's clear that this is the place where most of the people are going to hook up. There's a huge L-shaped couch that takes up a big chunk of the room, plus a double-wide chair, a couple of beanbags, and two video game rockers. Hayley Langer is taking advantage of one of them; she's straddling this guy Brent, practically sucking his face off while his hands make their way up her skirt.

Erin is watching the Hayley Langer spectacle, too, only she looks more sad than disgusted.

"I want to kiss somebody," she tells me.

"Oh?"

"Don't you ever feel like that? Like there's this ache inside of you, and you just . . . Never mind."

I want her to keep talking but I don't know how to tell her that and not sound like some sort of perv.

"It's hard to talk in here," Erin says. "Wanna go somewhere else?"

I nod. She starts to walk away and motions for me to follow.

We find a door that leads to a walk-in closet. This must be where Matt's family stores all of their sports gear. There are shoulder pads and skis and basketballs and about half a dozen pairs of sneakers. The whole room smells like feet.

Erin locks the door behind us. Interesting.

"Can I ask you something?" she says, her voice thick with whatever cocktail Lexi had me pump her full of.

"Sure."

"Why does she hate me?"

"Who, Lexi?"

"Yes. Her. Why?"

"She doesn't," I lie.

Erin shakes her head. "She totally does, Samantha. It's so obvious. And she doesn't even know me!"

"She's threatened by you," I say before I can stop myself. I regret the words even as they're leaving my lips. If this ever got back to Lexi . . . I'll just have to deny it. Who's Lexi going to believe anyway?

"No, she straight up hates me. I don't know what she said to Bobby, but now he's trying to wiggle his way out of Homecoming. It's so humiliating."

Erin kicks some shoes out of the way and plops to the floor in a decidedly ungraceful move. She reaches up and tugs on the bottom of my sweater. "Sit with me," she says.

So I do.

We sit side by side on this cold, stinky floor, so close that we're practically touching. The air crackles around us. I have to keep reminding myself that I must be misreading the situation. She likes Bobby, after all.

"It's hard being new," Erin says. "I really liked my old life. I had the most amazing friends, a super-cute boyfriend, and, you know, the whole Homecoming thing. There's a really good chance I would've won. And I know it's stupid, but, like, who doesn't want to win a crown?"

"Me," I say, holding up one hand. Erin chuckles. "And you could still win a crown," I point out. "That part hasn't changed."

"No, no, no," she says, shaking her head too hard. "I won't."

She starts to cry. Tears actually fall from her eyes, her head bobbing around like she's a floppy rag doll.

"I'm sorry," she says. "I'm so sorry, I'm so sorry."

Erin buries her head into my shoulder. I let my right arm reach around her in a side hug of sorts. She snuggles in closer, crying more quietly now.

She's sad, I remind myself. She likes Bobby. Not you.

"You're so nice," Erin says, her words muffled by my sweater. "So, so nice. And so pretty, too."

Okay, there's no mistaking that. Why is she commenting on my level of attractiveness? And lying about it?

Erin lifts her head slightly, her emerald eyes latching on to mine. "I really wanna kiss someone," she says again, staring straight at me. "I really want to, like, so bad—"

My mouth lands on hers before she can finish the word. She parts my lips with her tongue, gentle and firm all at the same time. She tastes salty-sweet.

She tastes like heaven.

We kiss for a long, long time. There are hungry kisses, soft kisses, sweet kisses. She touches my face. I touch her hair. We press closer together. I can feel her breasts against my own.

And then, just like that, it stops.

"Oh god," she says. "Oh, god, oh, god, oh, god." Erin's head drops into her hands, and she rocks back and forth. "I can't," she moans. "I can't— I'm not—"

"Gay?" I finish for her.

"No," she says. "It's not that. I'm not . . . *out*."

"Oh."

"I'm not *ready*."

Of course she's not. "I get it."

This closet feels hot. I can't take the stench. I start to stand up, but Erin pulls me back down.

"Don't go," she says. "Not like this."

Erin reaches for my hand, clasping it in both of hers. "Gimme time," she says, still slurring her words a bit. "I do like you, Samantha. I just need a little time."

I know what she's going to say next before she says it.

"Can you wait for me? Just until after the election."

I don't know whether to be excited or insulted. But I look at her, this girl I just made out with, this girl I kissed for longer than I've ever kissed anyone, even Lexi—

I decide on excited.

With one quick move, I put my hands on both sides of Erin's face, pull her close to me, and kiss her deeply. I try to say what I am feeling with the kiss: You are adorable. I want to keep kissing you. I don't care if it makes my best friend hate me. You might just be worth it.

"Wow," she says when we part. "You're really good at that."

"After the election," I say. "I can wait until then."

As I slip out of the walk-in closet, the significance of this isn't lost on me.

Erin Hewett isn't out yet, but she will be. She all but said so.

And maybe, just maybe, I'll end up with an actual girl-friend, instead of a friend who's a girl who lets me make out with her once in a while. A girl I know doesn't love me, not the way I love her.

And, really—I can be loyal to Lexi and lust after Erin at the same time, can't I?

Can't I?

THIRTY-SEVEN

Alexandra

It's well after midnight by the time the Puritan Party starts to wind down. The event has been a success by all counts: Ivy was a hit. Bobby Jablonski is totally hot for her. Sam kept Erin busy for a big chunk of time. When Hewett resurfaced, she was trashed, and let me tell you: Erin Hewett is a sad, ugly drunk. The girls who told me how much they admired what I was doing for Ivy were the same girls who looked at Erin Hewett like she was some rando skank that crashed their sacred party.

It gets better.

When I'm ready to leave, I can't find Ivy. I search the basement. I search the first floor. I check outside. I knock on bathroom doors. Matt's parents' bedroom has been marked off-limits, but I sneak in there anyway. It's the last place I can possibly look.

She's not in the room, but the door to the master bath is cracked open. I walk in to find Ivy Proctor passed out in the tub, skirt smushed up around her thighs. I can even see her panties.

But that's not all I see. Right by her hand, on the lip of the tub: a pink Lady Schick. Was she . . . ? Or is Matt's mom's razor just in the right place at the right time? It's up to me to make the most of this situation. As carefully as I can, I wedge the handle of the razor into Ivy's clenched fist.

I whip out my phone, make sure it's on silent, and start taking pictures. This is beyond perfect. It's bad enough she's so obliterated at a party, but to be passed out in a stranger's bathroom? Flashing her lady business? Holding a *razor*, no less? Frick will shit her pants.

When I'm satisfied with the number of pics I've taken, I tuck my phone away and start to rouse Ivy. "Sweet pea," I say. "Time to go home."

Ivy's eyes flutter open. "Oh, shit," she says, before promptly vomiting all over herself.

I don't hold back her hair. I just take more pictures.

I could clean Ivy up all by myself, or with Sam's help. Instead, I reach out to Matt. *Come quick,* I text him. *It's Ivy. Your parents' bathroom. Don't tell anyone.*

When Matt comes to my rescue, I lock the door behind him. "You can't say anything about this to anyone," I say. "Please, Matty. She'd be so embarrassed. She was just nervous, is all. She drank too much on an empty stomach."

"It's okay, babe," he assures me. "It happens. Look at me last weekend."

"I know you understand," I say. "But the others might not. And she's so close, Matty. I think she might actually win Homecoming Queen!"

He snags a long-sleeved T-shirt of his mom's and turns around, ever the gentleman, when I swap it in for Ivy's vomit-covered top. It's about two sizes too big and hangs low enough to hide the wet spot left on her skirt from me cleaning up the puke.

"How am I going to sneak her out of here?" I say.

"Wait here," Matt says. "I can clear everyone out in fifteen."

At times like this, I wish I loved Matt for real. He's a good guy. Not the brightest bulb in the box, but definitely decent. Plus, he's so damned good-looking. And buff. And totally in love with me, which may be his most attractive quality of all.

When Matt returns, it's with Sam in tow. "Jesus, Lexi," she says. "What the hell was in those drinks you were making?"

Leave it to Sam to screw up a near-perfect situation.

"Root beer," I say. "Like, ninety percent root beer."

"And what—ten percent crack?"

"She's fine, Sam," Matt says in a soothing voice. "We've all been there."

When he turns to lift Ivy out of the tub, I shoot Sam a warning look. *Shut up*, it says. *Don't blow this.*

She nods wearily. *Message received.*

It takes the three of us to get Ivy safely down the stairs and into the car. She's so tiny, but passed out, her entire five-foot-one-inch frame is nothing but deadweight.

"She's sleeping over at my place," I tell Matt. "I'll get her hydrated before I bring her home. I promise."

"You're such a good person," he says, before kissing me good night.

After he says this, I swear I can see Sam rolling her eyes.

Sam is the first of us to get up in the morning. I awake as she's putting her shoes on.

"Were you about to sneak out?" I ask, joking.

"I just need to go home," she replies. No joke there.

Something is up with Sam. I knew it from the minute she called me out in the bathroom. She was weird on the ride home, didn't want to recap the party with me last night, and now, this.

I could ask her. I could say, "What happened to you last night?" But it doesn't mean she'd tell me.

Better to give her some time to cool off.

"Take my car," I tell her. "You can pick me up on the way to church."

She considers this for a second, then says, "You have to get Ivy home. I'll just meet you there."

"But how are you getting home?"

"Wyatt," she says. "He's probably already on his way."

I don't like this. I don't like how she's talking to me, or how she's not looking at me, or how she's behaving with me. Seriously, what the fuck happened at that party?

I push back my comforter and slide out of bed. I'm wearing a tank top, no bra, and a pair of cotton boy shorts. Sam's eyes are drawn to my rack, same as always. I go to her and slip my arms around her in a hug.

But Sam doesn't melt into me like she normally does. She stiffens up.

Now I know something is wrong. I just don't know what, or how to fix it.

I whisper in her ear, "Thank you for last night. You were a rock star. I don't know what I'd do without you. But I know I never want to find out."

My plan is to let my lips graze hers as I pull away. It's a move I've perfected over the years. Only this time, Sam turns away. My lips land on her cheek, not her mouth.

I stand back, my eyes wide open in horror.

"I don't want you to do that," Sam says quietly. "Not unless you mean it."

She turns and walks away before I can even respond.

It's nearly noon before Ivy stirs. I consider waking her up hours earlier, as I usually attend the eleven-o'clock service at Second Presbyterian, but she was stone-cold out. I even texted her mom from her phone, to tell her that I (Ivy) would be staying late for pancakes. I don't need Mrs. Proctor getting all suspicious or worried.

Skipping Sunday-morning service the day after the Puritan Party is kind of a no-no. In Spencer, it's the day that gets the second-highest teen attendance all year long (the first being Christmas, of course). But it would've been worse showing up with Ivy so completely hungover. Matt's family attends the Family at Five service at Grace Journey; I'll just go with them later tonight.

I'll be honest: I don't give a crap about God. He certainly doesn't give a crap about me. Between stealing my father and saddling me with Natalie, I know for sure I've been forsaken.

But I'm a Midwestern pageant girl. God is not optional. So I play the part, and I play it well. Just the right mix of sinner and saint.

Just the right mix of everything.

While Ivy struggles to get conscious, I go brew a fresh pot of strong coffee. I bring her a mug with two Tylenol and four Tums. She takes these things silently, swallows the pills and chews the tablets, and drains half the mug. Then she digs into her purse, takes out a small handful of other pills, and slams those down, too.

"For my broken brain," she says. "I should have taken them hours ago."

"Your brain's not broken!"

"You don't know," Ivy tells me. "You barely know me at all."

"I know that you're a good person," I say. "And last night, you were the hit of the party. Seriously, Ivy, you've got this election in the bag."

She shakes her head like she's trying to clear cobwebs. "No," she says. "I did bad things last night. I'm not supposed to drink, Alexandra. These pills I'm on? I'm not supposed to drink *ever*, let alone get drunk. I *told* you that."

"Listen," I say, "I kept an eye on you the whole time. I would never have let you hurt yourself. When I found you with that razor, I took it away and everything."

At the word "razor," Ivy's eyes fly open and the color drains from her face. "What razor?" she asks.

"When I found you in the bathroom, you were holding a razor. But it didn't look like you cut yourself or anything. Believe me, I checked."

Ivy tugs the cuffs on the T-shirt even farther down her hands. "I don't know what you're talking about."

"Sure," I say. "Okay."

I ask Ivy which church she and her family attend. They don't go every week, she tells me, but when they do, it's Grace Journey.

"We used to be regulars," she says. "Before . . . you know. The incident."

"You have to stop calling it that," I say. "'The incident' sounds like something shameful."

"It *is* shameful."

"No," I say. "You need to own it. This bad thing happened, but you can't let it define you. You were hurting. You got help. You rebooted your life. Now you're on your way to becoming Homecoming Queen. You're a success story of epic proportions."

Ivy is looking down at her feet, but I see a small smile form on her lips. "I had fun last night, didn't I?"

"Yes," I say, beaming. "You one hundred percent did. I couldn't have asked for a better coming-out party for you.

"Now," I continue, "you just have to keep it going for two more weeks."

THIRTY-EIGHT

Ivy

High school sure is different when you are popular.

Alexandra told me this would happen. That after the Puritan Party, I would suddenly have a lot more "friends." She even used finger quotes around the word.

"They won't be real friends," she said. "Not like me and Sam. But they are the kind of 'friends' who can help you get elected."

Now people wave to me in the hallways, and talk to me when I am getting books out of my locker, and volunteer to partner with me on class projects, and invite me to sit with them at lunch. This was maybe the scariest part of all: eating lunch with different groups of people each day. Especially since Alexandra said it would be better if I did it on my own.

"We need people to see you as an individual," she explained. "Not my 'pet.'"

"Is that how people see me?"

She thought for a second. "Maybe 'pet' was the wrong word. More like my project."

I think that "project" is even more insulting than "pet," but I do not say this.

Alexandra says that we are real friends, but the truth is, there are a lot of things I think but do not say to her. The truth is, I still find her a little bit scary. Not like serial-killer scary. She is more like a hard-to-please teacher that you really, really, really want to like you. I often do things that disappoint her, and I can read this disappointment on her face. I see it in a slight frown, or a narrowing of her eyes, or a toss of her hair. I see flashes of irritation and anger, too. I worry that with one wrong word, one wrong move, she will cast me out of her kingdom and condemn me to a life sentence on the island of unpopularity.

This person I am now—desperate to hold on to my new social status—would make the old me want to vomit. I know this. I used to look down on people like me. Social strivers so desperate for approval that they treat high school like a job. Except, that is exactly what I do now. Every night before I go to bed, I spend at least half an hour picking out my outfit and accessories for the next day. And every morning, I wake up an hour earlier than usual to do my hair and makeup and put on whatever costume I selected the night before.

It is like an interview that never ends. I spend my days smiling and waving and making appropriate small talk. I am always on. At night, when I get home, I am exhausted from the effort.

But it is worth it. This Saturday, Bobby Jablonski and I are going on a date. A real one, just the two of us. Alexandra thinks he will ask me to Homecoming. There is this junior, Jake Tosh, who might be able to take Erin off Bobby's hands. This would free him up to go with me. "You're the one he wants to take anyway," she tells me.

I like Bobby. He is a nice, normal guy. Cute, but not so cute that I lose the ability to form sentences in his presence. Sweet, but not disgustingly so. What he lacks in intellect he makes up for in charm. Even my mom will like Bobby; that is the kind of guy he is.

The first major Homecoming court event takes place on Friday. It is part pep rally, part pageant, as Alexandra explains. I have never attended one of these, or if I did, freshman year, it did not make enough of an impression on me to remember it. But basically what happens is that the student body loads into the auditorium. Principal Frick will talk about the importance of Homecoming and what is and is not appropriate behavior for the game, the halftime parade, and the dance. Then the football coaches will come out and put the fear of God into anyone even thinking about pranking the rival team.

Finally, all of the candidates take the stage for a Q&A so that the students of Spencer can get to know them better. It is kind of a joke, Alexandra says, because most people just vote for the hottest boy and hottest girl. But this year will be different. I am in the mix, and most people do not know me. Even though I am currently experiencing a swell of popularity it is mostly with the seniors and some of the juniors. Since the whole school votes on the king and queen—or at least, anyone who attends the dance—this is my one big chance to win over the underclassmen.

We spend a lot of time talking about how to craft diplomatic answers—responses that, as Alexandra explains it, "straddle the delicate line between authentic and posturing."

"In pageant interview, there is always a right answer," she says. "Not one that's factually correct, per se. But the right answer is the one the largest number of judges wants to hear. The one that makes them smile. The one that hits them right in the feels."

She lobs me the first practice question: "What are you passionate about?"

"Um," I say. "Well. I guess . . . I don't know?"

"Seriously?"

I shrug. "Sorry."

Alexandra closes her eyes and takes a deep breath. Her hands are balled into little fists at her sides. A telltale sign of her irritation with me. When she has done this in the past she curled her nails into her palms so hard they left little red half-moons indented in the flesh.

I shift nervously from foot to foot, fighting the urge to chew on a cuticle. That would only make Alexandra more annoyed with me.

Finally, after a really tense minute, she releases the fists, opens her eyes, and exhales. "I'm going to be you now, okay?"

"Okay."

"Ask me the question."

I repeat, "What are you passionate about?"

She smiles warmly. "I am incredibly passionate about rescuing animals from kill shelters. Millions of pets are abandoned each year, often because the people who purchased them didn't think through their decision. I adopted my dog from one such shelter. His name is Butcher, and the love we share has helped me through some really tough times. In fact, I'd go so far as to say that *he* rescued *me*."

Her eyes well up with tears as she says this last bit, and for a second, I feel pretty choked up, too. But it was all for show; in a snap, her face is wiped clean of emotion, and she is simply Alexandra again.

"See?" she says. "*That's* how it's done."

She has a list of twelve questions for us to practice with—all questions that have been used in a previous Homecoming Q&A. Three are starred; those are the questions that were used more than once.

We run through each question until I am able to give an answer Alexandra finds satisfactory—not once, not twice, but three times in a row. It is exhausting. I cannot remember the last time I had to talk about myself this much. Maybe in the hospital, but even there, I preferred to listen more than I did talk.

This goes on for hours. So long that my mother ends up inviting Alexandra to stay for dinner. I expect her to decline but instead she says, "I'd love to. Thank you for inviting me, Mrs. Proctor."

My parents are thoroughly charmed by Alexandra and her pageant-perfect performance. I study her as she answers their questions and realize that she is adopting many of the techniques she was just coaching me on. Repeating the question in the first part of her answer. Smiling a lot, but not too broadly. Saying things she knows they want to hear.

Alexandra helps my mom clear the table. When she is out of earshot, my mom leans over to me and whispers, "Your friend is delightful!"

There are a lot of words I would use to describe Alexandra. "Delightful" is not one of them.

Back in my room, she is once again all business. "Now, where were we?"

Before we call it a night, Alexandra asks me to consider thinking about how I can talk about my past in a positive way.

"Everybody knows what happened," she says. "To not address it in some way would be foolish."

I tell her I do not want to talk about that time in my life. "I thought the point was to focus on who I've become."

"It is," she says. "But to do that the right way, you need to acknowledge just how far you've come."

"I don't know."

"Look," she says. "Your story could absolutely be your most powerful weapon. You just have to learn how to use it."

The idea of "using" my story makes me feel a little sick. I wish I had passed on a second helping of my mom's mashed potatoes.

"Trust me," Alexandra says. "And practice. Tomorrow's Thursday, so you're on your own. Make every second count. You're definitely going to need it."

THIRTY-NINE

Sam

My lips are bruised from kissing. Hot kissing. Secret kissing. The kind of kissing that is so intense, when you're not doing it the only thing you can think about is when you'll get to do it again.

I wasn't sure there'd be a repeat performance of what happened between me and Erin at the Puritan Party, but there was. The first time was at *church*, no less. We saw each other just before the service began. Erin caught my eye across the pews and nodded her head toward the doors. Then she got up, and thirty seconds later, I followed her into the ladies' room. It was empty, and after checking for feet, Erin pushed me into the handicap stall, locked the door, and stuck her tongue in my mouth. She was completely sober, too.

"I have to see you," she whispered.

"You're seeing me now."

"Tonight," she said. "Can I come over?"

"Sure. Come for dinner. My mom would love that."

She gave me one last kiss—deep and wet and everything

good in the world—before slipping out of the stall. I sat on the toilet, shaking. Erin Hewett *liked* me. She *wanted* me. *Me.*

That night, after stuffing our faces with my mom's famous fried chicken, Erin and I locked ourselves in my bedroom and kissed for over an hour. We did more than kiss, actually. There was some over-the-clothes boob touching on both our parts, and at one point, Erin directed my hand under her skirt but over her underwear. She rubbed up against it, moaning softly as we kissed.

Everything inside of me exploded all at once, a thousand points of starlight bursting from my skin.

"I didn't know it could be like this," I said softly.

"Me either."

Afterward, we lay back on my bed, holding hands and talking. Erin rested her head on my shoulder and sighed. "This is perfection."

"You can say that again."

That night, not long after Erin had gone home, Lexi texted me. *Can you be on Erin duty this week? I have Ivy covered.*

I started laughing. As if I needed her to ask.

But I had promised Erin that we would stay a secret until after the election. And part of keeping us a secret meant not tipping Lexi off to anything. The girl was sharp. She could read me like a book. Having her think that I was glued to Erin's side because she commanded me to be was our safest bet.

Sure, I texted back. *I'll take one for the team.*

Then, before I could talk myself out of it, I texted Erin.

Tomorrow after school. My place?

YES, she wrote back in all caps.

Tomorrow couldn't come soon enough.

The next day moved glacially slow. Whenever I saw Erin, my pulse would race and I'd get the tingles in my stomach. None of which I could reveal when Lexi was around. But there was something about this whole secret thing that made everything that much hotter.

That afternoon, we had to be careful, what with Wyatt right next door and my mom just down the stairs. Even with the door locked I jumped every time I heard footsteps.

By Wednesday, my mother was starting to get suspicious. She didn't know about the kissing, but me inviting the same friend for dinner three nights in a row isn't something that escapes her notice. When she asked me about all the time Erin and I were spending together, I told her we were working on a project for school.

"Maybe you can work on it at her house tomorrow night," Mom replied.

So I texted Erin, *Can I come to your place tomorrow?*

It was almost two hours before she responded: *Maybe.*

I texted back a question mark. It took her another half hour or so to write back, *I don't have a lock on my bedroom door,* followed by a series of smiley faces, kissy lips, and hearts with stars.

That's okay, I texted back. *We can just hang out.*

I got another smiling emoji in return, but no solid invite.

That night, I couldn't sleep. My brain wouldn't stop racing.

For five days straight, I'd made out with Erin Hewett. I'd touched and been touched by Erin Hewett. The hours between each encounter were excruciatingly painful as it was. What if I had to wait more than twenty-four hours? I couldn't even fathom it.

But where could we go? What secret place could we occupy?

Erin had a car—that was something. Could we drive out of town? Maybe go to a movie theater, or even just find a field to go park in?

My plan got more elaborate as the night wore on. It involved disguises and fake names—crazy things that, had I been thinking clearly, I would've known were crazy. If I slept an hour, I'd be surprised.

I arrive at school feeling completely strung out, with purple bruises under my eyes. "You okay?" Erin asks when she sees me. "You look like hell."

"Couldn't sleep," I admit.

"Make sure you caffeinate," she says. "Turns out my mom's got a work thing. She won't even be home until almost eleven."

I want to slam her up against the bank of lockers and mash my mouth into hers, but I can't, so I don't. I'll just have to save it for later.

As I head to homeroom, I pass by Lexi, who winks at me. A gesture that, one short week ago, would have turned my knees to jelly. Only this time, I feel nothing.

At long last, the spell has been broken. I am free of the evil queen.

She could be a queen. Erin, I mean. A good one. An *honest* one. The kind of Homecoming Queen Spencer High deserves.

Helping Erin would be risky. Not just for me, but for her. If I burn Lexi's and my friendship to the ground, there's no telling what Lexi would do to retaliate. I think about how she wrecked Sloane Fahey sophomore year. What she's about to do to Ivy. And she isn't nearly as close with either of them as she is with me.

If I did this, I'd have to be so, so careful. Leave no trace of my actions. Make it look like someone else was the mastermind.

And then it hits me: Why *not* Sloane Fahey? She's clearly got some agenda of her own these days. She's been stalking Lexi. Flirting with me. But what exactly does she want?

It's time I find out.

FORTY

Sloane

There are nine days until the Homecoming dance and I do not have a date.

Correction: I do not have a *proper* date. Instead, I have a horndog freshman who has asked me to said dance no less than four times since the Puritan Party. Apparently there is a clock on his invitation now. This morning, I found a note in my locker that read, "3 freshman honies [sic] have asked ME to Homecoming. If you don't say yes by 2morrow, I'm going w/ 1 of them. PEACE."

I'll admit, I find it kind of charming that James told me this via an old-school analog locker note and not, you know, a text message. But. Taking Matt's little brother to the last Homecoming dance of my high school career would be social suicide. It'd look desperate, for one thing. Although I don't know why, exactly. Plenty of senior guys date "freshmeat" girls (they actually call them that, too—I didn't make that up) and nobody says boo. But an older woman with a younger guy? Somebody call Olivia Pope, because that is a SCANDAL.

There is a part of me that wishes I was gutsy enough to just say yes to James. I mean, I didn't even *go* to Homecoming last year, because I didn't want to fly stag. It's too depressing to be at a dance all by yourself, unless a bunch of your girls are going by themselves, too. But even then we all sit around looking for some boy, single or not, to ask us to slow dance.

That was what happened freshman year. The following year, when I was a sophomore, Jonah Dorsey and I were already a thing, and I went with him. We had the best time. He asked me what color my dress was (sapphire blue) and bought a tie to match. He got me a wrist corsage of baby white roses and blue satin ribbon. He took me to dinner at Olive Garden before the dance. He didn't stop staring at me the entire night. At one point he whispered to me, "You're the most beautiful girl in the entire school."

I still miss having Jonah as a boyfriend. He was, like, the *perfect boyfriend*. Until Alexandra had to screw everything up, that is.

My plan to exact revenge on Alexandra has stalled. Nothing is going the way it should be. The idea to seduce Sam into giving up the goods on her has fallen flat, even though I've tried everything short of flashing her my boobs. Maybe she isn't really into girls.

Of course, just as I am about to give up, Sam invites me to have lunch with her. Well, "invites" is a strong word. It was more along the lines of her saying "See you at lunch?" in passing. But she was smiling when she said it.

So maybe my plan isn't dead after all.

~

As luck would have it, Sam is sitting alone at her usual lunch table when I make it through the checkout line. I scan the caf and see that Alexandra is cozied up to Matt (retch) and Ivy is somewhere altogether different, chatting with Jen Tyner and a bunch of juniors. Now is definitely the time for me to make my move.

"Hi, there," I say, casual-like, as I put my tray down.

"Hey, Sloane. What's up?"

I shrug. "Same old, same old. You?"

A slow smile spreads across Sam's face, lighting her up head to toe. Seriously, you've never seen a girl go from plain to pretty that fast. "Ditto," she says, but I'd bet money that's a total lie. Something is definitely up with her.

Neither of us is particularly good at small talk, which makes for an uncomfortable start to lunch. It doesn't help that I keep catching Alexandra eyeing us up.

"So," I say, "are you going to Homecoming?"

Sam nods. "Probably. Yes."

"Taking someone special?"

She doesn't respond to this. Instead, she arches one eyebrow in my direction.

"Sorry," I say. "I didn't mean to pry."

Sam creates a tall stack of Oreo cookies, then unstacks them in strange patterns, almost like she's creating shapes with checkers. It's weird, is what it is.

"Do you always play with your food?" I ask, trying to keep things light.

"Nervous habit."

"Why are you so nervous?"

Sam shrugs. "Homecoming, I guess."

"What about it?"

I watch Sam do an eye-sweep of the caf, like she's looking for hidden federal agents amongst the Spencer High student population. Then she turns to me and says, "Cone of silence?"

"Sure. Yeah. What is it?"

"I'm kind of worried about Ivy Proctor," Sam says. "Please don't tell anyone I said that. It's just . . . Well, she's been through so much already. I'm worried that the pressure of Homecoming is getting to her."

We both look over to where Ivy is sitting. Her face is animated as she talks to Jen. She must've said something funny, too, because Jen starts laughing in that loud, braying way of hers.

"I know she *looks* okay," Sam says. "But think about who's trained her."

Our gaze turns to Matt's table, where Alexandra is practically glowering at us.

"Sam?"

"Yes?"

"Why the sudden interest in Ivy? Alexandra, I mean."

Sam crams one of the Oreos into her mouth whole and crunches down. Then she pops another, which she chases down with a big drag off her juice box.

"I don't know for sure," she says, her voice so low I have to lean in to hear her. "But I think it might have something to do with Erin Hewett."

"Really?"

She nods. "Like I said, I could be wrong. But Lexi was really irritated when she found out Erin made the ballot. She said she would never let her win. I thought, when Lexi dropped out of the race, she'd chosen to be the bigger person. But now . . ."

"Now you think she's running Ivy to make sure Erin doesn't get the crown," I finish for her.

It's a solid theory. Alexandra Miles is exactly the kind of person who would sacrifice herself to make sure the enemy goes down. Only, in this case, it's not even a sacrifice. Sure, she may not win Homecoming Queen, but if Ivy does, then Alexandra will be branded a saint. And as long as she doesn't squander everyone's goodwill, she'll be a shoo-in for Prom Queen in the spring.

"Genius," I say.

"It would be," Sam says, "if it didn't mean hurting Ivy."

I don't follow this line of thinking.

"Lexi's really pushing Ivy to talk about what happened sophomore year," Sam explains. "Her breakdown. What led up to it. The time she spent in the mental hospital. She keeps telling Ivy that this is what's going to win her the election, and maybe it will—but then she'll win out of pity, and Ivy will realize that. Can you imagine what this will do to her self-esteem?"

I shake my head in disbelief. "She's that vindictive? Alexandra?"

"I've already said too much," Sam replies, before shoving another cookie into her mouth.

I think back to that day at play rehearsal, when I told Alexandra that she was due for a takedown. At the time I'd thought maybe Erin Hewett was the perfect person to do it, but I had no idea that Alexandra had it in for her. I just thought that, being new and all, she was the person most likely to give Alexandra a run for her money.

But now Sam's dropped this handy piece of knowledge straight into my lap, gift-wrapped and everything.

I knew my flirting was working.

I can use this to my advantage. I can campaign on Erin's behalf—use what Sam told me about Ivy and how she's concerned for her to help bolster the vote.

I can steal this election out from under Alexandra and her fake protégé, and I can stick it to her in the process.

"Don't give it another thought," I tell Sam confidently. "I've got this."

Nine days. Not a lot of time to accomplish something so big. Except, I know exactly where to start.

Guess I'll be going to the dance with James after all.

FORTY-ONE

Sam

Erin's house looks like something out of a Pottery Barn catalog. At least, I think it does. I don't get to look very long before she takes my hand and starts running up the stairs. I follow her into her bedroom, where she closes the door behind her. She was right—there's no lock—but she moves a pair of hand weights against the bottom, like some kind of hillbilly security system.

"Hi," she says, grinning.

"Hi," I say back.

"I want to see you."

"Hello?" I say. "You *are* seeing me."

"No," she says. "I want to *see* you." She steps closer to me and starts unbuttoning my shirt, slowly and deliberately, until my bra is fully exposed. Then she steps back, grabs her sweater by the hem, and pulls it off over her head.

We kiss, bra-to-bra. Her hands are on my bare skin. Mine are in her hair. When we break, Erin kicks off her shoes and yanks her skirt down. She's standing there, clad only in her lavender lace bra and matching panties. It's not all that revealing—no more than a typical bikini at the pool—but I can't take my jeans off fast enough.

There is more kissing, more touching. Erin guides me over to her bed, gently pushes me down so that I am on my back, wastes no time climbing on top of me. My heart is racing so fast I'm afraid it might explode. She leans over to kiss me, her bra in my face. This is when I realize that Erin's bra hooks in the front. Without thinking it through, I reach up and start to unclasp it. We both gasp when I am successful.

"I'm . . . I'm . . . I'm sorry," I say. "I—"

"I'm not," she says. She reaches down for my hands and moves them to her. She is soft and warm and I want to do more, so much more.

We kiss again.

This goes on forever. Long enough for the sun to go down and the room to go dark. At some point, we both take off our underwear. I don't know if what we're doing is considered sex or not, but it certainly *feels* like sex.

And yet it's so much more than that.

What it really feels like is *love*.

"I'm hungry," Erin says after a while. "Let's go heat up some dinner."

We put our clothes back on in the dark. I don't know about Erin but I feel sort of . . . I don't know. Bashful? I've never even let someone see me this naked before, not even Lexi.

Downstairs, Erin roots around the fridge and offers up a

bunch of leftovers: pizza, freezer lasagna, some chicken noodle soup. "Or," she says, "I could make you one of my semi-famous grilled cheese sandwiches."

"That," I say. "I want that."

I sit on a stool at the breakfast counter, watching Erin slice cheese, butter bread, and put it all together in a hissing-hot skillet. She is beyond adorable. I see the small brown mole on the corner of her neck and think, *I've kissed that mole. My tongue has been on that mole.*

"Did I tell you that I am officially not going with Bobby Jablonski to Homecoming?" Erin says.

"No. What happened?"

She turns and shoots me a look that says *you know exactly what happened.*

"Does this mean you're going solo?" I ask hopefully.

"No," she said.

No? Does she mean she's going with me?

"This kid Jake asked me," Erin continues, her words like little knives in my heart.

"Jake Tosh?"

"Yeah," she says. "Bobby was trying to orchestrate this weird double date with Jake and Ivy and him and me, but I know he wants to go with Ivy, so I just let him off the hook."

This shouldn't hurt as much as it does. Erin was always clear about us needing to be a secret until after Homecoming. And I knew she was planning on going to the dance with Bobby. What's the difference if it's Jake instead?

"Besides," Erin says, "it doesn't really matter who I go with, when the person I wish I were going with is you."

My heart doesn't warm when she says this. In part because it totally sounds like a line Lexi would drop on someone. It just has that air of calculation to it. Of unreality.

I clear my throat. "We could go together," I say.

"I thought we agreed to wait."

"We did. Until after Homecoming. But the thing is, at Spencer, the vote for king and queen takes place within the first half of the dance, so that they have time to tally the votes. Once it's closed, there's nothing anyone can do to change it."

Erin doesn't respond right away. She flips the sandwiches, lays the spatula down, and turns to face me.

"It's not about the votes," she says. "It's not like I'm going to win anyway."

"But you could," I say.

"How?"

"You could start by making a surprise killing at the Q&A tomorrow. Principal Frick approves the questions ahead of time—can't you get them from her?"

"No," she says. "I can't and I won't."

Erin grabs two plates from the cabinet, puts one sandwich on each, cuts them on the bias, and hands one over to me. The outside of the bread is crisp and toasted perfectly. I bite in, releasing tons of hot, oozing cheese. Some of it drips down on my chin, but I don't care. It really is the best grilled cheese sandwich I've ever had, and I waste no time in telling Erin this.

"You're amazing," I say. "And you deserve to be queen."

Erin grins. "You're only saying that because I let you get to third base."

"No," I assure her. "I'm saying it because it's true."

Here, I pause. Every fiber in my body wants to tell her about Lexi's plan—about what she has in store for Ivy—but if I do that, there's no turning back. I will be declaring my loyalty to another. And despite what just happened upstairs, I can't shake this niggling feeling that it all seems a little too good to be true. Erin, I mean. Or, rather, Erin and me.

Is there really an Erin and me? Or is that just part of *her* master plan?

Is she capable of being that devious?

"What are you thinking?" Erin asks, breaking my train of thought.

"Nothing."

"Bullshit," she says. "I can see it on your face. There's something you want to say. So, spill it."

The desire to tell her everything wrestles with the part of me that's afraid it's all a lie. Desire is winning by a narrow margin.

"To be honest, I'm worried about what this whole competition is doing to Ivy," I say carefully, not sure how much of Lexi's plan to reveal. "You didn't see her at the Puritan Party. She was . . . different. Not herself. And after everything she's been through . . ."

Erin nods. She takes a bite of her sandwich and chews thoughtfully. "You're a good person, Samantha Schnitt."

This, I think, is the worst possible thing she could say to me right now. Because I am so *not* a good person.

I tell her, "You don't know me as well as you think you do."

"I'm getting to know you."

"True."

Erin looks at me, not saying anything, with an intensity that makes me feel more naked than when I was actually naked.

"Stop," I tell her.

But she doesn't stop. She barely even blinks.

It makes me squirm.

"Am I the first?" I blurt out, not even sure where the words are coming from. "Girl, I mean. Am I the first one you've kissed?"

"No," Erin says. "Am I yours?"

"No."

She nods. "Full disclosure? I did know that you were gay. Before we even met."

"Frick told you?"

She nods again. "But she failed to mention how utterly adorable you are."

Erin says this last thing with a disarming grin, punctuating the sentence by biting into a triangle of grilled cheese. And just like that, I *know*. She's for real. This—whatever is happening between us—it's for real, too.

"She's setting her up," I say. "Ivy. Alexandra's setting her up big-time."

The story pours out of me before I can stop myself. Lexi's plan. Why she felt she needed a plan in the first place. The lengths to which I know she'll go, just to make sure she secures that crown. The path of destruction she'll leave in her wake. What I think it will do to Ivy Proctor.

"That poor girl," Erin says when I have finished.

"I know. Ivy doesn't deserve to be treated like this."

"Agreed. But I wasn't talking about Ivy."

"Surely you don't mean Lexi."

"I surely do," she responds. "I mean, yeah, she's hard-core evil. There's no denying that. But, like, people aren't *born* that kind of evil. That's learned behavior."

I think about Lexi's mom, who she was before Mr. Miles died, and who she became afterward. I think about how she's always tried to craft Lexi in her own image, and how even Lexi's way of rebelling—by becoming the anti-Natalie—is still pretty much a reflection of her mother.

But then I think about some of the truly terrible things that Lexi has done over the years, even before her dad passed away. I think about what she's got in store for Ivy, and how I was prepared to help her execute the scheme, just like I always do.

Like I always *did*.

"It has to stop," I say. "Lexi's reign of terror. We can't let her destroy Ivy Proctor all over again."

Erin arches an eyebrow, like she's asking me a question.

"I'm serious," I say. "We can do it if we work together. You. Me. Sloane Fahey. Nothing would make Sloane happier than being part of a plot to take Lexi down."

"So you want to fight evil with evil?"

I have a feeling I'm supposed to say no, but I can't. This is Lexi we're talking about. I swallow hard and say, "Is there any other way?"

Erin doesn't respond at first. Instead, she chews through the last of her sandwich. Then she wipes the grilled-cheese grease from her hands with a paper towel and sighs a weary sigh.

"Okay," she says finally. "When do we begin?"

FORTY-TWO

Alexandra

My calves are burning from tonight's practice, a self-directed one as Natalie was a no-show. After running through my talent repertoire—I always have five songs prepped, each from a different genre—I spent literally an hour going up and down the stairs in my new Tippy Top heels. Natalie used to have me start from the second-floor landing and head all the way down to the basement. There, I'd complete two full laps around the room, doing The Walk—only never doing it good enough for Natalie. When I'd strike my final pose, she'd launch into a blistering critique, every single one of which ended with the word "Again."

I never complained, though. Not once. And tonight, even though Natalie was who-the-fuck-knows-where, I ran through the whole routine twice. If she ever does decide to show up to one of our lessons again, I don't want her claiming I'd gotten lazy.

After I hear Natalie stumble in and retreat to the kitchen to pour herself a Blanton's, I hit the shower. I stand under the steaming hot water until it starts to cool, long enough for my creamy skin to turn salmon pink. I can't help it. It feels so good on my aching muscles.

I launch into my post-shower routine, which mostly consists of using two different body creams, a facial moisturizer, and no fewer than three hair products. Twenty minutes later, I emerge from the steamy bathroom, still wrapped in a towel, and almost run smack into Natalie. She's clutching the cordless phone and looking beyond furious.

"What are you up to?" she asks.

"Showering?"

"Don't play dumb with me, Alexandra. I just got off the phone with Frick."

"Can we talk about this after I get dressed?" I say.

I move past my mother and into the bedroom. To my dismay, she follows me.

"A little privacy, please?"

Natalie doesn't move. Instead, she says, "When were you going to tell me that you dropped out of the Homecoming race?"

"It's not what you think," I tell her.

"Oh, I'm pretty sure it's exactly what I think," she says. "Frick told me you've been behaving erratically at school. Hanging out with that girl who tried to kill herself a couple of years ago. She says you've been *coaching* her—that you're trying to get *her* elected Homecoming Queen."

Leave it to Frick to fuck everything up. Why was she calling my mother? There has to be some rule against that, right?

"What do you care, Natalie?" I ask. "You haven't been around for weeks."

"You don't understand," she says. "First you win Homecoming. Then Miss Indiana University, then Miss Indiana, then Miss America. That's how it has to be. That's how you get the hell out of here."

After everything, this is the thing that almost does me in.

I want to leave. I've always known that I'm too good for this life. But my dad's death nearly destroyed Natalie. When I leave, she'll actually be alone. Is that really what she wants?

"Fine," I mutter.

Natalie's eyes narrow.

"I'm watching you," she tells me. "So get your shit together, and get it done. On Saturday, it better be your name announced, or don't even bother coming home."

With that, she storms out of my bedroom, slamming the door behind her.

I don't really care about Natalie's empty threats. But what I *do* care about is Frick interfering with my plan. Calling Natalie the night before the Q&A has to be a calculated move on her part. Why? Did she think my mother would cause an ugly scene? Did she think that would throw me off my game?

I can't help but wonder what else she's going to be lobbing my way.

Guess I'll find out soon enough.

FORTY-THREE

Sam

The pre-Homecoming assembly used to happen in the morning, right after homeroom. But everyone would get so riled up that the teachers protested. Have it in the afternoon, they said. If you're going to get a bunch of teenagers all jacked up, do it right before you send them home so we don't have to deal with it.

At least, that's what I imagined they said.

So this year, the pre-Homecoming assembly is being held during last period. On a Friday. Everyone's loud and squirmy because the one thing standing between them and the weekend is a stupid assembly that most people couldn't care less about.

Lexi's cares, though. And now, so do I.

We are sitting together, near the front of the auditorium, as the king candidates take the stage. Matt and the two other football players up for king are decked out in their home uniforms, with green-and-gold jerseys and bright white pants with a green stripe running down the side. Joining them are Tyler Moses, a prepster soccer stud with swoopy, boy-band hair that always falls in his eyes, and Curtis Wilson, student council president and likely future president of the United States.

Frick is onstage, too, ready to ask them a bunch of stupid questions that supposedly will help the Spencer High student body get to know the candidates better. Only, we all know how this works: they'll listen to the empty answers, they'll make a lot of noise, and then the girls will vote for whomever they think is hottest, while the guys will vote for whichever one is their closest bud.

But with Erin and Ivy in the queen race, it isn't the same old, same old Q&A. People are genuinely curious as to how Ivy will respond; there are still some students taking bets on whether or not she'll relapse before the dance. (I may or may not be responsible for those rumors, at Lexi's request. Another item on the list of things I now regret.)

Finally, it's time for the queen candidates to take the stage. Ashley Chamberlain is in her cheerleading uniform. Hayley Langer is sporting a Spartan green sweater over a denim micro-mini and knee-high boots. Ivy's rocking a plaid skirt in school colors, topped with a fitted turtleneck sweater. And then there's Erin.

The wearing school colors thing isn't a rule. It's just something candidates typically do. Last night, we discussed the possibility of her wearing her cheerleading uniform, as would be expected. But we also talked about the need for her to stay under Lexi's radar. The girl misses nothing. If I was going to switch sides, and start working against Lexi, I'd have to keep her distracted. Or, rather, Erin would, by waging a hell of a queen campaign.

So instead of sporting her pep squad attire, Erin's dressed in head-to-toe white: white T-shirt tucked into white jeans over white kitten heels. Standing there, amongst a sea of green and gold, she looks like an angel. She practically glows.

Lexi is furious. She's muttering all kinds of things under her breath, but I know her well enough to know what's making her the most upset is that she didn't think of it herself.

The first two questions are recycled from previous years. Erin's responses are textbook perfect, only even better, because they come across as 100 percent genuine. Ivy's holding her own; she's more tentative than the other three candidates, but in a sweet, disarming way.

Then, Frick drops the third question: "Why are you proud to be a Spencer Spartan?"

Ashley talks about cheerleading (of course she does). Hayley talks about how it's her job as an American and God-fearing Christian to have school spirit. She gets slightly more applause, but I think that's because she managed to hike her skirt another half inch higher. And then it's Erin's turn.

She acknowledges her New Girl status right off the bat. "Although I haven't been a Spartan for very long," she says, "in the short time I've been here I've received such a warm welcome. . . ." She doesn't talk about being a cheerleader. She doesn't talk about America or Jesus.

Erin, sounding like the sweetest, nicest, most honest person in the whole freaking school, speaks from the heart. She talks about how difficult it was for her to leave California, pick up her life, and start over from scratch. And how, in the few weeks since she's enrolled at Spencer, she's already started to feel like she's home, only now home is here, in Spencer, Indiana.

"Corny," Lexi whispers to me. "She totally played that the wrong way."

But when Erin finishes by thanking everyone, and talking about how honored she is to even be considered for Homecoming Queen, she's met with thunderous applause. Turns out, Jake Tosh is the World's Best Hype Man. He gets the crowd totally fired up for her.

I swallow my smile. I can't let Lexi know how pleased I am. Instead, I whisper back to her, "Don't worry about Ivy. She's got this."

Lexi nods grimly, but she starts tapping one toe furiously, practically shaking the row of auditorium seats.

Ivy's looked too nervous this whole time to perform according to Lexi's standards, and I'm sure Erin's stellar display isn't helping alleviate her anxiety. When she walks up the mic, she leans forward just a touch too far, and the sound spikes dramatically, making half the kids cover up their ears.

She takes a step backward, her cheeks flaming red. Then she closes her eyes and breathes in deeply, letting the air out slowly, and finally starts again.

"There was a time when I wasn't proud to be a Spartan," she says, which makes Hayley smirk right there on the stage. "In fact, there was a time when you couldn't pay me enough money to come back to this school. I hated it. I hated what it did to me.

I hated the teachers for letting it happen. And I hated my class-mates for thinking it was funny."

The energy has shifted. The words Ivy's saying are making people feel uncomfortable. Even Lexi's squirming in her seat. If she could, I think she'd put her hands over her eyes so she wouldn't have to watch Ivy fail so spectacularly.

But, in another heartbeat, everything changes.

"I didn't think there was a place for me at Spencer," she says. "Not after my . . . my . . ." Ivy closes her eyes again, takes a few deep breaths, then opens them and says, in a voice much more strong and clear and full of conviction, "Not after my attempt. But I was wrong. Spencer, it turns out, is a place where anyone can get a second chance, even the kid who went crazy in the bio lab."

She smiles as she says this, and there are some chuckles from the audience.

"Holy shit," Lexi says under her breath. "She's pulling it off!"

"I made the choice—and it was just that, a choice—to shut everyone out," Ivy continues. "But as soon as I stopped doing that—as soon as I let my guard down enough for people to see the real me—I was accepted. I was made to feel like I am not tied to my past. You see me for who I am today.

"I'm not new to Spencer—" Here, Ivy nods toward Erin. "But Spencer is new to me. And I have to tell you, I love—absolutely love—what I see."

Everybody goes nuts when she says that. Bobby Jablonski, not to be outdone by the less-popular Jake Tosh, turns into a hype man himself, getting everyone all kinds of frothed up.

Ivy stands there, smiling, a single, perfect tear falling from her right eye. The stage lights catch it, but even if they didn't, there's no mistaking why she's running her pointer finger under her lash line.

When the volume lowers enough for her to keep talking, Ivy says, "You asked me why I'm proud to be a Spencer Spartan. This is why. *You* are why."

Ivy gets an honest-to-goodness standing O. The teachers, who are supposed to remain neutral, are cheering her on. Even Ashley, her fellow competitor, can't hold back the waterworks. She literally throws her arms around Ivy, giving her a hug. A real hug, not a fake one designed to win back some votes.

No, Ivy Proctor has managed to reduce one of the most popular girls in our entire school into a sad spectacle of blubbering.

It is truly like a scene from one of those clichéd teen movies where the loser gets a makeover and suddenly everyone loves her and wants to be her friend. Only it's not a movie; it's our high school. And that loser? She could win the crown, if my evil schemer of a supposed best friend wasn't hell-bent on taking her down.

That's exactly why we have got to take her down first.

FORTY-FOUR

Sloane

I have to hand it to Alexandra: she's managed to turn Ivy Proctor into a high school hero. Fact: The final bell has rung and there is still a ring of students surrounding Ivy, all clamoring to tell her just how awesome they think she is. And there's Alexandra, beaming from afar like a proud parent. Meanwhile, Erin Hewett, my dark-horse candidate who I was banking on beating Ivy out for queen, has slunk off silently without anyone even noticing.

I'm never going to get back at Alexandra this way. Ivy is now a lock for queen; there's no question about that. I was hoping that James would be able to rally the underclassmen for Erin—this was the condition I gave him for agreeing to be his date for the dance—but there's no way he'll be able to swing enough votes to pull off a win for Erin. That plan . . . did not work. In fact, I've been dead-ending all over the place.

Except when it comes to Samantha Schnitt. Because my top target? She's headed directly my way.

Before I can so much as wave hello, Sam asks me what I'm doing after school.

"Key Club," I say. "Alexandra asked me to run the meeting."

"Right. And after that?"

I shrug. "Nada."

"Shake my hand," she tells me in a low tone. "Now."

I don't question this. I just do it. And what do you know? She palms me a piece of paper.

"Don't open that now," Sam instructs. "Just come to that address tonight, after Key Club. But don't tell anyone where you're going. And make sure no one follows you."

She's so serious I can't help but laugh. "What's up with the cloak-and-dagger routine?"

"You'll find out tonight," she says. "I'm going to pretend like I'm irritated with you now. She's watching us."

Sam doesn't have to say who "she" is. I know without looking it's Alexandra.

"Whatever, Sloane," Sam says loudly, then spins on her heel and walks away.

I honestly have no idea what is happening. But I seriously can't wait to find out.

FORTY-FIVE

Ivy

She said I was going to win all along, but I never believed her. Why would I? I am Ivy Proctor. I am the basket case of Spencer High. The girl who punched through a window on school property. Who disappeared for nearly two years. Who did not have a single friend . . . until now.

"I owe you everything," I tell Alexandra. "Everything."

"No," she says. "*You* did this, Ivy. I was just here for support."

There is nothing true about that statement. Sure, I am the one who looked the part and charmed the right people and killed at the Q&A. But she was the one who taught me how to do all of it. She was the one who gave me the courage to speak up. To share my story with a room full of strangers.

"Everything," I say again. "All you."

Alexandra smiles warmly. She reaches for my hand, squeezes it inside of her own.

"Don't go home," she says. "Come to my place. We'll have some low-key girl time, get you ready for tomorrow night."

"I'd like that," I tell her. "I've never actually been on a date before."

She assures me there's nothing to be nervous about. Bobby, she says, is "kind of like boyfriend training wheels."

"Plus," she continues, "he's totally smitten with you, so the hard part's already over. Just be yourself. Well, you know. The new version of you."

It is this last part that I find less than reassuring. I am still not entirely sure if I have become the person I am supposed to be—the person Alexandra believes I should be—or if I have gotten really good at pretending.

Maybe they are one and the same.

I wouldn't be surprised.

FORTY-SIX

Sloane

"Run this by me again?"

I'm sitting at the breakfast bar in the kitchen of one Erin Hewett, listening to her and Samantha Schnitt spin me a yarn of epic proportions. Apparently, the wisdom nugget Sam dropped on me the other day—about Alexandra running Ivy to make sure Erin didn't win—told only part of the story. Because according to her, the plot goes much deeper than that. According to her, Alexandra's scheme ends with her trashing Ivy at the eleventh hour and snatching back the Homecoming crown for herself.

With slow, methodical precision, Sam walks me through the sequence of events for a second time. Erin nods along. It all *sounds* like something Alexandra's capable of, but this is Sam we're talking about. Sam, who practically doesn't exist outside Alexandra's shadow. I mean, everyone knows she's been in love with the girl forever. That she'd do anything for her. How can I be sure this isn't part of an elaborate scheme to set me up, too?

Before I can ask the question, Erin jumps in and says, "Sam told me about some of the shit Alexandra's pulled on you over the years. So I know you understand all too well what kind of havoc that girl can wreak. But put yourself in Ivy's shoes for a minute. Think about what she's been through. How it must've felt to her, to have someone like Alexandra catapult her from high school infamy to popularity in a heartbeat.

"Now imagine how she's going to feel if we allow Alexandra to pull the rug out from under her," she continues. "You're tough. *You* bounced back. But will Ivy?"

I don't actually know Ivy well enough to answer her, but my prediction is no. No, she won't. Because as tough as people may or may not think I am, the truth is, I bounced back out of *necessity*, not strength. Alexandra Miles came *thisclose* to destroying me entirely. But my mom works, so homeschooling wasn't an option, and she doesn't make enough to send me to private school. I am stuck in Spencer until graduation day. Then, if all goes well, I'm off to Chicago. I am literally counting down the days until I can put this place in my rearview mirror.

So, yeah, I feel for Ivy. I wouldn't wish Alexandra's wrath on anyone, but especially not her. And yet, something about what these two are proposing feels risky.

I know what you're thinking: *Sloane, this is what you wanted. And these are the exact two people you thought could help you execute your plan. So why are you hesitating for even a second?*

It's one thing to fantasize about destroying a girl's life. It's another to actually get the job done.

"Here's what I don't understand," I say. "How exactly is she planning on taking back the election in the first place?"

Sam and Erin exchange a look I can't decipher.

"Oh, god," I say. "Is it that bad?"

"If by 'bad' you mean 'unknown,'" Erin says, "then yes."

"How do you not know?" I say to Sam. "Is she keeping you in the dark? Is *that* why you're turning on her?"

She shakes her head. "It's not like that."

"So then what is it like?" I shoot back. "There must be a reason."

Erin reaches over and places a hand on Sam's forearm. Sam's head snaps up in her direction. Erin nods, but before either of them say a word, I know exactly what's going on.

"Holy shit," I say. "The two of you are together. Like, *together-together*."

Sam's face turns beet red. And are those tears filling up her eyes?

"Way to go, Schnitt," I say, trying to convey my utter lack of disapproval. "I see your tastes are improving."

They both smile at this, and I see Sam's stiff shoulders start to relax. "Nobody knows," she says. "Nobody can know. Not until after Homecoming."

"Sure," I say. "Makes sense."

"So you're in?" Sam asks in a hopeful lilt.

Knowing her secret—knowing *why* she's so eager to turn on

her supposed BFF—makes this entire proposition feel way more safe.

"I'm in," I affirm. "So now what?"

"Now we need to come up with a plan."

FORTY-SEVEN

Sam

After a good two hours of near-fruitless brainstorming, Sloane offers to give me a ride home. I turn her down at first, imagining that once she leaves Erin and I can get down to a different kind of business. But then Erin tells me her mom's due home any minute, and I know what that means: no privacy. I manage to sneak in a super-steamy good-bye kiss while Sloane's in the powder room. It'll have to hold me until tomorrow.

In the car, Sloane says, "So why haven't either of us mentioned Alexandra's Achilles' heel?"

"I don't know what you mean," I say, even though I do.

Sloane chooses to ignore my lie. "She thinks her mother is some kind of tragic figure. You and I know better. It's icky, going after someone's mom. But you can't deny she wouldn't hesitate to do the same thing to someone else."

She's got a point. Yet knowing what I know, not just about Lexi but about Natalie, too, I can't sanction a plan that will torpedo them both.

"I still think Matt's the way to go," I say, deflecting. "If he knew what she was really like, he'd dump her in a second. And that would humiliate the hell out of her."

"It won't work," Sloane argues. "Not with me involved. People will think I'm making stuff up just to steal him away from her. No, it's got to be something bigger."

I think about what Erin asked me the other night, about fighting evil with evil. Going after Natalie would be beyond evil, though, wouldn't it?

"Just think about it," she says.

Sloane turns the corner onto my street and my heart stops cold. Lexi's car is parked in my driveway.

"Keep driving," I tell Sloane, slinking down in the seat. "She's at my house!"

I check my phone. No missed calls. No missed texts. If Lexi's looking for me, why hasn't she let me know?

"Maybe she just got there?" Sloane guesses.

Sloane pulls into a gas station about a block outside of my neighborhood and puts the car in park. "What now?"

Lexi can't know that Sloane drove me home, or that we were even together. Talk about raising suspicions. I could have her drop me a block away and say that Erin was the one to give me a lift—I'm still on New Girl duty, after all—but then my mother will want to know why I didn't invite her in. Lexi doesn't know how much time Erin and I have been spending together in the first place. That's one enormous red flag I don't need to raise. Not now, when there's so much at stake.

Just then, my phone rings. Only, it's not Lexi. It's my mom.

"What do I do?" I ask, feeling panicky.

"Answer it!"

"Hey, Mom," I say. "What's up?"

She's just checking in, making sure I'm okay, and asks what time I think I'll be home. I tell her soon. She says not to take too long, as she's got an apple crisp in the oven and she knows how much I like it hot and bubbly.

What she doesn't mention is Lexi. Odd.

"Oh, hey," I say, trying to sound nonchalant. "Has Lexi stopped by yet? I left something in her car."

Yes, my mother confirms. Only, she's not sure if she dropped anything off for me. She said she came by to see Wyatt, to get a little help on a project she was working on for school.

"You just missed her," Mom says.

I should feel relieved, but I don't. Because if Lexi went to see Wyatt, it means that he's instrumental to the next part of her plan. And the fact that she didn't go through me, or even let me know she was approaching him, tells me that she is, in fact, keeping me in the dark.

"So," I say to Sloane, "how do you feel about helping me interrogate my brother?"

Sloane and I storm into Wyatt's room, gearing up for a battle. Only, none is needed.

This time she's gone too far.

"I won't do it," Wyatt says. "You can't make me."

"Make you do what?"

"You know," he says. "The pictures. I don't care what she promises me, I'm not sending them out to anyone. It's cruel."

"Slow your roll," Sloane says. "What exactly has Alexandra asked you to do?"

Wyatt's brow furrows. To me, he says, "Is she in on this, too?"

"*I'm* not 'in on this,' Wyatt," I assure him. "I have no clue what you're talking about. I swear to you."

He chooses to believe me. Then he turns to his computer screen, clicks a few things, and brings up a series of photos starring one Ivy Proctor, passed out in Matt's parents' bathtub.

"Of course," I say. "I should've known."

I fill the two of them in on what happened at the Puritan Party, and how I'm pretty sure Lexi roofied Ivy's drink. "I think she put something in Erin's, too," I say.

"She offered me one," Sloane says. "Thank god I turned her down."

"Well, now she wants me to hack into Spencer's database. Not just kids, either. Parents. Boosters. Everyone. She wants me to email these pictures to *everyone*."

"What did you say?" I ask.

"Told her I'd think about it," he says, a guilty expression plastered on his face. "She was standing, like, really close to me."

I shake my head. How could we both be such idiots? "That's good," I tell him. "Let her think you're going to go through with it. But you wouldn't, right?"

Wyatt shakes his head no. "I'm not a *monster*."

"Is there a way to prove those pictures came from her phone?" I ask him.

"Yes and no."

"Explain, please."

He sighs heavily. "Normally there'd be no way to trace them back to a specific phone. But, um, I jailbroke hers a few months ago. There's this . . . app in there. I can see stuff. Image stuff."

"You've been *spying* on her?" Sloane practically shrieks. "Can you, like, see her texts, too?"

"Yeah," he says. "I can see everything."

I simultaneously want to punch my brother and give him a hug. On the one hand, he's a disgusting perv. On the other, his disgusting perviness is about to come in real handy.

"So," I say to Sloane, "are you still interested in going after Natalie?"

Her eyes widen.

"Do it," I say. "Let's take this bitch down for good."

FORTY-EIGHT

Sloane

Once Sam gives me the green light, I waste no time in plotting how I'm going to get dirt on Natalie Miles. I figure I'll start early the next morning, when I know Alexandra will be with her pageant coach and therefore out of the house. I'll go there and make up some bullshit reason why I'm worried about her. This should at least get me in the front door. Once inside, I can snoop around until I find something incriminating.

Okay, so it's not a perfect plan. But we're running out of time. And fact: my previous attempt to get some goods on Alexandra's mom turned up nothing. The woman took a cab back to her house. Big whoop.

I arrive early enough to watch Alexandra leave. I see this from a unique vantage point: hiding in a thicket of her neighbor's shrubs. I wait exactly five minutes after seeing her drive away before extricating myself from the holly bush and walking up to the front door.

I ring the bell. I knock. I ring the bell again.

Nobody answers.

Of course, Natalie wasn't at the house last Saturday morning either, was she? That's when I caught her doing the walk
of shame. Now I'm faced with a dilemma: Do I stay here and
wait in the bushes until Natalie cabs it home, or do I drive back
downtown to see if I can catch her en route?

I opt for the bushes.

But there's still no sign of Natalie by the time nine o'clock
rolls around. Alexandra could be home any minute. Staying here
is about to become dangerous.

I call it a day.

When I get back to my car, parked a few streets away, I text
Sam to let her know my stakeout was a bust. She writes back to
tell me that according to Alexandra's calendar—which, thanks
to her creepy stalker brother we now have access to—girlfriend's
got a date with Matt tonight. He's picking her up at seven; I can
try again then.

But the nighttime shift yields nothing either. Let's face it: I
am not meant to be a private investigator. If I'm super-lucky, I
might be able to play one on TV.

Sam, Erin, and I make plans to meet up the next day after
church, to come up with a contingency plan. Wyatt says Alexandra wants him to email the pictures Wednesday after school.
That puts a seriously tight clock on our whole operation.

But there's four of us now—Wyatt has gone all in—so the
odds of us coming up with something successful have to be
good, right?

Right?

FORTY-NINE

Sam

Wyatt insists on going with me to Erin's for the brainstorming sesh. "I'm part of this now, too," he informs me.

I'm beyond irritated. I was supposed to get to Erin's an hour before Sloane. Erin's mom has some volunteer thing all day and we would've had the whole house to ourselves. Since that's clearly not going to happen, I text Sloane to let her know the time has been pushed up.

When the four of us have assembled in Erin's kitchen, we start bouncing around ideas. Wyatt thinks we should use the photos to force a breakup between Matt and Alexandra.

"He won't stay with her," Wyatt says. "He's actually a nice guy. He doesn't make fun of people, doesn't bully anyone. When he realizes who his girlfriend really is, it'll crush him."

"Maybe," I say. "But proving the pictures came from her exposes you, too, Wyatt. And there's no guarantee Lexi couldn't talk her way out of it, either. Matt adores her. It won't be easy to get him to believe she could be that cruel."

"I'm telling you, her mom is the key," Sloane chimes in.

"She'll do anything to keep that woman's crazy under wraps."

"Except we don't *have* anything on Natalie," I point out, feeling exasperated.

"Yet," Sloane adds.

To Erin, I say, "You're being awfully quiet."

"I'm thinking," she says. "But you're not going to like what I'm thinking."

"Spill it."

"We need Ivy," she says. "I don't think we can pull this off without her."

"Are you serious?" I say. "We're doing this in part to protect Ivy. Why would we drag her into the drama?"

"She has a right to know," Erin argues. "Plus, as of right now, she's got the most access to Alexandra. At least until the Wednesday deadline."

This is true. Lexi hasn't been the same with me since the Puritan Party. Probably because I haven't been the same with her, but still.

"It's risky," I say. "Ivy's a wild card. If we don't convince her right off the bat, she'll go to Lexi and blow the whole thing up. Then it'll be too late to save her."

We go in circles for at least an hour before Sloane throws up her hands and says, "Enough! We're not getting anywhere, and we've been playing this all wrong."

Sloane lays out a multi-pronged plan that involves the two of us doing most of the heavy lifting. She thinks I should be the one taking point on Natalie, since theoretically I'll have the easiest time getting inside Lexi's house. Meanwhile, she's going to use her connection to Matt's little brother to try to get inside his house, and maybe help Matt see the "real" Lexi.

Erin offers to connect with Ivy, but we all tell her that's too risky. "If you really want to help," Sloane says, "you'll work the Frick angle. She's your aunt, right?"

"What's my job?" Wyatt asks.

"You've got to convince Alexandra to hold off on the email until Friday," Sloane tells him. "That'll buy us a few more days. Oh, and you need to be campaigning for Ivy. Because at the end of the day, she's the only one I want to see wearing that crown. "No offense," she adds, in Erin's direction.

"None taken."

And with that, "Operation Crown Ivy" is officially born.

FIFTY

Alexandra

There's nothing quite as intoxicating as watching a sophisticated plan come together. And make no mistake—there are complicated machinations at work here.

In just a few short weeks, I have turned Ivy Proctor into a bona fide star. Now she's a star with a boyfriend, as her first date with Bobby Jablonski was such a smashing success, he asked her to make it Facebook official. Wyatt Schnitt is on board to leak the incriminating photos at my command. I'd originally planned on getting the photos today, but realized if I waited just a little bit longer, I could orchestrate a very public takedown at the Tall Oaks Mall, the night before Homecoming. Having an audience means I can play the part of Really Concerned Friend, and unofficially relaunch my campaign in the process.

It'll be cutting things close, but I've never been one to shy from a challenge.

Why start now?

FIFTY-ONE

Ivy

Two days before Homecoming I get a text from an unfamiliar number. It is a picture of me from the Puritan Party. In it I am doubled over in a bathtub, puking all over myself. You can't see my face but there's no mistaking whose teal skirt that is bunched up around her hips.

For a second I lose the ability to breathe.

Who is this? I text back.

A minute later, I get a reply: *Find out for yourself. Meet us in the faculty parking lot after final bell.*

Us? As in more than one person?

My instinct is to run to Alexandra for help. But she will be displeased to know there is photographic evidence of my transgression. "This could threaten everything," she would tell me. "Everything we've worked so hard for."

No, she must never know about the picture.

I must make sure of that.

It is easy to avoid Alexandra after school. We never hang out on Thursdays anyway. Even so, I wait a few minutes before heading toward the faculty lot.

My heart thumps wildly in my chest. I have no idea what awaits me outside. All I know is that I need to stop that picture from getting out.

When I walk through the double doors I am blinded by a too-bright sun. Squinting, I look around, but see no one. Was this all an elaborate joke? Or is this another one of Alexandra's lessons?

I am debating what to do next when a small white convertible rolls up to me. The driver is Erin Hewett. Samantha Schnitt is riding shotgun. And in the backseat, I see Sloane Fahey. Through the rolled-down window she says, "Get in."

So I do.

"We debated whether or not to let you know these even existed," Sloane tells me, after we have arrived at Erin Hewett's house. She is speaking of the two dozen pictures that exist of me in compromising positions. They are bad enough to have me disqualified from the Homecoming race. And the ones of me holding a razor? Those are bad enough to land me back in the hospital.

"What do you want from me?" I say, my shoulders shaking. I am doing everything I can not to cry. It is taking every bit of energy I have to hold back the tears.

"Oh, sweetie—nothing," Sloane says. "That's not what this is about."

"What Sloane is trying to say," Sam cuts in, "is that we're not responsible for the pictures. But we know who is, and we all agreed that you have a right to know, too."

No one says anything for a minute that feels like an hour. Finally, I blurt out, "Well? Who is it?"

"Alexandra," Sloane says. "Alexandra took them."

I gasp audibly.

"It's true," Sam says.

"How do you know this?" I ask.

Again, I'm met with silence.

"Well?"

"She was going to use them to destroy you," Erin says. "She tried to bribe Sam's brother to send them out to the school's email list."

"Why would she do that?" I say. "After everything she's done for me?"

"You were a distraction," Sam explains. "You took the attention off Erin. But she never meant for you to win queen. The whole time, she was planning on tearing you down in the end. Stepping in at the last minute. Picking up the votes that would have gone to you."

I hear the words she is saying but my brain cannot process them.

"Think about it," Sloane says. "In taking you under her wing, she earned a lot of good PR for herself. They all think she dropped out to support *you*. Like she martyred herself to make sure you had a dream of a senior year."

"I still don't understand," I say. "How does humiliating me help her?"

Sloane sighs. "Because if everyone were to find out that you were still this scary mental case, they'd all feel bad for her. Like she gave up everything for someone who clearly didn't deserve it."

"Sloane," Erin says sharply. "That's enough."

"What?" Sloane shoots back. "It's the truth, right?"

I feel as if I am going to be sick. This—isn't this what I feared all along? That my nomination had been some sort of sick joke. That people were out to get me. That I would unwittingly play the fool.

But Alexandra? My *friend*? The betrayal is almost too much to bear.

"It's going to be okay," Sam assures me. "Those photos—no one else will see them. Wyatt won't send them. Plus, he hacked into Lexi's phone and corrupted the files. If she tries to forward them to anyone, her entire system will crash. He'll delete them, too. He just can't do that yet or she'll get suspicious."

"Then why tell me about them at all?" I say. "If you've already taken care of it?"

The three girls exchange glances, concerned looks on their faces.

"You're supposed to go to the mall with her tomorrow night, right?" Sam says.

I nod.

"She thinks Wyatt's going to send the pictures out then. She's expecting him to. And when he doesn't . . ." Her voice trails off, leaving me to fill in the blank.

"She'll find another way, won't she?"

"That's what we're afraid of," Sam says.

Hot tears spill from my eyes. I cannot contain them.

"Well," I say, "thank you for telling me. I'll get my name taken off the ballot tomorrow."

"No!" the three of them cry, practically in unison.

"You have to *win*," Sloane says. "That's why we're telling you. We're going to help you protect yourself from Her Evil Highness, and come Saturday, you'll be the one wearing that crown."

"But how?"

"We're taking care of it," Sloane says. "For now, just be on guard. But don't act like you are. You can't make Alexandra suspicious."

Erin pushes a box of tissues toward me. "I know it's scary, but please, Ivy—trust us. We've got your back on this. I swear it."

Alexandra may have been playing me, but she *did* make me stronger. I have come too far to let her break me down again.

So I nod. I trust them. I have to.

FIFTY-TWO

Sloane

At eight o'clock, Wyatt Schnitt sends Alexandra a frantic text telling her that their plan might be in jeopardy. He needs her to come over, he tells her, so they can figure out how to fix the situation.

At 8:05, Alexandra squeals out of her driveway, headed for the Schnitts. I text Sam, *It's go time.*

Good luck, she texts back.

Once again, I approach the front door. Ring the bell. Knock. Ring the bell a second time. Still no answer.

This doesn't mean that Natalie Miles isn't home. At least, that's what Sam tells me. That she could be tucked in her house, three sheets to the wind. Or she could be sober but unwilling to greet an unexpected guest.

Sam told me where to find the spare key. Now I have to decide whether or not to use it. Because fact: even though I'd use a key, I'd still be breaking into someone's house. I could still get into a shitload of trouble.

Think of Ivy, I tell myself. *Do it for her.*

While I am strengthening my resolve, I see a car approaching. Panicked, I retreat into the neighbor's yard, diving into my trusty holly bush hiding spot. It's dark enough that I can poke my head up a little to survey the situation. The car does not belong to Alexandra, as I have feared. It's a cab, and my pulse quickens as I see Natalie stumble out of the vehicle, clearly drunk. She half walks, half runs to the front door, fumbles with her key, then disappears inside the house.

Score!

I'm trying to figure out how long I should wait before knocking on the door when I realize that the cab isn't going anywhere. The driver is idling. Almost like he's waiting for her to come back.

When Natalie reemerges from the house, she's holding something in her hand and shaking it around. Something small—I can't see what it is from here. Then she does her half-walk, half-run thing back to the cab. The door swings open for her. It's a male arm I see, clad in a sports jacket.

"Can we go to the Romper Room?" I hear Natalie ask loudly, just before the door closes. The cab peels away and I, without stopping to think, sprint off toward my car.

The Romper Room is a seedy club on the bad side of town. It used to be a strip bar until the city took away its license to nude. Now it's just this gross place where people go to behave badly. At least, that's what I've heard.

I don't have a fake ID, and I don't look nearly old enough to even try getting past the bouncer. But I don't care. If I can catch Natalie Miles looking like she's up to whatever she's up to outside of the Romper Room, it might be enough.

When it comes to betrayal, a little goes a long way.

FIFTY-THREE

Alexandra

It's Friday, and Ivy and I are in the final throes of Homecoming prep. We're practicing hairstyles and trying different eyeliner and lip color combos. It's all for show, of course. Within the next few hours, Ivy Proctor will go from hero to zero.

I've spent the past month elevating Ivy Proctor to near-legendary status. Now I'm going to take her down in a very public way.

It may destroy her, what I'm about to do. I know this. I know it, and yet it's not going to stop me. Ivy, like Taylor Flynn and Sloane Fahey and all of the other pathetics I've had to trample on over the years, is collateral damage. And honestly? I think Ivy's tougher than any of us knew. So maybe this will only help her grow that much stronger. I wouldn't be surprised if it did.

"Are we still going to the mall?" I say, as if I've had some kind of spontaneous idea. "Homecoming deserves a new lipstick."

"Sounds like fun," Ivy says. "Let's do it."

Oh, yes. Let's get it done.

~

Finding a parking spot at the Tall Oaks Mall on a Friday night is no easy feat. I have to circle the lot at least three times before snagging one that is at least somewhat near the Dillard's entrance. I'm taking Ivy to the Clinique counter to try out some new lip colors.

"Typically, I'm a MAC loyalist," I say. "But there's this one color Clinique makes that I think would be perfect for you."

I don't head straight to the counter, though. First, I do a lap around the store. "Scouting sales," I explain. Ivy follows, always a few steps behind.

I'm thrilled to see so many girls from Spencer milling around the store. I knew last-minute Homecoming shopping would draw a crowd. I spot Hayley Langer and her crew looking at costume jewelry and cackling up a storm. I wave to them. They wave back.

I couldn't have planned the timing any better.

We circle back to the Clinique counter. I ask the clerk for a sample of Black Honey. "It's kind of raisin," I say. "It'll look divine with your dress."

I pat some on her lips. It looks a little dark next to her ghost skin, but I pretend to like it.

"You know what you need?" I say. "A smoky eye. Don't you think?"

"Sure," the clerk says. "I can do that."

While Ivy settles in for her latest makeover, I pretend that my phone is vibrating. "Oops, I need to get that," I say. "Be right back."

I step away and speed-dial Wyatt Schnitt. "We're good," I tell him. "You can do the send now."

"Sure thing," he says.

I go back to where the Clinique clerk is going to town on Ivy's eyes. I supervise, anticipating my phone's vibration any second now.

Any second.

But by the time the clerk is finishing up a second coat of mascara, the pictures still haven't gone out. I text Wyatt a question mark. *Working on it,* he writes back.

We make another lap around the store. Near the perfume counters, we encounter Hayley and her minions.

"Let's try some out!" I say. "Every woman should have a signature scent."

"Sure," Ivy says. She seems tense. But she's always tense—being a lunatic will do that to you.

I pick up a few bottles and sniff. They're all so cloying. I find the least offensive one and thrust it in Ivy's direction. "You should try this one," I say. "It smells like winning."

While Ivy plays in perfume, I text Wyatt again. This time, I get no response.

"It's not happening," Ivy says to me. "At least, not how you planned it."

"Excuse me?"

"The pictures," she says quietly. "The ones you took of me? They're gone. Wyatt zapped them from your phone just now."

I'm staring at Ivy. No. What? What is she saying? I'm having trouble making sense of any of this.

Bright tears glisten in the corners of her eyes, but her face remains neutral. She continues to speak in that same calm near-whisper. "You have no idea what it took for me to do the things you've asked me to— no clue about what it took for me to trust you. You believed in me. So I believed you. I really, really believed you were my friend."

My mind is whirling. She knows. How does she know? How?

Wyatt? Did he trade what I gave him for everything I've vaguely promised him over the years? That disgusting little horn-dog. It probably only took a boob squeeze or two to get him to give me up. I'll squash that little acne farm like a pus-filled bug!

Ivy puts the perfume bottle down, reaches into her purse, and extracts her cell. She types something in. My phone vibrates. I look down to see a text from her. *There's more where this came from,* she wrote. And then a picture of my mother appears. It's kind of blurry and dark, but I know it's her. I just don't know *why*.

I look up. One of Ivy's fat tears is trailing down her cheek. But she's smiling. "There's video, too," she says. "Want to watch?"

"What have you done?" I practically growl.

"Me?" she says. "Nothing. But your mom, on the other hand . . ." She chuckles. "Hard when you find out someone isn't who you think she is. But, you know, it's all on the video. Are you sure you don't want to watch?"

"Listen to me carefully, Ivy," I say. "I don't know what you think you saw my mother doing, but it wasn't that. I can assure you. She's in mourning. She's never truly recovered from my father's death. And if you attempt to take advantage of her pain to besmirch her good name—"

"Let's watch," she interrupts. "You need the proof."

She queues up a video and holds it out for me to see. I reach for the phone and she snatches it back. "You're looking, not touching. And Wyatt has it backed up on three different servers, just so you know."

It's a dark, fuzzy video, but that is clearly Natalie, wearing the white fur stole my father got her as a wedding present. It's her signature fur. Everyone knows that fur.

She is standing outside some bar or something. She is not alone. She's wrestling with some sort of package—it's a little bag. She sprinkles some of the contents on the corner of her left hand and snorts.

My mother, the former beauty queen, is doing drugs. Out in the open. In front of a seedy bar. Captured on film, no less.

The camera zooms in on her companion. The sight of his face steals my breath away.

It's Douglas. Uncle Doug. My dad's best friend. The one who delivered the eulogy at his funeral.

He takes the bag from Natalie, sprinkles a little coke on her cleavage, and leans down to snort it up. She giggles maniacally as he does this. And then he starts kissing her, porn kissing with too much tongue, grabbing her breast with one hand and her ass with the other. I can't hear what they're saying, but I imagine it's something along the lines of "Oh, yeah, baby, right there."

Ivy Proctor is staring at me, and I want to slap her stupid fucking face.

"Why would you do this?" I ask her.

"This?" she says, tapping the phone. "That wasn't me. That was all Sloane."

"Sloane *Fahey*?"

"Do you know another Sloane?"

"Why?" I demand.

Ivy laughs so bitterly, it practically comes out a bark. "They say the best defense is a good offense, right?"

No. This isn't happening. It cannot be happening.

Everything I've worked for—all of it—crumbling right before my eyes.

"What do you want?" I ask her. "Name your price."

"I'm so glad you asked," Ivy says, sounding more like me than herself. "I want you to re-enter the Homecoming race."

"I don't get it."

"You told everyone you dropped out so someone more deserving could win," she says. "So I can't think of a better punishment than for you to retract that sentiment right before the vote. You want that crown so badly, don't you, Alexandra? Get back in the race, and let me beat you fair and square."

What she's proposing is akin to social suicide. And she knows it.

"I can't do that," I say quietly. "You know that."

Ivy *tsks* at me. "Then I think this video is about to go viral, that's what I think."

"You can't," I say. "That's my *mother*."

"And I'm somebody's daughter, but that didn't matter to you, did it?"

There has to be a way out of this. Has to. The photographs still exist. They could still get her disqualified. All I'd have to do is convince Wyatt to do what I'd initially asked. There's still time, and there are bargaining chips I've yet to use with him.

"Here's how this is going to go down," Ivy says. "You're going to call Frick—tonight, in fact—and let her know that you plan on competing tomorrow."

"And if I don't?"

"Then you know what happens."

I lean in closer. Our foreheads are practically touching. "You don't know who you're messing with, little girl. This isn't going to end well for you."

"That's where you're wrong," Ivy says. "We've made sure of that."

"Who? You and Wyatt *Schnitt*?"

"Don't forget Sloane. She's at your boyfriend's house right now, explaining everything to him. Don't worry. She knows to speak slowly."

I snort. "You think Matt's going to leave me for her?"

"No. But I think he'll leave you when he finds out who you really are."

This can't be happening. I have to think fast. Defuse the situation. What will it take to shut this down?

"Call Frick," Ivy instructs. *"Now."*

I pick up my phone, but it's not Frick's number I dial. It's Sam's.

"We have a situation," I say in a low voice.

"We sure do," Sam responds. "Because you are supposed to be calling Frick right about now."

Her words are like a sucker punch to the gut.

It's her. *She* did this. She's the only one capable.

How is this happening? How?

I end the call. Pull up Frick's number. Make the call.

"Hello, Ms. Frick," I say, trying to keep my voice steady. "I'm sorry to be calling you so late, but there's an urgent matter we need to discuss."

FIFTY-FOUR

Alexandra

I strand Ivy at the mall and hightail it home. On the way, I call Natalie. No answer. I call Matt. Same thing.

I have the sinking feeling that I am so totally fucked.

My brain is whirring a mile a minute, trying desperately to process everything that has happened. Trying to figure out what happens next. I'm usually three steps ahead, but right now, I'm ten behind.

Natalie is nowhere to be found. She's probably out getting wasted with Uncle Doug. I consider calling him but can't bring myself to do it.

I pace the house, feeling like a feral cat. Feeling like I'm about to explode.

I get back in my car and drive over to Matt's, but see Sloane's car parked in the driveway. Maybe Ivy was bluffing about that part. Or, even if she's not, maybe Sloane's plan to break us up has backfired. He hasn't called me. Hasn't texted. You can't break up with someone without telling them, can you?

That night, I don't sleep. I can't. Instead, I go into the basement and run until my legs are about to give out. No word from Natalie. No word from Matt.

It occurs to me that I am utterly, completely alone.

Is this how Natalie feels? Is this why she works so hard to numb herself?

I sit on the basement steps and let myself cry. Real tears, not the fake ones I can conjure up on command.

I cry until I have nothing left inside of me. Then I get up, wipe my eyes, and go to my room, where I lie awake until my alarm goes off the next morning.

At the game, I sit in the stands with Matt's family. If he is breaking up with me, they do not seem to be any the wiser. Doug is supposed to be there, too, watching the Homecoming game with us, but he already texted me that he's running late. Probably nursing an epic hangover. Natalie still wasn't home by the time I left. I can only imagine what the two of them have been up to.

The Spencer Spartans are winning, of course. We always do. So far Matt has scored two touchdowns, and we've barely begun the second quarter. I'm relieved to see that whatever transpired last night hasn't affected his performance.

My head isn't where it needs to be right now. It bothers me that I can't get ahold of my mother. She could at least pick up the phone.

At halftime, there's the tradition of parents walking the

candidates out onto the field for the final Q&A. It's kind of a dog-and-pony show for the alumnae. Natalie says this is a relatively new tradition—that back in her day, the king and queen were voted on in school the Friday before the game. There was a parade too, and the king and queen rode on the main float.

But several years back, the daughter of a big donor didn't win queen. He wanted to see his kid on the field, though. So they had all of the candidates trot out and do this dumb Q&A. The following year, they switched the election to take place at the dance, so all of the parents with candidates could see their kids honored. It's stupid and no other school in Indiana does Homecoming in quite the same way.

My freshman year, my dad was still alive. He walked me out as freshman class princess. I loved being on his arm, even though someone had the nerve to ask me why my grandpa was my escort. Sophomore year, just a few weeks before the accident, he was away on a business trip, so Natalie accompanied me.

Last year, I almost had to walk alone. But then Uncle Douglas stepped in at the last minute. He is once again my escort. And he arrives just in time. Alone.

The last thing I want to do is make an entrance with a man who apparently snorts coke off my mother's breasts. But I don't have time to find a replacement. So I swallow my disgust and delay confrontation.

"You look beautiful," Doug tells me, with a quick kiss to the cheek. I try not to recoil. "Shall we?"

I walk across the field on Doug's arm, feeling my stomach

churn. This is supposed to be one of the highlights of my high school career, and I can't even enjoy it.

The queen candidates stand in a row, clutching the bouquets of flowers our male escorts presented each of us with. One by one, we step up to the mic to introduce ourselves and answer a question posed by Frick.

I am the last to go. I didn't even really hear anyone else's answers. I'm too lost in my own head.

When it is my turn, Frick looks at me and very pointedly asks, "Who would you say is your greatest role model, and what would you do if you found out that person wasn't who you thought they were?"

The smirk on her face says it all. She knows. Somehow, she knows about Natalie.

I open my mouth to speak but no words come out. I am shaking. I am standing in front of hundreds of people, all of them waiting for me to say something, anything, and I don't have a single word.

The mic catches my sob, amplifies it out to the crowd. I drop my bouquet, cover my mouth with my hands, and run off the field. I don't stop running until I get to my car.

All that work. All those plans.

I rock back and forth, shaking, and am startled when I see a concerned Doug gesturing at me to roll down the window.

"I can't," I say. Then I start the car and peel out of the parking lot.

FIFTY-FIVE

Alexandra

I reach my house in record time. I can't believe I just did that. Me, Alexandra Miles. Turns out these colors *do* run.

As soon as I enter I can hear Natalie clanging around in the kitchen. Seething, I storm in there, ready to rip her a new one.

"You," I say, pointing at her. "You have ruined *everything*."

"What are you talking about?" Natalie asks. "Is the game over already?"

"It's all over, Mother. I've lost it all. To protect *you*."

"I still don't know what you're talking about."

I pull my phone from my purse, queue up Ivy's video, which she oh-so-graciously forwarded to me after I called Frick. "Here," I say, thrusting it toward her.

Natalie squints and pulls the camera closer to her eyes. When she realizes she's the star of this particular home movie, she lets out an "Oh, fuck."

"Is this your doing?" she asks. "You've been following me?"

"No," I say. "A classmate did. And then she gave it to another classmate who used this video to blackmail me. I gave up everything to protect you. And for what? So you could do drugs with Uncle Dougie? Jesus, Natalie. What the *fuck*?"

"You have no idea how hard it's been for me," she says. "You are young, and beautiful, and you have your whole life ahead of you. Me, I'm just a washed-up beauty queen."

I shake my head at her. "So that gives you the right to be a shitty parent? What if you'd gotten arrested?"

"It's not like that," Natalie says. "We play from time to time. But it's not like . . . I'm not an addict, if that's what you're thinking."

"I don't know what to think."

Natalie starts to pour herself a Blanton's.

"No," I say. "Don't you dare!"

"Can I at least sit?"

We move to the table. Natalie sighs heavily. "What do you want from me, Alexandra? In another nine months, you're going to college. You're going to leave me behind. Why do you even care?"

"Because you're my mother!" I say. "Of course I care."

"It's been three years," Natalie says ruefully. "You never noticed. Not once."

"What do you mean?"

"Me. Douglas. Three years. You were too self-involved to see what was going on."

"But, Dad's only been gone—"

"I know exactly how long your father's been gone," she says, cutting me off. "He didn't notice either."

Natalie starts talking, spilling a long, complicated story about how she married too young, to a man who was too old. She left the pageant world at his request. She gave him a beautiful daughter, played the part of the perfect corporate wife. In return, he allowed her access to his money.

"I was more like a prostitute than I was a wife," she tells me. "Except in the end, we weren't even having sex."

"Don't," I say.

She shrugs. "Douglas desired me. He always has. Even before your father and I got married, we . . . had some moments. And with your father gone, he could finally have me."

My ears feel like they're bleeding. None of this makes sense. My mother has spent the past two years as a sort of recluse. How could she have been carrying on some secret affair? With Uncle Douglas, of all people?

"You were so happy though," I say. "Right before Daddy died. You were inseparable."

"We were."

"But you were screwing Dougie the whole time?"

"No," she says. "Not then. That was real."

Suddenly, my lungs feel constricted and I am unable to breathe.

"The brakes," I say. "The rumors. You?"

"No," she says. "I would never. How could you even think that?"

"How could I *not*?"

Tears spill from my eyes. My mother's response? "You're going to ruin your makeup."

Is it any wonder I am the person I've become?

"He'll be happy you finally know," Natalie says after a while. "We won't have to hide anymore."

"Great," I say. "So now the two of you can smoke crack at our dining-room table."

"No, dear," she says. "Crack is for the lower class."

I think this is her attempt at a joke. At any rate, she offers a weak smile.

"You're going to leave me," Natalie says. "You're going to be somebody. You'll be the somebody I never was, and you're going to leave me here, all alone."

"What about Douglas?"

"He will take care of me," she concedes. "Until my skin gets too wrinkly, or my tits start to sag. Then I'll be alone again. But you, Alexandra—you will never need anyone. You are all that you need."

"I needed *you*," I say, my voice choking on the words.

Natalie has no response to that. She looks over toward the Blanton's longingly.

"Go ahead," I say. "Drink up. I'm done talking."

I walk upstairs and straight into the bathroom, where I take a long, hot shower. Trying to wash away all of the ugliness of today. I think of the shower water like a baptism of sorts.

It's time for the resurrection of Alexandra Miles.

FIFTY-SIX

Alexandra

Matt is supposed to pick me up at six o'clock on the dot, but he doesn't show. I've stopped trying to get ahold of him. I've never been a fan of futility.

I consider skipping the dance altogether, especially after this afternoon's performance. But to do so would be the ultimate show of weakness, and that's something I simply cannot allow.

So I do my hair. I do my makeup. I step into my lavender dress, a floor-length number with layer upon layer of diaphanous skirt. The strapless bodice sports literally thousands of hand-sewn crystal beads. It's a pageant dress, but not one I've ever worn in competition.

It's the dress I thought I'd be wearing when I became queen.

I drive myself to the dance. I plan to walk into that decorated gym with my head held high, daring anyone and everyone to ask me about what happened during halftime. I am going because not going would be sealing my fate. What Natalie said—about me being the somebody she never was—is spot-on. I am nothing like my mother. I will not hide in my house. I will not let a man derail my dreams.

I sit in my parked car as long as I can stand it. If I don't go in soon, I know I'm going to chicken out.

I can't let them win.

Even though I will leave the dance without the crown I worked so hard to win, I will still leave a winner. The crown is not the prize—I am.

Couples are still arriving as I make my way to the door. They look at me and they whisper. Yes, that's how quickly I replaced Ivy in the gossip mill.

Taylor Flynn is working the table, collecting tickets. "My gosh," she says to me. "I didn't think you'd be here."

"Um . . . thanks?"

She offers a tight smile that's so totally fake. "I need your ticket," she says.

Only, I don't have a ticket. Matt bought the tickets.

Taylor reads the expression on my face and says, "That'll be twenty dollars."

Is there no indignity I'll be spared tonight?

I pull some crumpled bills from my purse and thrust them in her direction. In return, she slides me a ballot. "Voting ends at eight," she says. "There's a box on each table to collect them."

There is music thumping through the gym, and a medium-size group of kids dancing near the DJ. I feel eyes on me from every direction. This is not me being paranoid, either. People are watching, and they are whispering, and I'd be lying if I said I wasn't second-guessing my decision to come.

Not that I let any of this show. To all those who are observing, I am my normal social self. Smiling, waving to "friends," making small talk.

I spot Matt across the room, chatting with Bobby and Ivy. Ivy, wearing a dress and shoes I picked out for her. Wearing makeup I paid for. Sporting a hairstyle that my former best friend gave her.

Ivy sees me before Matt does. She smiles and waves. Matt turns to see who she's waving at. When he realizes it's me, he turns, giving me nothing but back.

So that's how it's going to be.

I consider taking a lap around the room. I want to know what people are saying about me. I can't change the story until I do.

But before I get very far, Sloane cuts me off at the pass. "You showed," she says, not without admiration. "I'm impressed."

"Not now," I say, pushing past her.

She calls out after me, "Have fun tonight!"

I have never felt so humiliated in my entire life.

It is nearing seven thirty, which means I only have to stick around for another thirty minutes. Sixty tops, depending on how long it takes them to tally the votes. I've decided I'll stand to the bitter end, until that crown lands on someone else's head.

No one talks to me.

Not a single person.

At eight, Taylor comes around to collect all the ballot boxes.

It's almost over. The wait. Thirty minutes from now, the king and queen will be announced.

Over in the corner, I spot Erin Hewett. She's all alone, too. At least, I think she is.

But then I see her. Sam. She, too, is wearing a dress I picked out. She looks prettier than I've ever seen her. Happier, too.

In a second, I find out why.

Because there they are—Erin Hewett and Samantha Schnitt—kissing each other, right there in the middle of the Homecoming dance.

Son of a *bitch*. I didn't see it. How did I not see it?

At exactly nine o'clock, Constance Frick takes the stage to announce this year's Homecoming court. First, it's the senior class prince. That honor goes to Tyler Moses. Then, she announces the princess.

That honor goes to *me*.

This is worse than winning nothing at all. Because now it's clear that I am the runner-up. Now I have to stand on a stage and watch someone else take my crown.

Frick calls my name again. I have to take the stage. There's no getting out of this now.

Next, Frick announces the king. It's Matt, of course. He stands there, wearing a purple-and-gold plastic crown and holding an equally hideous plastic scepter. He doesn't look at me. He may never look at me again.

"And now for the moment you've all been waiting for," Frick says, looking downright cheerful. "Your Homecoming Queen for this year is . . . Ivy Proctor."

The crowd explodes. Of course they do. Of course.

Ivy locks eyes on me as she walks up the steps to the stage. I want to look away but can't.

"Thank you," she mouths. I fight the urge to rip out all of her hair with my teeth.

It hurts to watch Frick place the rhinestone tiara on Ivy's head, instead of mine. But I don't show it. I smile and clap and act like this is everything I wanted. She may have won, but I'm still claiming the moment.

The music starts for the King and Queen's dance. I watch Matt take Ivy into his muscled arms and I choke back a sob. Tyler reaches for my hand, gentleman that he is, and we join them on the floor.

It is the only dance I'll dance tonight.

As soon as the song has ended, I make a beeline for the door. Enough is enough.

But before I leave, I take one last look around the room. Sam and Erin are dancing together, and nobody seems to care. Sloane is dancing with James Leitch, and no one seems to care that she's pressed up against a freshman either. And there's Queen Ivy, tucked into Bobby Jablonski's embrace.

Looks like everyone got their happy ending. Everyone but me, that is.

It won't be easy, fighting my way back.

But I know I can, and I know I will.

I am—and always will be—Queen Alexandra Miles.

Winner.

Acknowledgments

First and foremost, I ~~want~~ need to thank my editor, Kristen Pettit, who never stopped believing that my words were worthy of being read. Working with you again has been an amazing experience. In fact, it never quite feels like work—more like fun. Always.

I'm grateful to the wonderful staff at HarperCollins, including Elizabeth Lynch, Veronica Ambrose (who, quite literally, is my favorite copy editor ever), Sarah Creech, Alexandra Rakaczki, Elizabeth Ward, and Gina Rizzo. Thank you all so much for the care you put into this book.

To my patient husband, who encouraged me to take on this project, and who cheered me on every step of the way, I say this: you are made of awesome.

And for Wendy Kinna, who's not only the best friend a girl could have but also the best beta reader ever—thank you for helping me find my ending. Again. And for loving even the most unlovable of characters every bit as much as I did. You deserve a tiara of your own.

Finally, I need to give shout-outs to my favorite writing partner, Carolee Kunz; my friend and mentor, Cruce Stark; and my lovely and talented Aunt Barbara, from whom I got the writing gene in the first place. I adore you all.